Pretend...

An Oxley College Novel

STACEY NASH

Pretend...

ISBN: 099424665X
ISBN-13: 978-0994246653

The right of Stacey Nash to be identified as the author of this work has been asserted by her under the *Copyright Amendment (Moral Rights) Act 2000.*

This book is a work of fiction. Characters, events, and incidents either are products of the author's imagination or are used fictitiously. Any resemblance to event or actual persons, living or dead, is entirely coincidental.

Edited by **Lauren McKellar**
Cover Art by **Sprinkles on Top Studios**

by Stacey Nash

Forget Me Not (Collective Series, #1)

Remember Me (Collective Series, #2)

Never Forgotten (Collective Series, #3)

Shh! (Oxley College Saga, #1)

Pretend... (Oxley College Saga, #2)

Stolen Sanctuary (Oxley College Saga, #2.5)

Wait! (Oxley College Saga, #3)

Dedication

For Tracey and Kellie

CHAPTER ONE

Savvy

I closed my eyes and drew a deep breath. It was just a beach party. Aunt Rosy and Uncle Trevor knew where we'd be. Kody was parked in front of some teen flick and everything was just fine.

The long strand of hair twirled between my fingers easily as I pulled it away from my face, up and back. Another pin into the twist did the trick to secure it in place. Fluffing out the ends and dragging the blonde mass over my shoulder, I assessed my appearance in the full-length mirror one last time for good measure.

"Hurry up," Tori complained from her room. "We'll be the last ones there."

"There's nothing wrong with being fashionably late." I swung my hips in a deliberate sashay as I rounded the bathroom corner.

"It's not our lateness that people will be talking about. You and I are looking fantabulous."

"Fan-bloody-tabulous." I threw my hands in the air and spun around, showing off my designer beach dress. Simple white linen, the Billabong number was the perfect outfit for tonight's party. Especially when coupled with my pale pink Havianas.

A car horn honked somewhere outside.

"That'll be Miller." Tori sighed.

"The elusive Miller? Are you telling me this boy—"

"Man, Savannah." She finger-raked her super short black hair. "Boys are for girls. Real women date men."

"This boy …" I wagged my finger, "…is not, in fact, a figment of your deepest desires and darkest secrets, but a real, live boy?"

"I told you he's been working flat-out all summer. Give me a break and prepare to be jealous, because he's far more real than any Pinocchio you would have met at college. Although … if his nose was as long as his di—"

I shoved a hand in her face. "T.M.I."

That scored a cheeky grin from my cousin, who turned and dashed down the stairs. She'd been talking about this Miller guy all summer, and even though I'd been home from college for more than a month I still hadn't met the first guy she'd dated since … well, in a while. And she called me her best friend.

I snatched my purse off the bed and followed the vanilla-scented path Tori had left as she fled. By the time I reached the front porch, my cousin was wrapped around a tallish, thinnish guy. By the way she clung to him as she kissed him hello, it was clear that

2

they shared something more passionate than each other's saliva. As if she sensed I was right behind her, Tori pulled back, keeping a hold of Miller's hand, and leaned into his side.

She grinned up at him. "This is my cousin Savannah."

"Hi." I gave an awkward fingertip wave and Miller smiled.

"I've heard a lot," he said.

"Likewise."

"I'm sorry about ..." He glanced away in that sympathetic way I'd grown to hate.

"Shall we?" Tori dragged him down the steps so fast that if he fell he would have snapped clean in half. Miller didn't seem to care. He let her drag him along like a puppy on a leash until they reached the curb, then he kissed her cheek and strode around the front of Tori's red Lancer parked in our driveway. Meanwhile, Tori beamed over her shoulder, mouthing, *Miller borrowed my car.*

Smiling at her giddy happiness, my fingers slid under the door handle and I let myself into the backseat while Tori climbed in the front beside her boyfriend.

Miller turned the engine over and my stomach flipped as he pulled away from our house. Up front, Tori giggled and I slumped in my seat, watching the streetlights zoom by the side window.

She spun around to look back at me. "Remember when we used to go to beach parties all the time?"

"Yeah ..." I sighed. Back in high school, they'd been a regular occurrence, and it seemed that they'd continued in my absence. She'd been trying to drag me to one all summer, and finally I'd given in.

"Wonder if any of my old friends will be there?"

Miller drove one-handed, his arm working overtime to turn the wheel while his other hand sat upside down on the console, cradling Tori's long fingers.

A good ten minutes after we'd left the lights of town behind us, Miller pulled the car into a dirt track. I pressed my palms against the coarse fabric of the backseat, bracing myself for the bumpy ride. In no time at all we reached a dark parking lot teeming with cars and suddenly I couldn't sit still, sliding from one window to the other to see who was there. Our headlights shone on at least a dozen other vehicles, all shapes, sizes, and makes. A shiny BMW was parked alongside a beat-up Combi van, laden with surfboards, and that sat right near an off-road motorcycle. But it was the black Outlander that caught my attention, sitting proudly amongst the other vehicles, despite its dust-covered doors and muddy wheels. Its presence somehow made this whole party a little easier to face.

As we climbed out of Tori's car, the smell of the ocean hit me, almost buckling my knees with its familiarity. The sounds of distant revelry danced in the air, but Tori's voice cut above it. "Shall we?"

"We shall." I eyed up the cooler bag in her hand.

Tori shot me a lopsided grin then unzipped the case and extracted a drink, which she passed my way. I uncapped the bottle and took a sip, the sweet raspberry flavour coating my tongue with its goodness. I hooked my arm through hers and we made for the path that led to the ocean. Five Mile Beach wasn't popular or crowded. In fact, it was more of a backwater beach that wasn't even patrolled. It had plenty of sand, with dunes that extended well beyond the beachfront. All in all, the perfect place for a bonfire party.

"I wish you didn't have to go back," Tori said, as we walked up the slight hill.

"You could always transfer schools and come with me."

She sighed. "You could've gone to uni here."

She'd never leave Coffs and we both knew it, which was exactly why I'd said she should transfer. I loved Tori to pieces, but being at college alone was the medicine I needed. The time away was better than anyone back home would ever realise, especially after what had happened.

Sand slid between my Havis and my toes, the grainy texture pure bliss on my feet that in just a fortnight's time would be confined to proper shoes. We crested the hill and the music hit me first, followed by the crash of waves. I stalled, my feet freezing in the sand as all five senses took in the scene below.

"Absence makes the heart grow fonder." I tossed the cliché over my shoulder as I flicked off my Havis and ran down onto the beach, where the orange glow of a bonfire cast a small crowd in silhouette against the evening sky.

Then it hit me. The scent of burning driftwood, coiling around me, suffocating me, dragging me back to that night.

His eyes sparkled in the firelight with laughter as I spun around them both, my feet kicking up sand with the dance. Other voices faded in and out, but it felt like it was just us. With one hand on her waist, he held the other up in the air and grabbing it, I spun around them both as if they were my own personal may pole. His smiling eyes never left mine as she sucked back on her joint, then when it was done, nuzzled into his neck.

A shrill beep invaded our moment and frowning, she reached into her pocket, took one look at the lit up screen and glanced toward me.

My stomach constricted, but Tori's hand snatched mine as she ran past. No longer burdened with the bag, she was like a whirlwind, dragging me toward the party. I laughed aloud in spite of the heavy feeling around my heart, and we ran right up to the fire's edge, with every damn soul here looking our way.

"Savvy's home!" Tori yelled. A few cheers followed, but mostly everyone ignored us, until a couple of girls I'd known in high school made their way around the fire.

"Hey girl. What happened to you? You disappeared to Oxley and dropped off the face of well, everything. Did you de-friend me?"

"Not just you. I shut down my Facebook." I didn't tell her I'd re-opened it with a fresh slate, only keeping people I was actually in contact with, like Tori. Even Kody wasn't on there, since she hated social media.

Pity bloomed in her eyes. "Ah. That makes sense ..."

Small talk ensued. I couldn't keep up with the conversation, my mind wandering. Their thoughts were practically painted on their faces; *the last time we saw you at one of these parties* ... It was just idle chitchat anyway. How was college? Did I like my major? When did I go back to Armidale? Was there a guy on the scene or was I single?

I cradled my drink while they buzzed around me.

"Shove over." Kody pushed her way onto the couch between Mum and I, popcorn spilling out of the bowl cradled in her arm.

I shifted a little closer to Dad, who said, "You all ready for the big game tomorrow night, chickpea?"

Kody laughed and tucked her legs up underneath herself. "It's a sure win."

The movie I'd picked out hummed into the opening credits, and I snuggled down into my spot on the couch.

"Don't be too cocky, now." Mum tutted. "Nothing's ever sure."

After a while, I found myself gazing into the fire while sipping my second vodka of the evening. Tori had disappeared, though I could guarantee there would be no mysteriousness about it. She'd be rolling around in the sand somewhere with Miller, for sure.

It was good to see her happy, but if I ever looked at a guy with that much blatant adoration, then the entire thing was over. I wouldn't be a fawning fool for any guy.

The girls I'd been talking to sat by my side, engrossed in their own conversation and me ... well, my mind wound back again, and that crippling feeling slammed into my gut. The waves crashing on the shore became a rhythm on which I forced myself to concentrate.

"Well, well ... Savannah West."

I looked up into Dane Beaumont's familiar face and smiled, once again in spite of the heaviness inside me. The guy was like sex on legs; he was so damn

7

good looking. It was a real pity he knew just how sexy he was. He smiled at me with the tummy-clenching grin that he'd perfected sometime over his past two years at Oxley, and positioned himself on the sand beside me.

"Hey," I said, ignoring the ridiculous giddy feeling that washed over me at his closeness. And, if I was being completely honest, the fact I hadn't set eyes on him since summer break started. One month, two weeks, and four days ago. Not that I was counting, because that would be beyond lame, and lame I was not.

"Hey, pretty girl."

I shook my head. The guy was the biggest flirt. And I wouldn't buy into it, not with the past we shared. My feelings for him needed to stay away, where I'd safely tucked them for years.

Thick and black, the plaited leather he wore around his neck hung in the hollow of his throat until he leaned forward, wrists balanced on raised knees. Then the Celtic disc that hung front and centre pushed his baggy T-shirt forward, affording me a glimpse of his tanned chest and just the lightest dusting of hair.

My tummy tingled for all it was worth, only the sensation was way too low to actually be in my stomach.

Ah crap. Why did Dane Beaumont, of all guys, have this affect on me? He was strictly off-limits.

"How's your summer break been?" An attempted cover of the fact all my brain cells had turned to mush.

"Not too bad. Yours?"

"Different. I hear Christian is at Olivia's place."

Gee, now I was the queen of small talk.

Dane chuckled, then planted his hands in the sand behind him and leaned back, his shoulder brushing my arm.

A stupid shiver rippled through my entire body, not leaving a single inch of flesh unaffected by his touch. Rolling, crashing, rhythmic waves. They were still out there.

"Savvy …"

"Yeah?"

"Don't be a stranger this year, okay?"

I snorted. "I wasn't a stranger last year, Dane. You were the one who ignored me." *While sleeping with every girl who walked Oxley's halls.*

Being around Dane had never been easy. In the four years we'd known each other, our relationship had always been complicated. I guess that was bound to happen when the only guy who made your skin buzz with more excitement than possible also made your heart clench with broken maybes.

"I'd never ignore you, babe."

"Don't use your sleazy lines on me."

His mouth dropped open in mock surprise and he leaned forward, motioning between us. "A line …" *fake gasp* "Savannah West, that was the truth."

He leaned in, bumping his shoulder against mine and leaving it there, the bare skin of his biceps, triceps, whatever ceps it was, smooched against my oversensitive skin. While his eyes, steady pools of green reflecting the firelight, caressed my gaze.

I gulped. *Again.* My stupid mouth had flooded with more moisture than the ocean before us held. Heat swallowed me in its warmth, radiating off his face that had somehow crept close while I was busy looking at his eyes.

Shit. He wasn't. Couldn't.

His tongue slid across his bottom lip and if I just ...

BOOM!

A squeal rang through the night air, then another loud bang, and suddenly fireworks bloomed in the blackened sky, which was bloody typical. They lit up the darkness with their beauty. And they bloody well matched the fireworks inside of me that I needed to ignore.

CHAPTER TWO

Dane

Driftwood Creations' inventory was low. There weren't any large pieces left, but we had a good display of lamp stands, bowls, frames, and even a few bigger pieces of furniture.

The old man had always loved creating things out of wood, and over the years he had turned his passion from a hobby into a mini business. Now, for the first time it was his sole income. He'd given away his day job at the pine plantation to focus on the art he was so damn good at creating.

I wandered out the back to his workshop where he sat on a wooden stool with Mum's little dog curled at his feet. The ornate base of what would probably wind up a coffee table rested between his thighs as he ran a battered piece of sandpaper over its limbs with long, sure strokes. The way he transformed each washed up log into furniture sure was something else; every single piece was a unique work of art.

"Si'down, kid."

I pulled up a stool, the scrape of its legs on the concrete earning pricked ears from the tiny terrier as Pa's calloused hands worked with great care. "That's gonna be sweet."

"Yup." He didn't take his eyes off the job. "It's all in picking the right bit of timber for the job. You need an eye for it; a piece like this, with plenty of sturdy branches ..." he tapped the limb he was working on, "... is perfect for a table. See how they all curve toward a central support? If you even them up, there's one hell of a strong stand with plenty of detail."

"You gonna put a glass top on her? Make the base a centrepiece?" I leaned back on the stool, my shoulders against the wall.

Smiling, the old man tipped his head toward a pile of raw wood. "You've got a knack for it, kid. Grab a chunk and get to work."

A layer of sawdust covered everything in the room, even the off-cuts littering the floor. "You know it's not my thing."

"Rubbish."

He tossed me one of his scraps, a small piece of timber no bigger than Roar, who'd just raised his head to look around. Little mutt probably thought he was missing out on something fun. I turned the piece over in my hand. There wasn't a lot to be done with a bit this size, maybe something decorative. I retrieved a sheet of coarse sandpaper from the floor, no doubt left where it last fell, and set to work smoothing down the wood. I'd been there the entire summer, helped him open the door for the very first time right before Christmas. Tourist season. It was coming to a close though, and things would slow down now until Easter. That slow period would be the real tell for the business.

We worked in silence most of the afternoon, only breaking for the bell indicating a customer had entered the shop. Not that we needed a bell, with Roar's excited friends-are-here yap. Usually I spent more time up front than out back and the old man did the opposite, both of us where we liked to be. Although it got boring, working the wood beside him held a certain solidarity, even if my efforts couldn't be called art. But his … he had an unmatched talent which meant this was a viable business. He just needed to run it properly for these first few years to get it off the ground. So it didn't become a statistic— failing in the first two years.

The bell jingled once again and I set my work on the bench.

"It's just me," Mum called from the front door. Roar ran circles around the dusty workshop floor, not stopping until Ma's rosy face appeared in the staff entry door a moment later. "I thought you two might be hungry."

She placed a wicker basket on the workbench and Dad set his piece down, scrubbing dusty hands on dustier work jeans. Good thing the old girl was on the ball; she plucked one of those cleaning wipe things from a packet in her bag and passed it to him. Dad cleaned his hands then took a look in the basket, plucking out a slice of bread which he offered to the dog.

"Smells good, darlin'."

I gave my own hands a onceover with the hospital-grade disinfectant. She passed me a plastic container that warmed my aching fingers, fingers that were used to pushing a pen at college, not working timber. Looked like some kind of stew—chunks of beef and potato swimming in brown gravy. It smelled more than good; it smelled bloody amazing. I dug in, shovelling a huge hunk of beef into my mouth. The muggy January heat might have had me sweating, but there was nothing better than a good feed, stifling weather or not.

"Is this your work?" Mum held the piece I'd been carving, its tiny branches like long fingers messed up in a tangled wooden knot.

"Yeah … just humouring the old man."

"It's hardly humouring, Dane. This will make a fine ornament."

Leaning against the counter, Pa gestured my way with his fork. "That's what I've been trying to tell him. Kid won't recognise his own talent."

I laughed around my last mouthful of rich casserole. "Give it up, already. I'm at the business end of this show, and you both know it. Got a head for it." It wasn't that I hated working with my hands—it just wasn't my thing. "You staying now, Ma?"

She nodded.

"Then I'm heading out." Pressing my hand to her shoulder, I kissed her on the cheek then gave the old man a see-ya-later nod.

I crossed to the back door and left the tiny shop, emerging into the equally small parking lot where my Outlander waited. The best thing about my black SUV was the fact my surfboard could slide in the back, so I didn't have to worry about it being strapped to the roof when I wasn't with my wheels. I climbed in, and the springs in the driver's seat sagged under my weight as I worked to wind down the squeaky window. Felt like a hot box in here, thanks to another almost forty-degree Celsius day. I cranked up the stereo and slung an arm on the open window, then peeled out onto the road.

With tourist season in full swing, my preferred beach was a little cove out of town. I zoomed along the highway for a good fifteen minutes before pulling into the road that led to the coast. My phone buzzed along the way, and when I brought the Outlander to a stop in Five Mile Beach's dirt parking lot, I grabbed the cell off the passenger seat.

Yo, Beauy. What's happening?

That was Logan; nothing for weeks, then a text out of nowhere. We'd been friends for a few years and had been through some serious shit together. The kind that shot the formalities out of the park. I flicked back a reply.

Nothing. Just about to hit the surf. What's doin'?

I popped the hatch and climbed out, taking my phone. It buzzed before I'd even reached for my bag.

Heading back to college this year. Don't suppose you're looking to move out of Oxley? Get a place in town? I could use another roommate.

I dragged my duffle bag over from the far corner and stepped out of my flip-flops, then dropped the boardies and pulled my spring wetsuit up over my arse while contemplating a response. The high pitch of laughter caught my attention, and I looked over to where a pair of chicks had just climbed out of the only other car in the lot. The curvy brunette offered up a smile.

And lose the free flow of ladies? Appealing as living with you is, it's my last year. Oxley's the place to be.

Grabbing a handful of shirt at the back of my neck, I tugged it off over my head then shoved the keys to the Outlander inside my towel and grabbed my board out of the car.

There was something about walking up the wooden path with Shea oaks on either side, sand oozing between my toes, that felt like home. I'd probably spent more time in the water than I had anywhere else over the years. Even as a kid I'd joined Nippers—surf lifesaving for kids—rather than the soccer team, like my mates. Saltwater was in my blood.

I crested the hill and sucked back a whiff of ocean air. In only a few weeks I'd be hundreds of kilometres inland. Should've picked a university based on location, not its course choices. There was no doubt I was enrolled in one of the best business courses this side of the big cities, and Oxley wasn't too far from home. Still, I missed this place when I was away.

I hefted the board under my arm, reshuffling its weight. Soft sand gave underfoot as I walked off the wooden steps and out onto the dune. A few people bobbed around out in the surf, but nowhere near as many grommets as you'd find at the beaches in town this time of year. I jammed the end of my board into the sand and dropped my towel, taking a moment to soak in the crashing waves, watching for where they were breaking, seeing which direction the swell pulled.

Satisfied I had the drag pegged, I dropped my towel on the sand and pulled up the top of my suit, sliding my arms inside the sleeveless top, and caught the long cord that was attached to the zipper between my fingers then pulled it up until it hit the top. I tucked my board under my arm and made for the water. The soft sand gave way to firm, and the moment my toes hit the shore I couldn't wait any longer. I jogged into the rolling waves until the water lapped at my knees then flopped onto the floating fibreglass belly first and paddled out to deeper waters.

As I pulled each arm through the briny waves, I realised that this was what made me happy. Made me feel the same way my dad felt when he was turning wood. Being one with the ocean, knowing which wave to catch, then the breathless six-second ride to shore—that was what life was all about. Following my gut always gave the best ride, and that was bloody awesome. Time moved in a different way out there. An hour could pass in the blink of an eye. A whole day in just a moment.

When the sun fell close to the tree-line, I paddled in to shore. My hair flicked off my forehead as I shook the water out and hoisted the board under my arm.

"Hey …" Giggling, the girls from earlier walked my way. One stepped forward. "Impressive surfing out there." Wearing a white bikini, and with a pair of flip-flops hanging from her fingers, the chick was damn hot. Her redheaded friend was of much the same calibre, if not better, thanks to her cherry locks.

"The swell was pretty mediocre, but thanks." Her swell sure wasn't average. I began my trek up the beach. They'd follow. The talkers always did.

"You from around here?"

Bingo.

"Sometimes."

"We haven't seen you before."

"You mustn't have been looking, babe. I'm here every day."

"Well then, I might see you tomorrow."

"Maybe."

The smile she offered said she'd be here waiting, available for the taking.

I unzipped my wettie and peeled it back to my waist, enjoying the warm air on my bare skin. I tossed my towel around my neck and looped the Outlander's keys into the tag on my suit before heading back up the beach and to the parking lot. It hadn't been an epic session, but it didn't need to be to sate my thirst for catching a wave. Those few seconds when I got up on a good one were unlike any other moment in life, and each wave … each wave told a different story. No two rides were ever the same.

I leaned my board against the Outlander and unlocked the hatch. Lifting it up and peeling off the wetsuit, I then changed back into my board shorts, feeling refreshed and alive thanks to the drying saltwater on my cool skin. I reached for my phone and woke it up with a thumb to the screen to see what Logan had come back with.

Mate, come on. There'd be just as many girls to bring home,
only you'd have a much bigger bed to roll them around in.

He'd need a roomie for the money, but as good a bloke as Logan was, I couldn't not be at Oxley. I'd made a promise to myself to watch out for Savannah West, and I might have spent the last year doing it from afar and through mutual friends, but there was no way I could it keep an eye on her all the way from town.

Soz, dude. No can do. Pumped you'll be back on campus though.

CHAPTER THREE

Dane

I'd been back at Oxley for a whole day, and already Christian had me lugging shit around for the social committee. I hefted the keg out of the back of my Outlander and stood aside while my mate grabbed the second one, grunting as he heaved it out of the car. Always the organiser, Olivia, the impeccably ordered redhead he'd been dating for almost a year, pushed the hatch closed, and led the way into the dormitory we called our college home. As we came around the corner, her screech just about killed my ears. "Savvy!"

Good thing I was paying attention or I wouldn't have pulled up in time to stop from barrelling their hug-a-thon over. "How was the summer? You never called, or emailed, and your texts were so …" Olivia blahed out a sound. "I missed you so much!"

"Likewise. Life sucks when I don't see you every day," Savannah bellowed in her friend's ear. Christian raised a brow, but I'd already noticed the way Savvy's tight shirt didn't quite contain her assets. Dude needed to keep his eyes locked on his girlfriend.

They kept jumping. I kept watching Savvy bounce. Christian kept gawk-grinning.

"How was your family?" Olivia bubbled. "I bet Kody was happy to see you. And your parents ... they good?"

Savvy never missed a beat, nor did she acknowledge my disapproving look. Instead, she placed her hands on Olivia's arms, her pretty blue eyes trained on the other girl as she lied. "Ecstatic. Now, tell me about your break. What happened? Who did you see? What did you get up to? Oh my god, Christian met your family. How did that go?"

My mate took that as his cue to heft the keg higher onto his shoulder. "This damn thing's too heavy."

Olivia's hair bounced with her shrug. "It was all right, I guess. My dad loved him and they went golfing every other day, so there was that."

"Oh ..." Savvy glanced toward his retreating back, and damn, if Christian wasn't right. My arm ached; best get the beer put away. I reshuffled the weight, shot them each a suave smile and took off while Savvy continued as if there'd been no interruption. "But it was good having him there, right? You guys got some alone time?"

Their voices faded, but the voice in my head, Savvy's, brushing off Olivia's question didn't. Shit, if everything about that still didn't sit wrong.

****

~Savvy~

Olivia turned around and grabbed a fat envelope off her desk, which she passed to me. "Here, I saw this and thought you'd love it."

The pink paper bulged between my fingers, thicker than just an envelope holding a letter. "You shouldn't have, Livia."

"Just open it already."

I tore open the delicate paper and a pair of hibiscus-shaped earrings, made from seashells, if I wasn't mistaken, laid within. "These are just gorgeous. Thank you!"

I unpinned the tiny diamond studs in my ears and replaced them with my favourite flowers, then kissed her on the cheek.

"I'm so glad you like them. I saw them at this lovely little boutique on the harbour and—"

"The harbour? Shut up! One of these days I'm coming home with you so we can hit the city shops together."

"That would be so nice, Savvy."

I threw myself onto her bed and watched Olivia move around the room with more grace than ever. She always seemed more refined after school breaks, as if she were taking more notice of how she moved. Her fingers moved over the paper laid out on her desk.

A peek over her shoulder revealed a huge calendar on the desk, already colour coded with several social events, hockey games, and term breaks. It looked like Olivia was facing another hectic year. The woes of being Ms Socialite. *Fancy dress courtyard party* covered one of the pink squares.

"What this?" I jabbed at the date three weeks from now.

"That's our first major function of the year. It's just a keg party in Front Courtyard, but we're dressing it up with a theme."

"Come on, girl. Give up the details. You know how much I love costume parties."

Olivia offered me a real smile, along with a pencil and notepad. "Occupations."

Squealing with delight, I snatched the stationery and started sketching a plan. Something fun, different, and just a little bit sexy. That was what I'd need to create the perfect costume.

"What are you wearing?"

"No idea. But Dane and Christian were talking bodyguard costumes."

She didn't talk much as she made the calendar look like a fluorescent bingo card. I didn't have a lot to say either, so when my sketch was complete, shopping list and all, I got up. The silence was a tad unusual for us, but I wasn't going to push her to talk about summer break if she didn't want to.

"Right, I suppose I'd better unpack. I'm in block L this year, mid floor. Swing over when you finish up here."

"Sure."

I bounded out of her room and down the stairs, then into a courtyard sprinkled with people. Waving to a group of fellow teaching students across the way, I felt pretty good inside—light—as if a weight had lifted off my shoulders since I'd left home this morning.

"Hey!" I yelled across the courtyard, my voice echoing off the brick walls that enclosed it.

"Savvy," someone shouted back. "Get over here!"

I ducked under the chain-link barrier and out onto the grass. Just as I stood up, my shoulder slammed into a rock-hard …

"Mother fu—"

Papers fluttered everywhere, but I straightened up, glancing into the same cool green stare I hadn't stopped thinking about for the past three weeks, even if I had pretended to totally ignore it just a half hour ago.

"Shit. Sorry, Sav." Dane's mouth curved around my name like he was happy it had passed his lips. Lies … all lies … The guy knew how to make a girl swoon.

"Dane." I fake smiled, scooping up my sketches.

"Now, now. Don't be like that."

"Like what?" I deadpanned.

"You know we're friends, right?"

I raised my eyebrow.

"You don't have *female* friends, Dane."

"Sure I do."

I went to move around him, but Dane's hands gripped my shoulders, holding me in place while his eyes searched mine. The connection was too much to handle, so I dropped my gaze, taking in his loose tank. The neck scooped so low the trail of his leather necklace led right to the stupid smattering of hair that peeked out the top of his shirt.

"We've been friends for a long time, and that night—"

"No." I held up my hand. "Please, just no."

He dropped his arms to his sides, sucking in his lips as if he knew he had no right to mention what had happened *back then*.

"Kasi," I shouted to the friend who'd waved me over earlier. "I missed you SO much."

I didn't look back as I shot across the courtyard, away from the only person at Oxley with whom I couldn't pretend.

"Get your arse over here, Savvy," Kasi called. "I've got so much to tell you."

CHAPTER FOUR

Savvy

Music pumped through Front Courtyard, bouncing off the walls so loudly it was near impossible to hold a conversation. They were the perfect party tunes to shimmy along to as I worked my way through the crowd, holding a plastic cup in my hand. It felt like my head—too light. Whatever they put in the stuff they called Go Gas sure was potent. I swallowed another mouthful of the sweet, strong liquid.

"Looking good," a low voice growled in my ear, and I spun around, facing my favourite ex-next-room neighbour.

"Dono, how are you?" Setting my empty glass on the ground, I threw my arms around his ample shoulders and pulled my friend in for a hug, as if I hadn't seen him just yesterday in the dining hall.

"Better now I've seen you."

Tossing him an eyebrow waggle, I said, "I bet that's what you tell all the gals and guys."

"Just you, baby, just you."

Looked like he'd decided cross-dressing was the name of the game for tonight's occupations theme. He had on a plaid school uniform, the fabric of the pinafore stretched taut across his round belly, while a wig, its ginger locks pulled into two braids, covered his short, spiked hair. I twirled one of the woollen braids around my index finger, but Dono was oblivious to my harmless flirting. The guy was as gay as a Fruit Loop, yet his gaze was fixed on one spot through the crowd, where the boob patrol surrounded Dane like a flock of seagulls chasing a lone chip.

My teaching classmate Kasi was there, giggling like the schoolgirl Dono had dressed as. Her hand rested on Dane's chest, and I'd bet she was copping a good feel through the tight button-down he had on. My fingers twitched to be in her place. I clamped them around my cup tighter. True to his word, Dane had dressed as a bodyguard, and it looked damn good on him. All black and white, his shirt was coupled with an honest-to-god suit and some kind of ear piece that connected to a tiny microphone at his mouth. That mouth moved with slow purpose, probably uttering just the right thing at just the right moment to keep the boob patrol's attention. He must have said something funny, because laughter surged through his little flock.

"Savannah!" The squeal pulled my attention away from the scene across the way and to Becca, who'd lived on our floor last year, too.

"Becca, bo-decca. How's my girl?" Dono tossed the leggy blonde a wink and smiled.

"Not bad. Love the dress, pretty boy!" She bent to kiss his cheek, then grabbed my hand. "I can't believe we haven't caught up yet. How was your summer? What did you get up to?"

"Pretty good," I answered. "I didn't do much really, just hung out at home."

"Good to see your parents?"

I shrugged, tamping down the pang in my chest as I flat-out lied. "Always."

"You've got a sister too, right? I bet you guys hit the beach together every day." She scanned the crowd. "Gee, I'd love to live on the coast."

"Yeah …" An image of Kody sprung to mind— parked in front of the TV all summer, watching reruns of *Glee*. "I miss the ocean when I'm here. Everything else though"—I swept an arm through the air, indicating I meant Oxley—"I miss when I'm at home."

"You're the sweetest," Becca said, as if it were a personal compliment.

"No, you are." I forced the last of my drink past the aching lump in my throat, and placed a hand on her elbow to move past. "But my bladder isn't. It's time to pee."

Edging my way around her, I tried not to stab anyone's feet with my pointed heels. Those shoes may have topped off my police costume perfectly, but gee they were deadly.

The crowd was extra thick tonight, so making it to the edge of the courtyard was hard work. Once I reached the fringe, my exit grew easier, and even though people had spilled over into Back Courtyard, I managed to make it upstairs to my floor and my own bathroom without anything more than a wave and hello as I trotted past.

I lingered up there longer than was absolutely necessary. Probably because the mention of home had brought a lump to my throat that I needed to get under control, pronto. I twisted the manufactured curls back into the ends of my hair using my fingers, then reapplied a fresh coat of cherry lipstick. My police cap had somehow twisted, so I repositioned it back into place too, slightly off centre.

Feeling more composed, I was ready to head back downstairs, but first I ducked into my room and checked my phone for messages. There were no pockets in the tiny black dress, and Aunt Rosy always went on about the danger of sticking a phone in one's bra. Too much radiation, or some such business, could cause breast cancer. It was probably just an urban myth.

No new messages or calls. Things sure were different to last year; it seemed that Miller kept Tori well occupied. I pulled the door closed behind me, glancing at its empty timber. The whiteboard alone wasn't much to look at. I really should get around to decorating that sometime. The blank canvas was so un-me. I scrawled my name across the top and added a few flowers to pretty it up. That'd do for now.

My heels clipped against the brown tiles as I descended the echoing staircase. The bass of the music thrummed, even from here. Happiness seeped into me from the beat, and I tapped my fingers against my thigh. There was nothing more grounding than a good courtyard party. I really did love being around these people.

"Sav-aaaaan-nah!"

Throwing an arm into the air, I waved at whoever lingered across the courtyard as I walked past. Stopping to mingle back here was just too far out of the fray.

"Come join the masses," I shouted back.

When I reached the edge of Front, the gathering grew mighty loud. No wonder they'd upped the music's volume. A crowd had assembled around one of the wooden picnic tables, and it looked like beer races were on. Christian Allan and Blaine Stratford stood up on the table, each chugging down giant yard glasses. I struggled to catch a glimpse through all the people, but after a bit of ducking to see through the gaps yup, sure enough, Flirty McFlirt Dane was there too. If Christian was playing drinking games, then his surfer sidekick was usually in on it, too. Dane held a glass stein he'd procured from god knew where, and despite his raucous talking and laughter, he was still the plaything of Kasi and co. If the well-practiced panty-dropping smile he tossed their way every minute or so was any indication, he looked to be loving every moment of their attention.

Glancing up at his mates, he said something to Christian, but one of the boob patrol used long fingers on his chin to force him to look at her. She said something sexy-looking and swayed just a little while Dane dropped a kiss on the corner of her mouth.

My stomach clenched.

By morning there'd be another notch in his renowned desk.

Heat flushed through my entire being as if it were

trying to cleanse the image from my eyeballs. Pity it was too late.

Then two things happened at the exact same moment.

"Savvy!" Dono shouted from the circle of keggers, and Dane glanced right at me, while his lips were still on Ms Boob's. Spinning around before my flushed face drew any attention, I fled the voices, Becca's earlier questions, and the courtyard. Walking at top speed until I reached the back parking lot, I dropped to the gutter, my legs no longer willing to fight against the vicious pang in my chest. I was stronger than this. I didn't let anything get to me. But something about tonight was different. Maybe it was the fact I'd been flitting around alone rather than with Olivia, or maybe it was Becca's questions, or it could have been that since the memories of the beach party had resurfaced, I couldn't shake the heavy cloud that hung over me.

"Hey, girl."

I closed my eyes at the deep cadence of Dane's voice. Why in the hell was he out here when his gaggle of girls was inside? A nudge on my shoulder shifted my weight slightly off centre. "Move over, princess."

I sucked in a breath of fresh country air. God, I missed the saltiness of home. I could almost … I sniffed at the air as he lowered himself onto the curved gutter beside me … yep, it was mingled with the tang of beer, but I could smell it. How in the hell he managed to smell like the beach this far away from it was beyond me.

That scent made my stomach wriggle all too enticingly.

"What is it, Dane?"

He stretched his long legs out in front of him and leaned back, just like he had that night of the bonfire. His answer was so long in coming, I thought he wasn't going to say anything at all, but finally he broke the silence. "Talk to me."

He couldn't be serious. What did he want me to say? There was a plethora of things I could say to him, but nothing I'd ever actually utter aloud, let alone in his presence. Tamping down all the mixed emotions being around Dane caused, I pulled on my bubbly persona. "What are you doing out here? The party's inside."

"I want you to talk to me." He shoulder-bumped my arm. "What's bothering you?"

God, he was persistent.

"Nothing."

We sat in silence for several moments, just the sound of his even breaths between us, while the party buzzed in the distance. His feet tapped against one another to the beat of the fading music. The scuffed Converse he wore were out of place with the rest of his costume. I swear he'd been wearing those same shoes since high school.

"Couldn't give up the Cons, huh?"

Dane uncrossed his feet. "They're black. They work."

I closed my eyes and drew in a deep breath. It wasn't like I hadn't seen him sleazing it up before, or like I hadn't seen him kiss the same girl over and over again. Nor was it like I hadn't lied to myself before either. I'd had definite feelings for Dane Beaumont for years, no matter how hard I tried to ignore them.

"I'm serious about us being friends again." He

dropped an arm around my shoulders, the tang of beer noticeable on his breath with his nearness. "I'm here for you, Savvy. You don't have to be strong all the time, you know. Life sucks, and it's okay to let it all out once in a while. Hell knows you should, after what you've been through."

My dumbarse throat swelled, my tongue forgot how to work, and oh my god, was I sniffling? Bringing my knees up and wrapping my arms around them, I mumbled, "I know."

"I don't think you do know. I don't think you know how to drop that damn wall you've built around yourself for long enough to let anyone ..." He groaned.

"Let anyone what?"

Dane sighed, pulling me against him. "Let anyone in."

"I have friends—"

"And your so-called best friend has no idea about your folks. Let me in, Savvy."

I pushed out of the warmth of his arm, and my dumbarse heart protested at the necessary distance I placed between us. "You don't want in, Dane. You barely said two words to me last year."

"Because after that night—"

"We're not talking about it."

"Damn it, Savannah, you need to talk about it sometime." His voice rose, and as boozy as Dane sounded, it carried more conviction than I cared to hear. "You don't talk to Olivia about it. What about Victoria? Anyone?"

Footsteps approached from behind us, and my heart jumped into my throat. "Keep your damn voice down," I growled.

A confused look rippled over his features, but I wasn't about to explain that my life here at Oxley was a precious bubble that excluded my past.

"Not bothering this girl are you, Beauy?" Sarcasm dripped off the guy's tone.

Everyone knew girls liked being bothered by Dane, but I wasn't the typical Oxley girl. I was aware of his ways. Not that he was trying them out on me.

Dane staggered upright, his hand held out, which the other guy grasped. Placing his free hand on the dude's forearm, Dane said, "Good to see you tonight, mate. It's been far too long."

I didn't recognise him, but I knew everyone at Oxley, even the newest flush of first years who'd only been living here for three weeks. He must have been from off campus.

The guy's gaze briefly slipped to me, then he gave Dane a smile. "You know where I live; come 'round sometime."

Dane offered his mate a lazy smile. "All right."

Resting my forehead on my knees, I listened to the hum of the music, all the while ignoring the voice in the back of my head that said I *should* talk to Dane. He'd been there that night, after all, but then I feared that kind of heart-to-heart would only make us closer, and I wasn't sure how much pushing away *my* heart could take.

"Walk with me, Sav."

Raising my head to a hand two inches from my face, I had no idea how to take this boy. Surely this wasn't one of his games; he didn't just want to add me to a list of conquests. Surely he was seriously offering friendship.

Shut up, brain.

Why did I have to complicate everything with stupid thoughts? Dane was a good guy; I knew him … and the way he was now at Oxley wasn't how he'd always been.

I placed my hand in his, and Dane pulled me to my feet and turned back toward the residency hall. "I'm starving. Let's eat."

I groaned as he walked down the path, tugging me along behind him. "Of course you are. Got the drunken munchies?"

"I'm not drunk." He hiccupped. Obnoxiously loud, it was clearly fake.

We both chuckled. Dane dropped my hand and continued through the gates and into Oxley. At this time of the night, the dining hall would be closed, so he must have a stash of food somewhere. My stomach grumbled at the thought. This was the second year I'd lived in this residency hall, and as we walked through Back Courtyard, I felt almost at home. I'd always loved being here, but home was an empty house back in Coffs. A place I hadn't lived in for over two years and would never live in again. Not where I'd resided the past year—not this dorm swarming with people who didn't really know me. Something felt different tonight, though.

Dane led the way around the fringe of the still pumping party and up into block B, which was where he'd lived last year. It must have been where he was again. We trudged up the stairs all the way to the top floor, and he veered toward the mini kitchen. Turned out Dane's floor was one of the lucky ones that sported a kitchen stocked with all kinds of appliances. But it wasn't the pie oven, the microwave, or the espresso machine he reached for. It was the electric kettle he flicked on. He reached up to a shelf high on the wall and extracted a Styrofoam cup of two-minute noodles.

It felt a little weird being up here in his space, where he hung out and slept and showered. It was almost too intimate. I couldn't help but glance over my shoulder at the empty hallway.

"Where are you living this year?" Dane spoke over the boiling kettle.

"L, facing into the courtyard. It seems like a decent floor."

"Cool." He peeled back the lid and poured steaming water into the bowl of noodles. He grabbed two forks, and his chest rubbed against my arm as he shuffled past me. Dane swaggered to the very end of the hall, where he kicked open a door without so much as pushing a key into the lock. *Well, that was secure.*

"C'mon." He tipped his head toward the entrance.

With butterflies weakening my knees, I walked along the hall, my gaze set on the light shining out of the open door. Sucking in a deep breath didn't settle anything down; if anything, my head lightened, as if I were about to float away.

How ridiculous.

I walked into the room to the view of his holy hotness sitting on the desk, one leg balanced on the seat of his chair, his noodle-holding hand resting atop. His jacket lay across the bed, discarded, showing off a skin-tight white tee that didn't leave a single contour of his toned chest to the imagination. The earpiece was still in place, though he'd swung the mouthpiece down, out of the way. Not knowing where to sit, I stood in the doorway while he poked at the food with a fork.

Dragging the fork through his cup, Dane scooped up a heap of noodles and held them in the air over the container, watching the steam rise.

"So," he said, "let's talk."

My gaze slipped to the open door behind me.

He placed the noodles and forks on the desk, and grabbing my wrist, towed me forward, kicking the door closed so hard it banged against the frame.

"People will talk."

Dane smirked at me as he moved with arrogant laziness back to his perch on the desk.

"Sav, who cares? Everyone knows ninety per cent of gossip isn't true anyway." He grabbed a bowl from the corner of his shelf and dished noodles into it. "Besides ... you've had your fair share of hook-ups."

"What? No I haven't." My voice sounded a little screechy, but nipping that in the bud, I said, "I hooked up with two guys last year, Dane Beaumont, and that has nothing on your catch of ..." I eyed the desk which OMG, *was* notched! "Many."

His gaze followed mine, and he chuckled. Walking across the room, he passed me the bowl from which a fork protruded, and picked up the cup for himself.

I wasn't quite sure what to say, so I ate quietly while sneaking glances at Dane, shovelling steaming noodles away like no man's business. His hook-ups comment wasn't all wrong. I'd made out with a couple of different guys last year, but that chemical zing which made it fun had always been lacking.

Looking down at my bowl, only a few odd strands lingered in the bottom.

"How's Dakota?"

My fork stopped halfway to my mouth at the

mention of Kody. Swallowing my surprise, I pulled together an answer. "It's a huge adjustment, and she has her moments, but mostly she's okay. Well, as okay as okay gets."

"And you?"

Building tears stung my eyes. No warning, just bam and there they were, along with an aching throat. I dropped onto the edge of the bed, my stupidly high shoes falling off my feet. The tears didn't come, but gee, it felt as if they would.

Warmth settled over my shoulders and a hand cradled my head, and sitting there in Dane's room, my walls burst. The emotion I'd been suppressing since *that* night all washed out at once like a flash flood. The sadness, the devastation, the way my life had changed—it was more than I could coherently think about, so I thought of nothing and just felt. In his arms it was easy, like I was less alone. Like for that instant I didn't have to hold it together, and not managing didn't matter. Dane held me tight against his chest, my cheek pressed against his firm body, so much like another night so long ago.

"I'm okay," I croaked out.

His hand on the side of my head lifted then resettled, smoothing back my hair with gentle strokes. I inhaled his scent, the beachy goodness that was just like home. Like the place I'd lived with my family, overlooking the ocean from high up on the hill.

My eyes fell closed, and leaning against him, my body relaxed. More tired than I'd been in an awfully long time, I melted into Dane, taking comfort in his nearness.

After a while Dane's breathing evened out, as if he were growing sleepy. I lifted his arm from around me, and he fell onto the bed, rolling onto his side. He could have been awake or asleep; I wasn't really sure. He'd had a pretty boozy night.

I scooped my shoes off the floor and hooked them over two fingers, then with my other hand I reached for the door, but my arm caught a snag.

His hand grasping my elbow, Dane peeked up at me out of one eye. "Friends?"

"Friends."

I exited his room, pulling the door closed behind me, and as I did so, a small group of girls peered up at me from where they sat in the hall, their backs against the cement wall. I offered what I hoped passed for a friendly smile, and slipped down the stairs. Why did he make it so hard not to fall for him?

CHAPTER FIVE

Savvy

Other than running into Dane on the way to the dining hall the next night, I hadn't seen him around. Oxley was always bubbling with life, and he was usually at its centre, but he was conspicuously absent all day Sunday and on Monday morning, too. He wasn't the only one. Olivia had been god knew where, no doubt hiding from the world after the ugly fight her and Christian-the-jerk had apparently had on Saturday night; I hadn't been able to get a hold of her for two days now, not by phone, nor email, nor by bashing her door down. My entire world felt a little out of whack. At least Tori had called me, though.

Dragging the teensy brush over my thumbnail, I cradled the phone between my shoulder and cheek for the second time in as many days. "Ah-huh."

"It just wasn't working. He was super sweet and seemed into me, but then it just kind of waned off. Like once he'd gotten laid that was it; he lost interest."

"Gah. I swear that's all boys ever think about."

"Boys ..." Tori echoed. "He wasn't a man after all. Sleazebag."

It must have been the week for man troubles. At least Tori didn't sound upset. That was something.

"Why is it so hard to find a nice guy? There hasn't been a single genuine guy that I've really connected with since Dane."

She sighed and I swiped the brush over another nail, leaving a pretty deep red—Shining Crimson, according to the label on the bottle. Holding my hand against my boots confirmed the colour was a perfect match.

"Speaking of sleazebags," Tori said, "have you met any Pinocchios lately?"

"Nope."

"Whoa, quick answer. Not a Pinocchio then, but a real man?"

A laugh burst from me. I hadn't so much as looked a guy up and down since returning from summer break, unless I counted Da— "Not unless you count Dono."

"Savvy, I haven't even met the guy and I know you've got too many girly parts to be his type."

I glanced at my watch—nine-o-eight. Education Studies started at nine-thirty, and this conversation needed killing. Real man or not, Dane wasn't for me. "Shut up. Dono loves my girly parts. Cuz, I've got to go. Talk to you soon?"

"Always."

"Perfect. Love you."

I hit *end call* and, careful not to bump my freshly painted nails, slung my messenger bag over a shoulder and since today was a little cool shrugged into my red coat. This year's classes were already looking a little more trying than the ones I'd taken last year, but all of the info on education was rather interesting. It seemed new age compared to the work experience I'd done in grade ten with Mum. That was a lifetime ago. Sighing, I jogged down the stairs and into Back Courtyard, then out to the parking lot and onto Elm Avenue.

I'd always enjoyed the uphill walk to campus. It was a pleasant stroll along the winding footpath, with views of the town sprawled below and the huge shade trees overhead. I glanced toward the bus shelter at the bottom of the street, and I'd be damned if it wasn't Olivia, standing there with her arms wrapped around herself as she studied the road as if the bus was twenty minutes late.

Thank god, she was out of hibernation.

"Livia!"

Her attention swung my way, and I waved. After a quick glance in either direction, I ran across the road to give her a hug. There was no doubt that she'd need it after the fight she'd had with Christian. I threw my arms around her shoulders and squeezed extra tight. Those types of hugs were so comforting. I could still feel the one Dane had given me only two days ago. Heat rushed to my face, and I buried it in Olivia's shoulder.

"Where have you been? I've called by a dozen times and you never answer, then you're not at meals either, or answering emails. I've been worried about you, and I'm so sorry about Christian."

She held on to me. "It's been weird. Everyone's been weird." Her voice sounded a little tight, poor soul. I pushed her back so I could get a good look at her and boy, the girl had breakup written all over her pretty face. Dressed in jeans and a baggy sweater, with a completely nude face, she wasn't Olivia at all. This whole look was not the best way to approach their epic fight. It practically pinned a sign on her forehead that said *beware, broken heart*. I felt for her, I really did, but she needed to smarten up, show Christian what he was in peril of losing, and I was just the friend to help.

"You look terrible. Where's all your style ... and your ... your makeup?"

Liv glanced at the approaching bus. "That's me. I've got to go, but I need to talk to you. Tonight?"

"I've gotta talk to you, too."

And that was the truth. I needed to pull her out of this funk. There were far better fish in the sea than Christian Allan. Guys who would treat her right, because Liv, she was one of those rare kinds of people that were pure goodness. She was so damn giving, and she deserved that in return. She deserved someone who'd love and cherish her, treat her like a queen. And Christian had never fit the bill.

She climbed on the bus and walked down the aisle, then slumped into a seat, looking miserable. I thwacked the window, and when I had her attention shook my head. Olivia was worth ten Christians. We'd fix this tonight; I'd pull her out of this and make her remember just how amazing she was.

As the bus pulled away and rumbled off into the distance, I resumed my walk. No point in crossing back over the road as there was a path on this side too, and it was probably nicer, with more of those leafy elms overhead.

'Savannah." I turned to see who'd called me, and Kasi jogged up the footpath. "Wait up."

I stopped in the middle of the path until she caught up, then started walking again.

"So, is it true?" she asked. I shrugged. God knew what she was talking about. "Did you hook up with Dane on Saturday night?"

"No." I cast her a sideways glance.

She looked right back at me. "You're lying, and I'm jealous as anything."

I shook my head. As much as I'd like to tap some of his epic hotness, there was no way I'd ever act on it, let alone admit it. The sisterhood was stronger than that.

"Yes!" Was she trying to convince me or herself? "It's true. You did shuffle out of his room in the middle of the night."

"What? It was not the middle of the night, and I was not shuffling. And hell, I didn't sleep with anyone."

My pulse rose, thumping in my ears. My red boots pounded the pavement with force. I'd known locking myself in a room with McFlirt would lead to this, and yet I'd still let it happen. No one to blame but myself.

Kasi dropped it after, that and the conversation turned toward class, not that I paid much attention. My thoughts were too focused on the *what ifs*. What if I hadn't gone up to his room? What if we hadn't had that conversation? What if I had hooked up with him?

We somehow reached the education building in record time, and as I slid into my seat, Kasi smirked, as if she'd confirmed the stupid rumour. A sinking feeling settled in my stomach.

What if Tori heard that I'd hooked up with the guy she'd thought would be her forever?

****

I climbed the stairs to block K and rapped on Olivia's door, waited three seconds and knocked again. Only silence greeted me along with the unmoving wood. "Livia," I spoke loud enough that she'd hear through the thick timber. "I know you're there."

An even harder knock still resulted in nothing. Surely once she heard my voice she'd open up, since she wanted to talk. I waited another minute, glanced down the empty hall, then tapped a third time.

"Olivia Dean, it's dinnertime."

It was like a minute's silence on Remembrance Day; the hall was so quiet.

Either she'd had second thoughts about talking, or she'd headed to the dining hall already, even though it was only five-thirty. I gave the door a lingering look, then headed back to the stairs. There was no sign of her in the courtyard either, so I ducked into the dining hall, where a few people had already claimed their evening meal. It was peopled sparsely enough that I didn't even need to scan the tables to know she wasn't there. But he was.

Dane smiled at me from where he sat on his lonesome. It was that panty-dropping smile that made my tummy flip. Flip upside down, inside out, and back the front. Eating wouldn't be such a bad idea, since I was already here and all, so I shuffled through the servery, settling for a plate heaped with steamed vegetables. After grabbing cutlery, I made my way to Dane, who grinned up at me as I set my plate on the table.

Checking out the Quicksilver tank that showed off his impressive arms, I said, "Heya."

Dane continued smiling. "Hi, pretty girl. How are you doin'?"

"Not, bad. Do you want a top up?" I nodded toward his empty glass.

"Please."

I grabbed his glass from the table then hit the drink machines, where I topped up his cordial and filled another glass with chilled water for myself. When I turned around to head back, two of the bustiest members of the boob patrol sat on either side of Dane. I swear if Ella Parry's shirt were open any farther, her girls would have fallen right out and into his face.

I slid our glasses onto the table and took a seat behind my plate of veggies, right opposite my friend. Dane spared me a quick glance then returned his attention to Ella, who had vomited a string of questions I didn't care to pay attention to. No way was I buying into her games, so I picked up my fork and speared a carrot.

"What are you doing later?" Dane asked.

I was used to ignoring McFlirt's displays from a distance; up close it was impossible to block out, even with focusing every iota of my attention on my plate. I stabbed a piece of broccoli and shoved it in my mouth, taking the slowest, most thought about chew. This was what people did. They flirted, they picked up, and they wound up in bed together. The broccoli lodged in my throat on the way down. I reached for my water.

"Savvy, what's happening?" Dane asked.

"Me?"

"Who else?" Ella mumbled. She may have been an old friend of Olivia's, but boy did she set my radar off … There was just something about the haughty way she held herself, and the snide comments she uttered when she thought no one was listening.

"You okay?" Dane said.

"Dandy."

"Then what are you doing tonight?"

Shit, that question was directed at me? I shrugged, playing it easy. "I need to catch up with a few people."

Ella's head snapped my way, no doubt hoping for a scrap of gossip, but no way in hell was I about to divulge a single thing.

"I was hoping you'd catch up with me." Dane winked, and by god, my fluttering heart needed to be still.

"What's on offer?" I asked. "It'll need to be good."

His smile turned sultry as he leaned across the table, stopping right in my space. "It'll be better than good. It'll be fucking awesome."

The dumb flips moved to my heart. Ignoring them, I said, "Game on."

Dane slumped back in his seat, his arms spread across the chair beside him. Ella must have thought that was all right, because she leaned back so far it looked as if his arm were around her. But Dane? He just pushed his plate aside without even turning to face her, and said, "Later ladies."

"Yeah, later," Ella answered.

Then the king of smooth tossed a wink my way and pushed his chair back to stand up. "Let's roll."

"Let's," I answered, suppressing my shit-eating grin. This display would only make people talk more, but it was hard to care when I'd just won out over Ella Parry.

Once we were outside, I turned to Dane. "Okay, spill."

A sound somewhat like a chuckle on steroids spewed out of him. "I'm playing cards with the boys. Wanna come with?"

A quick glance at my watch revealed it was only six o'clock. "I wish I could, but there's something else …"

"Are you ditching me, Savvy?"

"You say that like it's never been done before."

He shook his head, an amused smirk on his lips as he sauntered away in that lazy rolling gait of his that oozed confidence. The guy sure knew how to move; it was like watching a celebrity on the red carpet. Dragging my attention away, I shot around the back way to block K, scaled the stairs again, and rapped on Olivia's door.

Still nothing.

Where had she gone? If she wasn't in her room, at the dining hall, or chatting in the courtyard … It was Tuesday and not a hockey day, so where else could she be? The library maybe. It wouldn't be the first time Olivia had stayed on campus late.

Returning to the courtyard, I doubled back to my room in case we'd crossed paths, only she wasn't there either. Flicking a quick text her way produced the same radio silence as knocking on her door had.

I fluffed out the brand new flowers I'd tacked to

my door earlier that day, and a thought struck me.

Surely she hadn't. She wouldn't. From what I'd heard from Dono it had been an epic fight, and right there in the middle of the courtyard party, but she'd been with Christian for more than a year, so maybe …

It was worth a shot. About facing, I strode to the staircase and this time, instead of heading down, I went up. The door to Christian's room stood wide open, filtered light splayed across the dim hallway, and the noise. Holy heartbeat, the noise spilling out of the room sounded like a party turned nasty. No way was Olivia in there. Curiosity had the best of me though, so I continued along and peeked inside.

Half a dozen guys were sprawled on the floor in a circle, all hollering to be heard over one another as they laughed, shouted, and threw down cards.

Well hello, I'd found Dane's game.

"Trumped! Ha ha you're all mine." Laughing, Christian slapped a handful of cards into the centre of the ring, face up.

Dane groaned, and he wasn't the only one. Dragging a hand through his sandy mop, he glanced up and caught me watching. "Savvy! Just who I need. Come park your sweet arse right here. I could use some help."

I should have said no. I should have kept looking for Olivia, but when it came to Dane Beaumont, I was a complete sucker, so I picked a path across to him and sat in the only free space; jammed between his warm body and the cold wall. Tilting my head allowed a good view of his cards. Goosebumps broke out along my shoulder, from the cool concrete wall or his skin burning against my bare arm, I couldn't be sure.

I shuffled in a little closer to escape the freezing wall. "Let's whoop some arse."

"Atta girl." Dane slung an arm over my shoulder, guiding my attention toward the fresh hand of cards he'd just scooped up. It was just his arm, but it weighed as much as a ten-ton car. The spot where his elbow hooked around my neck prickled with glee. With each second, I waited, tensed, for his side to bump against me. "This here ..." Dane pointed to a pair of jacks fanned in his hand, "... is a good start. Now what we need is ..." he tilted his head so it almost touched mine, and lowered his deep voice, "... is either the other two of those or three of something else, preferably picture cards."

"Got it."

We won that hand and the one after, by a landslide. I think we were working with Blaine as a team, because the other guy slammed his cards down and shouted, "Five hundred, suckers."

He and Dane fist-bumped mid air, then laughing again, Dane smacked a kiss right on my mouth.

One of the guys hollered. "Must've been good if you're gonna tap that again, Beauy."

"Twice the charm, huh?" echoed Blaine.

"Maybe she's—"

"*She* is right here," Dane growled. "Show some goddamn respect."

Unable to form my mouth around a comeback, I was too gobsmacked to react. He ... he hadn't set them straight about Saturday night. Dane glowered at the cards, his jaw clenched in a way that made a pulse jump in his cheek.

Everyone laughed, but then *bam*.

A fire blanket of silence smothered the room.

Half the guys studied the floor, while the rest stared at the door. It was a pretty big room, one of the hugest in Oxley, but from where I sat I couldn't see what the big deal was. I leaned around Dane, and oh shit … the look on Olivia's face as she stood in the doorway said it all. She was pissed. More pissed than I had been a moment ago when Dane had let them all believe we'd had sex. Olivia's arms were like a barrier to her heart, crossed tightly over her boobs while she glared at Christian. "We need to talk, and don't give me any of that 'not now' crap. It's happening. Now."

Well, that made everyone shift uncomfortably. I shouldn't be here. I should have kept searching until I found her. What a traitor. Leaning forward, I shifted my foot underneath me to rise.

"Dude, I think you better talk to her," he said to Christian, then Dane climbed to his feet and tossed his cards to the floor. He reached back and grabbed my hand. Confused at first, I wasn't sure what he was doing, but he tugged me to my feet, and as the room emptied out, he steered me toward the door.

I needed to check Liv was okay though, needed to make sure she was right to be alone with Christian. I paused as we got closer to her, but Olivia's gaze never left her boyfriend Dane tugged on my hand.

"Liv …" My voice sounded weak.

She barely spared me a glimpse—the look on her face pure war. Now was not the time to check on my friend; she needed to have this out with Christian. As I slipped past her, I mouthed, *I'm sorry*.

Christian groaned. "I'm sorry about Saturday night. It shouldn't have gone down like that. I was—"

"Drunk, Christian. But you weren't that drunk," Olivia said.

"Yeah, I was …"

Now out in the hall, I spun around, my sights set on the jerk who hadn't defended my virtue. Not that I cared about virtue, but still. What if the rumour somehow reached Tori? Things like this always travelled far and wide and she was the only one from home who was on my Facebook friends list. Two steps ahead of me, Dane was almost at the stairwell.

"Dane Beaumont," I called.

Half turning, he looked back at me over his shoulder, that stupid flirty smile in place. "Savannah West?"

"What the hell was that all about?"

His foot dropped onto the first step, then stopped. "What all about?"

"Letting them all think we hooked up."

"Oh." He jogged down a few stairs and grinned back at me.

"Are you for real?" I demanded, my feet thudding against the tiles.

By now he'd reached the landing, and framed by the entrance to my floor, he shrugged, smile still in place. He either thought this was a joke, or got off on big-noting in front of his mates. I reached the landing and strode right past him, down the hall.

"Come on, Savvy," he called behind me.

I didn't stop until I reached my room, where I jammed the key into the lock. Tori was more than just my cousin, she was like a sister, and the past her and Dane shared meant that I could never be with him. In rumour or otherwise.

"What if I didn't set them straight because I wish

it was true?"

I froze, a second from opening my door. "Drop the charm, McFlirt. We're friends. Not friends with benefits and that's how it's staying."

He'd followed me, and now, standing in front of my room, I could feel him right behind me, hovering far too close. So close that the back of my neck broke out in a cold sweat.

If I thought I'd frozen before, now I didn't even draw breath. His arm slid past me, nearly touching my shoulder, but not quite, as he grasped the handle and pushed my door open. There was something about the air as I finally dragged it in—thick, as if I were in the tropics.

I stepped back, putting some distance between us so I could think straight. Only Dane cocked that panty-dropping smile, evaporating any chance of rational thought.

"Goodnight, Dane." I closed the door before I did something stupid, like kissed the boy my cousin once thought she might marry.

CHAPTER SIX

Dane

"Run. Run. Run!" Logan jumped to his feet, fist punching the air. "And SCORE!"

Cheers erupted around us. For an interschool's comp, this game sure was tight. With ten minutes left in play, Jordan's team held the lead by only one point. Both teams had been neck and neck the entire game, with Logan's little brother a star player. The kid was damn good. Not that I knew a whole lot about rugby, but he sure could run like the wind, and that seemed to be keeping his team on point.

"Did you see that?" Logan fell back onto the grass beside me. "He grabbed the ball right out from under that winger. Did you see it?"

My mouth kicked up at his enthusiasm. "Kid's sure got game."

Scores of spectators surrounded the field, most of them high schoolers here to support their teams. Even though I wasn't a student spectator now, it felt like a lifetime ago I'd worn a school uniform and watched home games just to get off class.

My phone vibrated in my pocket. I fished it out. *Mum.*

"Hey," I answered.

"Hi, sweetie. You called me."

"I just rang to check in, see how everything's going with you and the old man."

Another cheer surged through the crowd, people jumping to their toes for the last minutes of the game. One of our guys tossed the ball and Jordan caught it on the full, running down the sideline to the thunder of *run, Haysie, run.*

Mum sighed down the phone. "How's everything with you? There's a lot of noise in the background."

"I'm at a footy match with Logan."

"That sounds lovely."

"It's good to have him back in town." I glanced at my friend, his face flushed with excitement. "Shop doing all right without me there to stop Pa giving shit away for free?"

A long pause. "The shop's just fine, honey."

"Glad to hear it. You keep him in line, okay?"

Her voice cracked. "Always. Now, you go and enjoy the game. I love you, Dane."

"Love you too, Ma." I ended the call and slid my phone away just as the crowd erupted again. Seemed Logan's enthusiasm was catching. The ref blew his whistle for time and my mate fell to the ground again, shooting me a strange look as he got comfortable. "Everything okay back home?"

"Yeah. Mum likes to talk every couple of days."

"You've got a good family there, bro."

I smiled. I really was lucky, unlike my mate. Logan had copped the raw end when they were dishing out parents. With not one, but two suck-worthy no-hopers, he was a real credit to himself. "Ain't that the truth. Business seems to be taking off, which is nice."

"Yeah? The shop looks good?"

"It's nice to see him doing what he loves. But shit, the old man wants me to turn wood." I chuckled.

"What's so bad about that? It's great he's keen to have company."

When he put it like that, maybe the old man really did need me around … Still, it wasn't the thing for me. "Not on your life, dude. I'm all about the business end of things. Once I've got this degree, I'll try get a job close by so I can help him out some, but not in the workshop."

Seemed the game must have ended, because Logan's attention swung back to the field, where Jordan jogged toward us, chugging down water from a plastic bottle.

"Nice game, Bro," Logan yelled.

The kid pulled up right in front, his chest heaving against his sweaty jersey. "Sure was a tough one."

"You pulled through though. Held that team up on your own."

"I dunno about that." Jordan flicked dark curls off his face. "More like the team held me up. Couldn't have made that last run without Jacko's pass."

One of the other players called out Jordan's name from centrefield and he yelled back, "All right, all right." He extended a hand, which I shook. "Thanks for coming."

"No worries."

"And me ..." Logan grinned. "I came too."

"You're always here, but you too."

While the younger Hays brother jogged back to his team, Logan gathered our rubbish and we walked off toward where we'd left the cars. "He needs to play in the town comp. I reckon they'd bump him up to first grade."

"Doubt it. He's only seventeen."

"Doesn't matter. He's good enough to play with the pros."

It was nice to see Logan so damn proud. After the year he and his brother had just lived through, they both needed some good shit to fly their way.

We reached the side street out by the school, where we'd each managed to nab a park, and Logan stopped by his red Corolla, leaning against the door. It looked like he wanted to say something heavy, because he just stared for a moment, but then his blue eyes lightened in a dead giveaway that this was about something simpler.

"Olivia Dean ..."

Well, I'll be damned. Wonder how he met her. "Is not the type of chick you take home for a roll in your huge bed then toss out before sunrise."

"You know her then?"

"She just bailed from a long-term thing with Christian."

Logan opened the door and leaned against his car, his brows drawn. "That's the bloke I met at the courtyard party?"

"Yeah."

He started up the engine and I thumped on the roof by way of goodbye.

"See you later, mate," he said with a parting chin tip.

I scooted around to climb in the Outlander. So, he was keen on Liv … She didn't fit his usual easy-to-screw type, but then it'd been more than a year since he'd played pilot to my wingman. Maybe things with him were different now. But hell, what was it with that chick? First Christian, now Logan. At least Logan wouldn't screw her over. He was a good bloke. Christian, on the other hand, needed his arse kicked.

Thinking of Olivia filled my mind with thoughts of Savvy, and she stayed there, taking up prime real estate for the remainder of my drive back to Oxley. Damn, flirting with her was too fun. We'd talked about a lot of shit recently, but the way she'd shut down on Tuesday night just when I'd been sure she was going to let me in … hopefully I hadn't overstepped the boundaries when I'd followed her to her room after cards. I might have made a promise to myself that I'd look out for her when she turned up at Oxley last year all alone, but that wasn't the only reason I was worried. She'd been my friend, too, and still was.

I pulled into my usual parking space and locked up, then made the trek inside. Fidgeting with the keys in the pocket of my pants, I walked through the courtyard. For a late Thursday afternoon, it was damn quiet. Only the usual suspects hung around, those just back from classes or sports. There was no sign of Savvy. She usually lingered, chatting with whoever was around when she got back from school. Yet, she'd been absent since the night of 500. It wasn't like I'd been specifically looking for her, but I hadn't been *not* looking, either. And Savvy was one of those people you couldn't help but notice, so when she wasn't around for two days it was obvious.

Not ready to hit the books, I went to the common room to see if anyone was about and sure enough, the boys were shooting a game of pool. Christian leaned over the velvet, cue all lined up to sink the last ball on the table while Cade, the fresher who lived on his floor, propped his weight against the other cue.

"Beauy." Cade pointed a gun finger my way.

"Cade." I mimicked his gesture. "I'm up next."

Neither of them answered; Christian was still eying up the perfect shot in one hit. Other than my mates, the common room was almost empty. Not silent, though; the TV blared with some stupid home-grown drama.

"You see Olivia up top today?" Christian smacked the cue into the ball.

"From a distance. You two make up?"

He scoffed out a laugh.

"Mate, that damn rumour flying around about her … not cool."

"Hey ..." He leaned his cue against the wall and started retrieving balls from the end pockets. "I was smashed and talking out of my arse." He didn't look that remorseful as his grinning gaze snapped to mine. "Speaking of chicks, what's this I hear about you and the blonde pocket rocket?"

This time I laughed and looking around the common room for a potential pool partner, caught on Savvy's friend watching us instead of the communal TV. "Hey, Dono, I need someone to help me wipe the table with these losers. You in?"

"I'm your man." The big guy pushed out of the lounge and sized up the table, which was now set to start a new game. "We breaking?"

"Go ahead," Christian offered with the plastic triangle, then placed it back on the wall rack. Cade passed Dono his cue and shuffling his bulk into place. Dono took aim behind the triangle of balls and slammed the chalky tip into them. Straightening up, he flipped the cue my way.

"I wouldn't mind taking the rocket for a spin," Cade said.

The wooden stick slipped through my fingers and bounced off the carpet.

"Who the hell is the blonde rocket?" Dono asked, watching my fumbling fingers.

Cade opened his mouth.

"Some fine piece of arse these losers think is up for grabs." I plucked the cue from the floor.

"Well, is she?" Christian smirked.

"Yeah, is she free game?" Cade asked. "'Cause I'd sure as hell like to tap that."

"Sure she is. Not like I'm about to let a bird tie me down." I threw in a laugh.

Sure, I liked Savvy. She was a decent chick, and 'pocket rocket' wasn't a stretch at all. She was plenty short and fiery. I'd been attracted to her for longer than I could remember, and she'd been pushing me away the whole time. But damn, I was growing tired of staying in my place. I'd thought it might be different when she followed me to Oxley, but no. After being shot down the first time I'd seen her here last year, I'd kept my distance. She wouldn't even let me within her massive circle of friends, but screw it. Maybe it was time to stop playing games.

CHAPTER SEVEN

Savvy

Dakota isn't well.

Those three words got me on a bus and out of Oxley quick smart. When Aunt Rosy's message arrived on Wednesday morning, it only took a few phone calls, some reshuffling of my schedule and half a day before I was home. Pity I could only stay the one night.

I pushed dinner around my bowl. Aunt Rosy was a pretty fine cook, but her fried rice was not designed to be eaten with chopsticks, no matter how authentic she thought it made the meal. There just wasn't enough glug to keep the tiny grains on the sticks.

Uncle Trevor set his chopsticks on the edge of his bowl. "How was school today?"

I glanced across the table at my sister, who didn't

seem to have the same utensil issues. With one hand cradling her bowl under her chin, she expertly shovelled the rice into her mouth.

"Dakota?"

Her shoulders rose and fell, and I just about choked. No one ignored my uncle, ever. He continued watching her, and Aunt Rosy shook her head so minutely I doubt anyone else noticed. "Sister Mary called."

That raised Kody's blue eyes to the conversation.

"Skipping class isn't responsible—"

"I don't care," Kody growled.

"Disrespect will not be tolerated, Dakota." Uncle Trevor levelled a glare over the rim of his glasses and Kody pushed off the table, leaving while we all watched. Red rose in Trevor's cheeks, Tori shoved food in her mouth as if nothing had happened, and I tried to make sense of it all. Kody was one of the innately good kids. Always had been. This behaviour was more out of character than Olivia turning hermit. Mind you, I'd been home for a day, and nothing Kody had done had been like her. She was shouting, yelling, cutting class. Heading back to Oxley tonight would be hard, especially when I'd made no ground. Leaving her like this ... it hurt.

Aunt Rosy pushed her plate aside. This must have been what she meant by not well. "She's just so upset, but she won't talk. At least not properly."

Tori caught my attention with an eye roll, but her mother was right. Whatever was going on with my little sister needed attention. Excusing myself, I pushed back out of my chair and reached the living room just as the first angry notes belted out of the baby grand. I didn't approach Kody, but rather flopped on the couch, pulling my feet up beneath me. It didn't matter how my sister played, it always sounded professional. Soft and gentle, hard and loud, happy, fast and upbeat—every song that seeped out of her talented fingers sounded as if it was being played just as it should. Right then the tone was angry, the notes short, sharp, and shrill. Her head swung with the movement of her hands, her entire torso thrown behind the notes she played. Whatever was upsetting her, it seemed to be pouring out of her fingertips.

The music ended as abruptly as it had begun, and Kody pushed loose blonde locks back into her hand, holding the hair off the back of her neck.

I wet my lips, trying to find the right words. "Life sucks, huh?"

Her hand dropped. Lazy curls fell against the back of her chequered school tunic.

"As if the stares, the can-I-help-yous, the people who help without asking,"—she blew out an angry breath—"aren't bad enough ... do you want to know what happened in music today?"

I nodded, even though her back was to me.

"Ms Morrit refused to let me play 'Riders On The Storm' for my assessment. That song ..." she banged a fist on the keyboard, "... best piano solo ever and not an easy piece." She raised her voice in a screechy imitation, no doubt of the teacher. "Only hymns or songs from the prescribed school song book are allowed, Dakota Jane. There will not be any 'spirit music' within these walls. What a load of bullshit. You know where they can stick their religion? Right where—"

"Chickpea." I hauled myself out of the couch and

laid a hand on my sister's shoulder before Uncle Trevor appeared with one of his respect-the-lord speeches. "They don't mean anything by it."

"Well, there is no goddamn god, and if by some miracle there is, then he's an asshole." Her fingers slammed into the keys, and she resumed her angry musical outburst.

****

A few hours later an obnoxious horn beeped its farewell as my bus pulled away from the curb. Spotting Tori's car, I waved and settled down against the window for the trip back to college. The guy two seats down had his headphones so loud I could hear the music's beat, and the rattle of a page turning came from somewhere behind me. Closing my eyes, I drifted.

Beep. Beep. Beeeeeeep.

I shot out of the house, pulling the front door closed behind me, and ran down the path right to the red Lancer sitting on the curb. Tori grinned over her shoulder as I climbed in the backseat. "Buckle up. We've got a party to hit."

"Better than a boring basketball game."

She turned to face the front. "You can say that again."

"Better than a boring—"

This time, the look wasn't a grin. I got an eye roll. She set her hand on the console, palm up, and directed her grin to Dane.

The whirlwind trip home had me strung tighter than a set of fake pearls. Sighing, I pulled myself back into the here and now. The bus came to a stop and pulling out my phone to look at the time: eleven forty-eight. It was a ridiculous time to climb off a bus, yet I stepped out onto the curb and hefted my overnight bag onto my shoulder. Two cabs waited in the rank, which was lucky, since I was the only person disembarking. Standing around in the dark at the station wasn't exactly a good idea. I climbed into the front seat of one, and told the driver to take me to Oxley.

As we pulled into the college car park, my gaze instinctively went to the curved window on the second floor of block B. Pity the light was off. It would have been nice to talk to someone. I trudged through both courtyards and for a Thursday, it was pretty quiet. Traditionally a big night on campus, there weren't many people about. I guess anyone out to socialise had already headed into town. As I cut across Back, a loan figure emerged at the base of block K with a stack of books pressed to her chest. Wearing tights and a white Henley, Olivia paused, her attention fully on the phone in her hand.

Panic swamped me and I ducked my head, taking god almighty strides to reach the door to my block before my best friend spotted me sneaking back into college. What she was doing awake and wandering Oxley after midnight was beyond me, when she'd always been an early-to-bed girl. Maybe she was still cut up over Christian and couldn't sleep. Maybe she was on her way to see him. Maybe they'd fixed things that last night I was there. Guilt sliced through me; here I was trying to dodge her, and I hadn't been there when she might have been in need of a friend, but I had my own issues, and Kody had to come first.

"Hey you ..." Damn, not fast enough. I plastered

on a smile and turned to face her. "Is that a suitcase?"

"Ah yeah ..." I glanced down at the faded red fabric, its Guess logo all scratched. "Gotta lug the books around somehow."

Olivia's brows scrunched together, but I wasn't hanging around for question time. I yawned without covering my mouth. Purely impolite, but it did the trick.

She glanced toward the way I had faced, block L's entry. "It's pretty late. See you tomorrow, Sav."

"Night." I climbed the stairs with the heat of her gaze burning my back and a nasty taste in my mouth for treating my friend so horridly.

CHAPTER EIGHT

Savvy

Grains of sand slipped through my fingers, their texture caressing my skin as I sat away from the main party, staring at the white foam. The crest of each wave was pretty much all that was visible on such a dark night.

"What's happening, princess?" Dane's black Cons appeared beside me, and I closed my eyes and took a deep breath.

"Just catching some air."

He laughed as his butt hit the dune, his long legs pushing through the soft sand to create a little mound on which he propped his feet.

"Do you ever think about how tiny we are in the grand scheme of the world?"

He scooped up a handful of sand. "Like one tiny little grain." His hand moved to allow the sand to drain out like water. *"Doesn't mean each grain isn't important."*

"I guess."

We sat together, watching the waves for a long time. Dane and I were like that ... we could talk all night about heavy stuff, or hang without the need for words. It wasn't until the grey of morning threatened the night sky that something changed.

"What are you two doing all the way over here?"

I shoved over to allow Tori room to squeeze between us. She hooked her arm over Dane's knees and smiled back at me. "You're not stealing my man, are you, cuz?"

I grinned at her. "Of course not."

"Then let's get home before my mum discovers we stayed out all night."

Someone had turned down the thermostat on this ice box of a town overnight. I pulled my jean-clad legs underneath me and glanced across at Kasi's notes, spread from one end of the wooden picnic table to the other.

"You said the module was Learning Through Art, right?"

"Yep." She reached across, flicking through pages in my textbook. "Just there."

"Thanks." No matter how long I looked at the words, I couldn't get it together. Guilt had me glancing to Olivia's room, even though I knew she would be at class rather than inside. And that was only in the gaps in between thinking about Kody, and trying not to think about Kody, since I was supposed to be catching up on classwork. Spurred on by the thought of my younger sister, I slid my phone across the table and woke it up. Still no messages, but perhaps that was a good thing.

"So, Savvy …"

I looked up at my study buddy. "So, Kasi …"

"Was he as good as they say?"

It took a moment and a wink from her before I clued in that she was back on the Dane Beaumont gossip train.

"I told you—"

"You betcha. The rumours about how good I am are nothing compared to the reality." The voice that came from behind me wasn't one I was expecting. Cade Matthews, resident footy-head fresher, scooped up my notes from the bench by my side and dropped them onto the table, making room for his rear next to mine.

Kasi's eyebrow arched suggestively, but I just smiled. So what if she thought I'd hooked up with Cade? It might just dispel the Dane rumours, and that wouldn't be bad. I couldn't risk the rumour about Dane and I reaching Tori—Cade was a good distraction. Well, it wasn't bad until I spotted McFlirt himself swaggering out of the entrance to my block, his gaze trained on me. He strode right up behind Kasi. "Where have you been, Sav?"

The goosebumps I'd felt earlier sprouted all over my skin anew and twice as huge. No way was I going to let it show, so I kept my hands on my work, the pen steady in my quaking fingers. My body shivered involuntarily under his steady stare.

"You a bit cool there, babe? Here, I'll warm you up." Cade's arm dropped over my shoulder, and he pulled me into the warmth of his body.

"Around," I answered Dane's earlier question about where I'd been.

His expression darkened.

"Yeah, why'd you miss so many classes? Been too busy in bed to drag yourself up to campus?" Kasi winked, and Cade rubbed my shoulder.

I glanced up at Dane, and even though I hated lying—letting him think Cade and I were a thing—it was easier than telling the truth in front of other people. Who knew what Kasi would say on Facebook. "Something like that."

Directing a scowl at Cade's arm, Dane tore off his college rugby jersey and tossed it at me. I shrugged the footy player's arm off and balled up the jumper to throw back at Dane, since I wasn't really cold after all. But the beachy boy-smell hit me, and instead of hoicking the thing at him like I should have, I found myself raising it to my face and inhaling like a crazy person. I pulled it over my head and slid into the cosy warmth.

"Better?" A slow smile spread across Dane's face, his Celtic surfer pendant glinting in the afternoon sun.

"Mmm …"

"Possessive much?" Cade mumbled, then rose his voice to ask, "You ladies hitting the uni bar later tonight? I could use some good-looking company."

"Maybe …" I said.

Kasi watched me with a narrow-eyed gaze, then craned her neck to look back at Dane. "Well, that all depends. Are you going out?"

McFlirt directed his answer my way. "Maybe …"

She looked from him to me and I shuffled closer to Cade, wrapping my arms around myself and the snugly jersey. Dane and I weren't doing this. Couldn't be seen flirting. If Kasi thought there was anything between us she'd post it on social media, tags and all. That knowledge didn't stop the stupid fluttering inside me though, so I dragged my attention back to the books. "Hate to be rude, but I've got a ton of work to do."

"Don't let us stop you," Cade said, eyeing off Dane sliding into the seat opposite him, his glorious biceps now on full display.

Ignoring them both, I looked over the prescribed reading again. After a few minutes of silence, Cade pushed out of his seat. "See you tonight then."

"Sure. Tonight," Kasi cooed.

"Later." I didn't take my eyes off the work at hand, even though I could feel the weight of Dane's attention on me. Whatever the hell he wanted, he needed to back off in front of Kasi. Perhaps a pointed glare would send the message. "You right there?"

"Nope. Let's talk."

"I'm trying to study here."

Kasi looked back and forth between us, but I didn't care. There wasn't anything to say. After a long look that morphed from weighing to accusing to questioning, he nodded and rose to his feet. As soon as he'd disappeared down the path toward Front Courtyard, I let out an almighty sigh.

"That good, hey?" Kasi chuckled.

She didn't know the half of it.

We settled into a comfortable silence, and this time I actually managed to work. The two education classes I'd missed didn't seem overly complicated. I caught up on all my reading, carried out a few exercises, and even made a start on our upcoming assignment. Well, picked out a topic, but hey, that counted.

As the buzz of people in the courtyard grew, so did a gnawing in my stomach. I closed up the books and started packing all my notes away, the sun was just about gone anyway. That was the lure of studying out here … the sunshine just brought out the best in me. Woke me up even.

"All done?" Kasi asked.

"It's dinnertime."

She raised her head and looked around, taking in the thickening stream of hungry students headed toward the dining hall. "I guess you're right."

I ducked upstairs and dumped my stuff in my room, then made my way across the courtyard and climbed the stairs to Olivia's. I hadn't seen her get back from classes, but maybe she'd ducked in the back way. I rapped on her door only to be met with silence again. Sure it was kind of early, not yet six p.m, but that was our usual time to head to dinner. So either she was ignoring me or was putting in even more hours at the library. Then again, maybe she was at social committee; god only knew when they met. It seemed pretty haphazard.

My tummy let out an almighty growl, so I hustled down the stairs and to the dining hall without her. I found a seat with Dono and set my pasta down. No sooner had I returned from grabbing a drink than Dane had decided that the best place to sit was right beside me. Obviously missing us eating together the other day, Dono gave me a what-the-hell look, which I shut down with a don't-ask look of my own. While training one hundred per cent of my attention on twirling pasta around my fork, I tried to eat without looking like a spaghetti-loving pooch from *Lady and the Tramp*.

"How's block B this year?" Thank god and Dono for small talk.

Dane's fork clinked against his plate. "Not bad. Front Courtyard is a hell of a lot quieter than Back."

"So I've heard."

I concentrated on my carbonara, tuning out their conversation. Eventually, Dono got up to get a second helping and in a low tone, Dane said, "Don't think about running away when that plate's empty. You and I are going for a walk after dinner."

"A walk?"

"Absolutely. Now eat up, princess."

What in the hell? I shot him a wide-eyed look, and he grinned in return. This was getting out of hand. If he thought being friends meant he could boss me around …

"I hate pasta night." Becca folded her long body into the seat next to Dono's empty one, slapping her plate on the table.

"S'not so bad," Dane mumbled around a mouthful.

She tossed me a wink and a knowing smile. Him sitting next to me didn't mean a thing. This damn rumour needed to be laid to rest before it reached anyone back home. My insides turned icy. "Didn't happen. Not happening now, or ever."

"That so?" Becca grinned like Alice's damn Cheshire cat, clearly not believing a word.

"What's not happening?" Dane twirled the last of his pasta around his fork.

"Yeah, what?" Smirking, Dono slid back into his seat with another humongous pile of spaghetti. Who knew how he managed to fit so much food inside himself? The guy ate like a starving lion.

As if he knew exactly what Becca meant, Dane dropped his fork onto his empty plate and extended an arm over my shoulders. My stupid hormones took off, dancing a joyous tune trough my system, and as much as I wished I had the willpower to push him away, that was all it was—a wish. Because I had absolutely no control over my stupid body. The proof was in the way I squirmed in my seat.

"Quit it," I growled.

Dane just chuckled. I swear he got some kind of sick enjoyment out of making me uncomfortable. "You ready?"

Dono and Becca both stared at us, all but open-mouthed at him acting all coupley. Everyone knew Dane Beaumont didn't do relationships; he was strictly a one-night stand kind of guy. Ignoring them, Dane piled his plate on top of mine, and standing, picked up both the dirty dishes. I pushed my chair out, rushing to get away before my friends could start an inquisition now that he was gone. Just as I reached the double glass doors leading out to the courtyard, a warm arm dropped over my shoulders again, steering me toward Oxley's front entrance.

"God, you're persistent."

I kept both arms firmly by my sides, despite wanting to curl the one pressed against Dane's side around his solid body. A glance back to my friends revealed just what we didn't need, Dono and Becca staring.

Shit ... I was still wearing his jersey.

Over the arched bridge we walked and out onto Elm Avenue where we turned right, heading away from campus. Dane's hip bumped against my waist. His closeness multiplied his smell tenfold from when it was just his sweater. There were most definitely tingles running along my entire left side, and I was most definitely ignoring them.

"Talk to me," he said.

"About what?"

"Where'd you disappear to?"

I tensed, stepping out from under his arm and picked up the pace.

"Home?"

Why could he read me like this? Oxley was my sanctuary, and I didn't need the past invading it. We rounded the corner, now on the road that led toward the outskirts of town. Inhaling the fresh evening air, I yelled behind me. "Come on, slacker. You wanted a walk, so keep up."

I put in long strides, my sights set on the running track up ahead. My jeans and boots probably weren't the best attire for a stroll, but whatever. Like I cared. Just as I was about to cross the road, a firm grip on my wrist pulled me to a halt.

"Stop running," Dane said. "Stop running from everything and just talk to me."

"I'm not running." Heat coursed through my arms, my legs, my head, my entire body, until I thought I might just explode from the pressure. My entire being was tenser than a tightly bound, overcooked leg of lamb. "NOT. RUNNING!"

Dane's arms swept around me. His strong hold encased every part of me, pressing me against his firm form. Talking … talking wasn't easy or simple. It brought all the nightmares back, dragged them to the surface so they could play out again. They were better buried where I could keep them locked away. Dane's chest rose and fell against me; his secure arms didn't let go. He held me like his body could block those nightmares from mine. And *my* body, wound so tight for the past few days, melted. My knees buckled and my cheek fell against his chest. His arms tightened a little more and finally, I could breathe. Strange that being held as tight as a Boa Constrictor was what finally allowed the fresh air to reach my lungs.

His lips brushed over my temple. "I know it's hard, princess, but you don't have to carry this on your own. You've been doing that for too long."

His arms loosened, and I released my death grip on his torso. Dane studied me for a moment, then tugged me across the road and onto the dirt track that sometime, someone had worn down into a path that was now known as the long running track. As we resumed our walk, the sun began its descent below the horizon, and just like on the night of the party, I found solace in the fact I couldn't see him clearly. Or maybe it was that he couldn't see me, walking side by side with our faces cast in shadows.

"Kody needed me."

Dane didn't miss a step. We kept walking along the path, long dry grass tickling the tips of my fingers as I let it brush over them. Neither of us spoke until we reached the halfway mark, where the long track swung back around. The sun had fully set, and luckily my eyes had adjusted well enough to see the path.

"She started at St Bridget's High this year, and it hasn't been easy on her. Rosy thought it would be better for her to switch after all the troubles at East Coast, but I guess it wasn't, or maybe it wouldn't have made a difference. There'd be sporty kids, bullies, athletic carnivals, unsympathetic teachers … all of it, no matter where she was."

"What is she, year ten?"

"Yeah."

Dane focused on the track, which made it easier to keep talking. "St Bridget's is a great school, but that's probably the worst grade. Kids can be pretty screwed up at fifteen and sixteen."

"St Bridget's isn't the best school …" I couldn't help the dig. The rivalry between St Bridget's and East Coast High had always been strong, and Dane and I came from opposite sides of town. It lightened the mood for a moment, and Dane shot me a sideways smile.

"I'm glad I ducked back to see her, even if it was just overnight. Kody doesn't open up to anyone else."

"What about Victoria?"

"Tori's not around much. Her degree's pretty full on. Besides, you know how she is …"

If Tori knew where I was right now, the fact I was in his room the other night … *Don't finish that thought.* We walked in silence for a few moments and it wasn't until a jogger overtook us that I realized we'd slowed right down. The end of the path loomed up ahead, but I wasn't ready to head back to Oxley.

"Kody's a tough kid. She's been through so much that I just want to scoop her up and make everything right again." The path narrowed and Dane's shoulder brushed against mine. "When I finish this degree and get a teaching placement, I'll be able to support her better."

"You're a good sister, Sav."

I wasn't anything like a good sister, but I tried— hell did I try. I had a lot to make up for. I'd been the world's worst sister once, and now Kody was paying for my mistakes. I'd also been the worst daughter, but I was studying for a career to be proud of just like my mum. We turned and started back the way, the silence enveloping us in a peaceful cloud. The jogger passed us again and as we neared Oxley, the bass of whatever music was cranked up thumped through the evening air. Sounded like people getting their Friday night drinks on before heading out a little later. I pulled on my bubbly persona. "You going to party with everyone fun?"

Dane cast a sideways look my way. "Are you?"

"Well, that depends ..." on what I wasn't sure. On if I felt like it—I didn't really. On if knocking back a few drinks would help me loosen up—Dane's chat had already done that. On if he was going—oh, crap. "On if I can talk Liv into it."

Dane grimaced. "Tough job."

"What do you mean? She loves socialising. A few drinks, lots of chatting ..."

"With the way everyone's talking about her and Christian? Olivia's all about playing it cool, right?"

This wasn't making a lot of sense. "She's not going to hide away in her room because they broke up. She's not that precious."

"Yeah, but that rumour about her masturbating—"

"Hold up." I grabbed his arm. "What rumour?"

"How can you not have heard it? Oxley's bloody grapevine—"

"Tell me the goddamn rumour, Dane."

We started walking again, and now at the end of the road, we turned into Elm Avenue.

"The night they split, Christian was pretty messy, and he might have said something about her teasing him in bed ... all look, don't touch, or some shit. I guess everyone picked up his dumb-arse comment and ran with it. Now she's copping the backlash."

"Oh my god. Poor Olivia. I'm the worst friend."

With Oxley in sight, I took off toward the building, jogging through the mass of partygoers in Front Courtyard and up the stairs to my best friend's room. It seemed that I wasn't the only one who'd had stuff to deal with, and Olivia truly was suffering alone, since I'd been AWOL for too long.

CHAPTER NINE

Savvy

Talking to Dane might have caused my two worlds to collide, but it was manageable. Outwardly, I was still bright, happy Savvy with the perfect life. Once we were alone though, the real me crept in, and all the issues and problems back home dominated our conversations. With Dane, talking was easy, not difficult like it had always been with Tori, or easy to pretend like I'd always done with Liv.

Liv … since my walk with Dane exactly a week ago, I'd managed to push my stuff aside and concentrate on my best friend. The rumour mill had sure done a number on her, but apparently there was a new guy on the scene, and that seemed to perk her up somewhat. The night I had planned for her should skyrocket that perk into something spectacular.

"Hurry up and get dressed already." I flipped through the clothes in her wardrobe, looking for the perfect outfit, one that oozed confidence and was sexy yet stylish. It was just a Friday night up at the bar watching some unheard of band, but the guy she'd been crushing on was going to be there, so she had to look fabulous. Besides, this would show the rumourmongers around here they should find someone else to talk about; my girl was back on the rails.

"I'm not going."

I stopped searching, poking my head around the wooden door. "Yes, you are. You need this, Olivia Dean. You need to get out, experience life, have fun. Be a college student for once."

The look she pierced me with said she was barely tolerating my bossiness, but too bad. She needed to move forward from this Christian mess.

Before she could protest, the door flew open.

"Never fear, the drinks are ..." The girl I'd earlier seen harassing Liv about this gig tonight barrelled into the room. Wearing a red non-designer dress with white polka dots, she had her hair in a ponytail. "Sorry ... I ... ahh ... didn't realise."

I'd seen her around Oxley last year, and this year too. No idea what her name was though. She was one of the quiet ones that mostly stuck to herself. I shot her a grin, eying off the Raspberry Cruisers in her hand. "Did you say drinks?"

"Sure did."

Yep, she was going to be an insta-friend; my partner in this Save Olivia mission. "I'm Savannah."

"I know. Everyone knows. I live on your floor, remember?"

Oops.

Ms Polka Dot announced, "Wasn't sure what drink you felt like, Liv, so I got everything."

"Right." I closed the cupboard. "Excellent choice."

Olivia sighed as she took in the outfit I'd picked for her—a sheer Witchery blouse, coupled with some awesome black capri pants. "Why do I feel like you two are conspiring against me?"

"Because we are, or at least we would have been if I knew I had a co-conspirator, right … umm …?" *Can't exactly call her Ms Polka Dot.*

"Molly?" Liv glared at me.

I put on a fake laugh to cover up my epic fail. "Right. And you're going to have fun tonight."

Molly handed Liv a Cruiser, and I clinked mine against it. "To new beginnings." I sure needed one of those. *Not lusting over boys that need to be friend zoned.*

"To new beginnings," Molly chimed in.

I knocked back a few mouthfuls.

"Fine," Olivia said, "to new beginnings."

Molly slid onto the desk. "So …" She wriggled her eyebrows suggestively at my best friend. "Logan Hays."

"It's not like that. We're just in the same Sociology class."

Molly grinned around the bottle pressed to her lips. "And he wants you to go see Quiet Renegade tonight."

"Won't you let up? It's nothing. Not a date or even an invite to meet him there. It's just one friend telling another about a rad gig. That's it."

I raised a brow at Molly; the girl was good. Livia liked this guy, I could tell by the crazy grip she had on that drink, the way she was downing it faster than her usual measured sips. Definitely masking the boy-like, maybe even to herself. I knew what that looked like; I'd done it for long enough.

"What's going on with you and Dane?"

Abort conversation. I wasn't walking into that one. "Nothing."

"That's not what I saw the other day."

Flip ... what had she seen? I'd kept my feelings under wraps. "It's nothing. I'm not interested." I scooped up her outfit and tossed it at her before the inquisition turned to questions I couldn't answer. "Go get dressed, we're going out."

By the time she returned, I'd knocked back my entire Cruiser, and Molly had cracked open a bottle of wine. My new partner in dragging Livia down the path of have-a-good-time shoved a wine glass in my best friend's hand. Insta-friend indeed.

****

Quiet Renegade weren't too bad, if you liked older-style pub music. Lucky for me, I had enough of a buzz happening that all I needed in order to dance was a decent beat. I swayed my hips, bumping against Liv to catch her attention. She'd been staring off toward the pool tables since we'd hit the dance floor. She grinned and bumped her hip against Molly's with a mile-wide smile. What a laugh. I hadn't seen her this tipsy in ... well, in forever. Liv generally didn't let her guard down. Her gaze wandered over my shoulder again, so I shimmied across to the opposite side of our little circle to see what all the fuss was about. Pity I wasn't tall enough to see over the crowd; too many heads bopped in and out of my line of vision to really figure out what she was looking at. Her attention was probably just snagged on that Logan guy anyway. Wondered what he was like ... he'd have to be a darn sight better than Christian, the jerk.

The crowd split; it was like Moses had parted the Red Sea to reveal Dane and his boys across the way. From this far away I couldn't be certain, but I'd bet the collared shirt he had on was Stussy. The surfer was laughing and smiling, knocking back a schooner, but his gaze ... those mint green eyes rested on me, and even from this distance I could feel the heat in his stare. A heat that turned me inside out, that made my toes curl, and totally shouldn't be there.

Leaving Liv and her wandering gaze, I danced across the circle again to stand between Molly's friends, my back firmly to the man I could never have. A couple of songs later, a slow tune hit and there'd never been a better cue for a trip to the bathroom. I leaned across to Liv. "I gotta go to the ladies."

"Me too," she shouted, then said something to Molly.

I snaked my way through the crowd and once we were out of the writhing dance floor, I hooked an arm through Olivia's. "If that's Logan Hays that you've been making eyes at all night, wow, tell me how we've never met him before." Not that I'd seen who she was looking at, but it did the trick.

"I haven't ..." she blushed a thousand shades of red, "... making eyes at anyone. Looks like Dane's mate."

Sure enough, Dane was chatting to a few guys, only one of them I didn't know. The blond hottie I'd seen once before at Oxley. Pretty sure he wasn't a resident. "I've seen him around though, since school's been back. Maybe he's a fresher …"

Two girls moved into the circle, and they wasted no time. The blonde rubbed up against Dane with a do-me-now smile and he … he … looked at her like maybe he was considering it. She popped a finger in her mouth then trailed it around the rim of his schooner while talking into his ear. I shoved my hair out of my eyes, my elbow colliding with solid flesh on the way back down, but I didn't look to see what I'd hit. I couldn't take my eyes off McSlut's hand. Trailing along his arm, over his … "Who is that bitch?"

"Table Thief," Liv answered.

"What? I meant the girl."

"Doesn't matter." Liv pushed through the bathroom door, totally oblivious to the foreplay happening across the way.

Mumbling under my breath, I shoved the door and it slammed against the wall, flinging back so fast I had to slap it open again. Half a dozen girls stood and in a queue and I groaned. The entire line of girls turned my way, but I slumped a shoulder against the wall and ignored them. When we reached the front of the line I went about my business, then emerged from the cell to straighten up. I flicked the water on, and the stream hit the basin, sprouting up all over the place to create a watery mess. Stupid faucet. I was burning up anyway, so the cool water felt all right. I patted down my damp shirt, applied a fresh sheen of gloss, and smoothed down my hair, taming the flyaway strands into place. Then, staring at my reflection in the mirror, I puckered my lips.

I was pretty. I was gorgeous. I was better than the tramp who had her arms all over Dane.

I'd show her.

Olivia looked at me all funny-like, and said, "It's so hot in here."

"Yeah, it's like they've got the heat up." That would explain the flush of heat running through me.

Another hair smooth and we were out of there and straight to the bar; I needed one more drink to cool me down. Then I'd show her.

I ordered two more vodka raspberries, which arrived in good time. I scooped up both plastic cups, and dodged first this person then that. The drinks sloshed in their cups, cool liquid trickling down my hand, and there Olivia was. I passed off one to her, my gaze wandering back to Dane, and hell did he have his flirt on. Bitch-face was now draped all over him, her boobs smooched up against his arm while her fingers toyed with the back of his collar. The room was suddenly ten times hotter than before.

That was *my* man, McSlut.

Only Dane wasn't, couldn't …

Something stuck into my side. *Olivia.* "Talk to him."

I nodded. "Yeah. I ought to, right? I should tell him … tell him …" *That I want him. Have done since I was sixteen.* I passed her my drink. "I'm going."

Only I didn't move. I stared at Dane and Bitch-face, glanced at my feet, and looked at him again. *What if Tori …?*

Screw Tori.

I placed one foot in front of the next, stepped out and brought the other foot forward. *Yes, Savannah, that's it. Shit, don't stumble.* I straightened up, and held my head high despite its drunken spinning, keeping my eyes on the game. Strike that—eyes on the prize.

The prize that was being licked along the length of his ear.

I took bigger strides. My shoulder slammed against a solid body.

"Hey! Watch where you're going."

Whatever, mate.

I edged my way past the dude, a leggy brunette, and another guy, then slipped into the circle next to Dane. Bitchface continued her game, and no one paid me a lick of attention.

"Hey, baby." Planting my palm right over the centre of his chest, I rose onto my tiptoes and smacked a loud kiss on Dane's cheek, then teetered to the side.

His attention immediately swung my way, along with that of every other person in the group.

"Princess." His tongue slid along his bottom lip, and his mouth kicked up a second before he swooped in and ... and ... and ... his warm lips touched mine. Pressed up against mine. He smelled like beach and beer, and those lips puckered against my mouth in the most heavenly, tummy-flipping ... *gone.*

An almighty smirk played on his handsome face. "Good to see you."

I licked lips that still tasted like him.

Wow.

Bitch-face cut me a pissed look, so I plastered on a sweet smile just for her. *Suck it up, love. Not yours.*

Not mine either ...

"You're late," Dane said, threading our hands together. Sweet Jesus, his soft palm felt like warm heaven.

"Sorry, I got held up." I leaned into his side, my fingers tracing over the warm metal pendant resting against his throat. Bet that looked all cute and couple-like.

I needn't have bothered. Bitch-face didn't even notice. She was looking behind us, wide-eyed.

"Shit," Dane cursed and dropped my hand. Then suddenly, I was left standing there with the tramp troop. Logan was nowhere to be seen as Dane rushed toward some commotion over by the bar. Well, this was awkward.

"Is that …?" The brunette who'd been talking to Logan craned her neck. "Are they fighting?"

I spun around and sure enough, Logan was laying into some tattooed guy twice his size while Dane tried to get between them. Fists flew like crazy, someone started shouting *fiii-ght, fiii-ght,* and the chant rose above the music, loud and clear. I pushed through the swelling crowd, but it thickened so quickly even my slight frame couldn't squeeze between all the sweaty bodies.

Then I spotted her: Olivia, her face drawn, her expression stricken.

Putting my elbows to good use, I surged forward, blazing a path to my friend. When I reached her, she grabbed hold of me with a shaking hand. "God, Liv. What happened?"

She stared at me, her eyes glassy and wide for a good few moments before she finally spoke. "This douchebag … Logan came, and then Dane …"

Raising myself onto my toes, I couldn't see either of them. Wait, no. Over by the door a bouncer had Logan by the arm as if he were escorting them out.

Liv's face blanched, and she swayed a little, sweat

coating her brow. I had to get her out of here before she threw up all that vodka Molly and I had plied her with earlier. "How about we go get you some fresh air?"

Liv nodded, and I took her by the arm, propelling us toward the front exit. A solid bouncer manned the door, his chunky arms crossed over his chest, resting on his oversized belly. He gave us a onceover, clearly writing Liv off as plastered. "You leave, you're out, girls. I can't let anyone back in."

"Thanks." Liv waved. "Awesome night."

I held her up by the elbow as we exited the stuffy club and emerged into the cool night. My head had a bit of a spin happening too, but I was in much better shape than her. I wasn't tottering on my heels, for starters. Olivia pulled away, and this time I was the one who stumbled, my heel clipping the step. Her weight disappeared from my arm as she toddled off toward the fountain where Dane and that Logan guy were talking. Waving arms, they both paced, and Logan shoved his hands through his hair; it didn't look pretty. Dane's bulky form moved, blocking Logan from walking away.

I shivered, wishing I were still curled into his side. It had been so cosy and full of awesome toe-curling—

The freezing air snapped my senses right back into place.

He wasn't my man.

Never would be.

Zinging chemistry be damned.

I dragged my phone out of my pocket and concentrated on looking at nothing on the screen.

"Shut up!"

The shout snapped my gaze to them, and Dane

looked right at me while his mate glowered at him, and poor Livia extended a hand toward Logan as if she was about to intervene. Although he was talking to his hothead mate, Dane's stare stayed on me, and wow, did it send tingles through my tummy. Or maybe that was just the vodka.

I diverted my attention back to my phone. Anger still throbbed through my temples from earlier, but now it wasn't only at that other girl, it was at myself, at Dane. It wasn't fair that he was the one guy who could make me feel. I shifted through my contacts until I found his name then changed it to McFlirt. The constant reminder would do me good.

They kept talking over by the fountain, Logan's movements sharp and angry. The two of us made a good pair.

"Hey." My head snapped up at the nearness of Dane's voice. He was standing so close my forehead just about clocked his chin.

"What was that all about?" I rolled my eyes toward his brawly friend.

"Some dick tried to force himself on Olivia."

"Whoa—"

Silence settled over us while I concentrated on my phone, ignoring Dane's heavy gaze. "Sav—"

"Mate ..." Logan led Olivia toward us, their hands linked. "I'm going to take Liv home."

I raised a brow. This guy wasn't another Christian, surely. She was off her face; now was most definitely not the right time to be making a move.

"Home to Oxley." Glancing away, he rubbed a hand along the back of his neck. "To her room, where she needs to go to bed, alone. Not anywhere else."

Olivia giggled. Maybe that last vodka hadn't been such a good idea.

I nodded, smiling at Logan's good intentions. "Okay. Well, I'm going to head home too."

My friend pouted at me, but I didn't care. I didn't know this guy from a bar of soap. Sure he sounded sincere, but there was no way I was leaving her drunken arse in his care.

"So, princess ..." Dane winked at me. "Let's walk."

And by walk he more than likely meant talk, and by talk he probably meant open up ... dear god.

"Don't go home because of me." The way he looked at me made my heart do stupid things. I swallowed. "Go find that chick you were ..." *foreplaying with* "... I'll be all right tagging along with these two."

"Really?"

That one word was full of so much meaning that the smile he threw my way squeezed my heart. I hated the fact he could always tell what I wasn't saying, yet I held firm. "Really."

Logan tipped his chin to Dane, then took Liv by the shoulders and turned her around to face the right way. They walked down the footpath in the direction of Oxley, and without waiting for me to protest again, Dane trailed behind. I watched the three of them walk away, my heart crashing against my ribs because Dane wanted to talk, wanted to walk, had played along with my pretence we were together.

Get a grip.

He glanced back over his shoulder as if he were about to say something, but instead he dropped that famous smile. I sucked in a breath of frigid air and steeled my heart against unwanted feelings, then jogged down the path to catch up while his smile turned into a cocky grin.

"Took your sweet time, princess." He slapped me on the butt. "Lucky I'm a patient man."

"Ha!" I laughed, landing a solid thwack to his rear. Nice one it was too. Those jeans, although a tad baggy, hid the perfect shape and firm ... *abort all thoughts of Dane's perfect butt.*

Think of sunshine and beaches and waves and board shorts and wetsuits. Wetsuits that fit bodies nicely. I'd seen him dressed for the surf plenty of times over the years, and the way that rubber clung to his toned muscles ...

Ah crap.

"Whatcha thinking about, Sav?"

I pressed my cool hands against my burning cheeks.

"Nothing."

"Jealous looks good on you."

"I am not jealous."

Dane let out a loud laugh. "No? So you played the girlfriend card up there just for entertainment?" He shot me a sideways smirk. "It had nothing to do with Lana looking for a fun time?"

The girl had a name, and McFlirt knew it. Well, I'd be damned. But there was no way I was jealous; that would mean I had some sort of a claim over him. I pointed toward Olivia and Logan up head. "Who's the new guy?"

"Logan was the first person I met in O-week my first year. He had some stuff to deal with back home, so took last year off. He's a good bloke."

"That's what you said about Christian."

"I never said that."

"He's your mate, right? You telling me you hang

out with scumbags on purpose?"

"Of course not. Christian's situation is complicated ..."

"I'll bet."

We fell into silence, slowly catching up to the lovebirds up ahead. Well, Olivia looked all loved up, with her head resting on Logan's shoulder as she clutched his arm. I wasn't too sure how he felt about that, though.

The twenty-minute walk seemed to be over in no time. Just as we reached Oxley's parking lot, we caught up to our friends.

"Can you get this thing opened?" Logan pointed to the locked gate.

Dane extracted his card and swiped for it entry. As the lock clicked back, Olivia pointed my way. With rosy cheeks and sparkling eyes, she seemed a little more with it than she had been earlier. "This is the one I was just telling you about; my bestest friend in the whole of Oxley and I love her to pieces ..." she flourished a hand toward me, "... Savannah."

Logan offered up a smile. "I'm Logan."

"I've heard all about you," I said, "but please, it's just Savvy."

Savannah was a different person to Savvy ... one who belonged in the past.

"We're home!" Olivia skipped through and into Back Courtyard. Logan rushed ahead and grabbed her arm a second before she attempted the stairs.

"I've got her." I slid my arm around her waist.

Liv stuck her mouth near my ear and in anything but a whisper said, "Take Dane to your room and have life-altering sex."

The ground needed to open up and swallow me

whole. Yesterday would be good.

Dane moaned suggestively. "That's the best idea I've heard all night."

"See?" Olivia said. "He wants to."

Logan chuckled somewhere behind us, and Dane's gaze burned my back, but I didn't stop for either of them. I didn't even look back. I just marched us through the courtyard and right up to Livia's room, where I deposited her drunken self on the bed.

She slipped her shoes off and started peeling off her clothes, while I tidied away all the bottles and mess from our earlier drinks. She changed into her PJs and flopped back on the bed. "Logan's so dreamy." She sighed and I pulled the covers over her. "Buuuut ... Dane's in love with Savvy and Savvy's in love with Dane."

"Shut up." I opened her door and stepped out into the hall. "Go to sleep, Olivia."

I snicked the door closed behind me. It was past time I was in bed, too. Just as I reached the landing, an almighty crash came from somewhere behind me. I poked my head back around to see Olivia strutting down the hall, PJs all skew-whiff. "Just going to tinkle," she said as she passed, then swung back around with a serious expression. "Do him. Tonight."

Shaking my head, I jogged down the stairs. No wonder she normally didn't drink. Her inhibitions and barriers weren't just down—they were obliterated.

Halfway across the courtyard, a deep, "Sav" caught my attention.

Blowing out a breath, I changed directions, heading toward where Dane and Logan leaned against the brick wall.

"Get her to bed all right?" Logan asked before I'd

even reached them.

"I daresay she'll have one hell of a hangover tomorrow."

"It'll do her some good. She needed to let loose tonight," Dane said, his gaze wandering up toward Christian's room. We fell silent then for a moment, as if no one wanted to acknowledge the horrid rumour. Maybe Logan wasn't aware. I shuffled my weight, leaning against the wall beside Dane, and stifled a yawn.

"I'm off," Logan announced. "See you guys around."

"Later." Dane tipped his chin.

Logan walked away, and as I turned to head upstairs Dane caught my arm. "About that life-altering sex ..."

I whacked him across the chest.

"How about a coffee then?" He hedged.

I shouldn't. Couldn't, but those big eyes batted and my resolve turned to mush. "Just a quick cup. I'm beat."

"Nothing's ever quick with me, baby." He winked.

Incorrigible. That was what he was. A dirty flirt who took every opening he saw. I walked away, heading toward my room.

My tummy fluttered with each step closer to my block. It somersaulted with each step up the stairs and by the time I reached my door, forget about butterflies—freaking hummingbirds zoomed around inside me. Because I knew he was right behind me. I might not have been able to see him, but I could feel it in that spot between my shoulder blades, between my hips, between my thighs. The tingle was everywhere.

I set a shaky hand to my lock. The key missed the hole, and I held my hand steady with the other one to guide it home. Still the key shook. Bloody hell; why did he have this effect on me? Dane reached over my shoulder. His warm fingers closed over mine, slid the key home and turned. The door gave way, yet his hand never moved. Strong fingers encased my fist, another arm snaked around my waist, and I could feel every place we were not touching but could be if I just leaned back against him.

Ah, what the hell?

I pressed my back to his front, rocking back on my heels and, like a paperclip to a magnet, his body caught mine. His heart beat against my shoulder, as fast as mine—a rapid, solid thud. The entire back of my body burned, from calves to butt to shoulders.

I slowly swivelled around.

We stood toe to toe, nose to nose ... almost. This time it wasn't the alcohol that made me dizzy. He bent his head just slightly to look me in the eye, and his stare was full-on. Moving slowly, he inched closer still until his mouth grazed my lips.

The staccato in my chest tripled.

He lingered, our bodies barely an inch apart, our faces even closer.

My stomach jittered.

My nether regions felt as if they'd caught a fever.

I moaned.

My eyes fell closed. I'd had a crush on this surfer boy since I was sixteen and now, now he wanted to kiss me? After all that had happened in the past four years? After I'd been dodging his flirty arse for the past few weeks? As if he could hear my doubts, those sinful lips brushed across my mouth again, this time slightly harder. His hands settled on my waist, holding me so gently I felt like I was delicate. I breathed out, and on my exhale his lips pressed against mine, not leaving.

Unable to take this torture any longer, I grabbed him by the waist and dragged him inside. Our hips smashed together and Dane's hands shot to my face, holding my cheeks as he consumed me and his mouth moved against mine with a heady fierceness that wasn't there a moment ago.

This was a kiss that had been building inside me for years.

CHAPTER TEN

Dane

My entire body burned hot, standing to attention with the need for more. Savvy took a step back and the new space between us felt like ice. Dropping my hand to her waist, I tugged her against me and she whimpered again. My heart raced. My hands ached to feel her skin.

Reaching past me, she slammed her door closed. Her lips, sweet and fierce, moved fast. My blood sang as it surged through my veins in a heady southward rush. Her hands slid up under my tank, and my breath hitched. She could probably feel the thunder that was my heart trying to bang the shit out of my rib cage. This moment had been building between us for long enough. For whatever reason, she'd been holding back, but finally she'd given in, made it clear I should have put the real moves on her sooner.

Her hands raked over my chest. Long nails against my skin trailed an excruciating path all the way to the band of my jeans and back up until her palms flattened against my pecs, hard. I stumbled, my back slamming against the wall, and now we were talking. There was nothing sexier than a girl who knew what she wanted.

I needed her sweet arse closer. Needed to feel her skin against mine. Savvy was with the game, and before I could reach for her waist, her chest crushed against me, her mouth still slanted over my lips. I deepened the kiss, gliding my tongue along the inside of her cheek, over her tongue, battling to show her just how much I'd meant it when I'd told her I wanted this. She tasted so damn good. My hands roved from her hips under her shirt and up the curve of her waist. That only made her kiss me harder. I ventured to lift her dress, and Savvy broke away long enough to duck her head through the opening, then she pulled the thing off and kissed me again.

Every bone in my body hummed to her tune. Those long nails pressed against my skin, scraping their way up the back of my neck until her fingers twisted in my hair. Even though I'd nursed a single James Squire all night, I felt drunk. Drunk on this damn amazing girl.

Satin slipped against my chest, her bra rubbing against my exposed skin, and I groaned, unable to take any more.

Using my hips, I pushed against her and she pressed back. Not what I wanted, but shit, everything was perfectly aligned, despite our few-inch height difference. I set my hands on her hips and lifted her off the ground, then deposited her on the bed.

She shimmied out of panties designed to make any man want to rip them rip off and my heart just about stopped. God, she beautiful.

Completely naked, Savvy looked up at me, the fire in her eyes blazing a trail right to my heart.

****

I woke to the warmth of a body snuggled beside me, the smell of coconut strong. Smiling, I blinked my eyes open to see a blonde mess of hair across my chest and a tanned arm slung over my abs. I didn't do the morning after. Waking up with a chick in bed was an awkwardness I could live without. But this … she needed to be closer, not gone once the fun was over. With the arm curled around her, I trailed my fingers along the length of her side, over her hip, into the dip of her waist and along her ribs, then back down.

She didn't stir, didn't so much as change the rhythm of her breath. I, however, couldn't lie still. Couldn't not hold her closer. My fingers continued their lazy trail, daring nearer her naked arse while my heart beat as if I'd just run a marathon. Surely the sound of it whacking into the flesh beneath her cheek would wake her.

Finally, she curled further into me, bare chest pressed against my side, the crown of her head under my jaw. I pressed a kiss against her blonde halo.

Savvy froze.

Rigid as a bloody surfboard. Even her fingers stiffened, rising off my body.

So much for mornings that weren't awkward.

"Morning, princess."

I felt her swallow against my chest, then swallow again.

"Dane ..."

"Who else?" *Play it cool, Beaumont.*

I waited for her to giggle, brush off her sleepy confusion, and wrap that sweet body around mine in the same way it had done last night.

"Right." Even her voice sounded like a tin soldier. "About that coffee ..."

"About that life-altering sex." Shit, I couldn't help myself, could I?

She pushed herself up, clutching the sheet to her chest to hide that perfect body from view. "Dane ..." She wouldn't even look me in the eye. "Last night was great, but it can't happen again. I ... I ... I think you should go."

Sitting up, I swung my legs over the side of the bed and grabbed my jeans off the floor. It took all of half a second to pull them on, followed by last night's shirt. I didn't even bother with the laces on my Cons.

She never said a word as I reefed open the door and strode out. It was pretty damn clear she just wanted the moment over. Lucky I was good at walking away.

CHAPTER ELEVEN

Savvy

The dark room didn't mask Tori's soft sobs. I was certain she thought I couldn't hear the hiccup-sniffs she choked on every few minutes, but I could. Just like I knew her and Dane had split yesterday. She hadn't told me yet that their two-year relationship was over, but I'd run into him at Coasties Fresh Fish & Seafood this afternoon, and he looked a wreck. I probably shouldn't have hugged him, shouldn't have felt the lust I did at our close contact. Nor should I have told him I was always here if he needed a shoulder.

I shouldn't have had to tamp down a pang of he's-single excitement either.

A rough cough masked another sad murmur.

I climbed out of bed and crossed the room to where my cousin slept. It was one of those nights where not a single skerrick of light was about, so I couldn't actually see her. That meant I had to shuffle until my knees came into contact with Tori's bed, then I lowered myself onto the mattress. She sniffed again, and I found her hand fisted in the blankets and covered it with my own.

"Want to talk about it?"

The silence lasted so long, I thought she must have fallen asleep. I squeezed her hand, ready to retreat to my own bed and guilty thoughts. Her whisper broke through the silence, "I ended it."

"You broke up with Dane?"

She pulled her hand away from mine. "I cheated on him and it was the biggest mistake of my life."

I couldn't think straight, couldn't walk straight. I couldn't even sit straight in a damn chair. Because every time I tried to actually do something, my mind wandered back to Friday night and that made me all kinds of fidgety. I really hadn't thought life-altering sex was a thing ... but when one night could make you question every last moral you thought you had just so you could go back for more ... well, that was pretty damn life-altering. Not to mention how I'd felt in the moment, when nothing else mattered, just me and him. Us.

Us was the problem I couldn't get off my mind.

More than anything else, I wanted there to be an us, but it just wasn't that easy. It didn't matter that I felt things with Dane that I had never felt before. That hanging out with him felt like being with my best friend ... that he had indeed became a best friend, one I constantly wanted to jump. Dane and I had a shared a past that couldn't be ignored.

Now here I was, chucking a Liv and hiding out, but it couldn't last forever. I had to face the fireworks, or more accurately, I had to face Dane. So I pulled myself together and threw on the skinny Levis that gave my butt the best shape, then pulled my hair into a perfectly styled messy bun. It was Monday evening, and for the first time since Saturday morning, I exited my room without checking the courtyard first.

Luck must have been on my side, for I scored a clear run all the way to the dining hall. Sure, I passed plenty of people, even stopped and had a couple of chats, but there was no McFlirt in sight. I climbed the steps into the dining hall, and spotted Molly and Olivia halfway down the line. Perfect—less chance of a confrontation if I was surrounded by friends. I put on the walk I knew dripped confidence to cross the crowded hall.

No sooner had I reached her than Molly whispered in my ear, "Ask Olivia how her day was."

"I can hear you," Liv complained.

Oh, this sounded like fun. I turned to face a furiously blushing Olivia. "Then how was it?"

She got all defensive, arms holding her breasts hostage. "It was all right."

"All right?" Molly hummed. "She skipped class to hang out with Logan."

Liv studied a knot in the floorboard. "The whole of Oxley doesn't care, Molly."

Molly's gaze shifted behind me, and that was the only warning I had before that salty, sandy scent hit me and an arm slid around my waist. "What's this about Loges?" Dane asked.

"Nothing," Olivia said, at the same time as Molly announced, "Liv here skipped class to spend the day with him."

"Interesting." Dane pulled me into his side.

The girl in front spun 'round. "Have you seen all the notches in the bench of his old room? Becoming one of Logan Hays's conquests isn't exactly difficult."

Geez, did all the guys around here mark their desks?

"Shut it, Abigail," Dane snapped.

"Oh, come on, Dane, I'm doing her a favour."

Molly used her back to block Abigail out of our conversation.

"Is it true?" Liv asked softly.

Dane glanced away, his jaw ticking. "It's an old dormitory. Do you know how many people have lived in that room?"

Even though she was facing the other way now, Abigail laughed, then muttered, "Says the other guy with a notched desk."

Bloody hell, and now that was what I was too—another notch on his freaking desk. My stomach dropped, and I pushed Dane away like I should have done when he'd first arrived. We moved through the servery, and Dane stayed with us all the way to the table, where he plonked himself between Liv and Molly, dead opposite me. Our knees touched and I shrank back, focusing on that stupid intricate metal knot hanging from its leather thong around his neck. At least it kept my eyes off his annoying smirk.

"What'd you think of the band on Friday?" Thank god for Molly and her small talk.

Dane cleared his throat and I looked up, right into those too-damn-pretty green eyes. Keeping his gaze glued to me, he answered, "The after party in Savvy's room was the highlight of that night."

A stray foot slid up my leg.

"But didn't you leave with Logan and Savvy left with Liv—" Molly's eyes widened. "Oh."

Dane grinned.

I just about swallowed my tongue, and it wasn't because his stupid Con was almost above my knee. Concentrating on my roast dinner, I mumbled, "Quit it, McFlirt."

Molly laughed.

"McFlirt, hey?" Dane's foot pressed against my inner thigh.

I swallowed the flood swamping my mouth. "It sums you up rather nicely. Don't you think so, Molly?"

"It is pretty close to the mark."

"Come on." Dane pointed a potato-laden fork at me. "You love my flirting."

"It's not your best trait."

"No? That my charm or my perfect pecs?" He danced them under his tank, and that damn tingle that had been building in my tummy since he'd first sat down spread to inappropriate places. "No …" he pursed utterly kissable lips, "… I got it. It's my smile." He dropped that sexy-as-all-hell smile that made girls everywhere fall to their knees.

"Well it's definitely not your winning personality." I pushed up out of my chair, which squealed as it scraped across the wooden floor. My cheeks burned as I walked across the dining hall to dump my plate and tray. Dane Beaumont could be so goddamn conceited … but all those things he mentioned were true. Screw him.

I headed outside with full intention of going straight to my room to resume my hide out, but just as I reached the turn from Front to Back Courtyard footsteps thundered down the path behind me. It wasn't Dane—they weren't heavy enough, and no way in hell would he run after any girl.

Molly panted out a strained breath and held up a finger, asking me to wait. I watched her catch her breath for several moments, and finally she fisted a hand on her hip and glanced back over her shoulder, then around the corner. She grabbed my arm and dragged me behind the back of block L.

"Look, it's probably none of my business, but—"

"But you're going to stick your nose in anyway?"

She offered up an almost-shy smile. "Well ... I couldn't help but notice that you like the guy, and he's obviously crazy about you, too. So, maybe you should embrace it."

I slumped a shoulder against the brick wall. Molly was so sweet I knew she was coming from a good place. "It's not the simple ... Dane and I ... well, Dane ... there's a history there."

"All the more reason to hook up." She sounded a bit exasperated, which was exactly how I felt. How I'd felt for the past few years. Longer even.

I let out a long sigh. "I know you mean well, but Molly ..."

"I'm sorry. I've overstepped my place." She started backing away.

"It doesn't matter how much I like him, or he likes me. We can't ..."

Her hand poised on her outthrust hip, Molly turned back around. The look on her face spoke volumes. She thought I was full of freaking excuses.

"Are you even listening to me?" I asked.

"You need to get over yourself, Savvy. He wants you, so go get him."

"Dane is Tori's ex."

"And Tori is?" She raised a who-the-hell-cares brow.

"My cousin; my lifelong closest friend. We're like sisters."

"Oh …"

"Yeah, oh." I dropped my other shoulder against the wall and slid down to the ground, my butt landing with a thunk. "It was serious. They dated for two years, Molly. Two. Whole. Years and I don't think she's completely over him."

"Oh …"

The look on her face said everything her lack words didn't. There was no way I could be with Dane, and she knew it.

CHAPTER TWELVE

Savvy

I'd been keyed up for tonight for the past week. With Easter break officially starting tomorrow, Central Night was the last Oxley social event until next term. I was all packed to head home tomorrow, and dressed for tonight already, so I trudged up to Olivia's room only to discover she'd bailed on me to hang out with Logan. Just watching a movie, she'd said—yeah, right. I'd seen the way they were the last time we were all together; there wouldn't be much attention on the screen.

It was a good thing Molly was up for the social. We'd been spending a bit time together lately, and I really liked the shy girl. Across the room, I gave my partner in partying a onceover. The jeans and baggy shirt wouldn't cut it. Maybe for studying in her room all day with the door closed, but for a night out? Ah, no.

Molly thrust a hand onto her hip, dishing me a pointed look. "This is what I'm wearing."

"No, it's not."

"I'm not a doll, Savannah. You aren't playing dress-ups with me."

I hooked my arm through Molly's and tugged her out of Olivia's room. Liv laughed, shouting, "Have fun, you guys."

"Okay," Molly relented. "I'll let you play dress up if you let me keep the Docs."

"Boots, Molly? Really? There's no way I can put you in a dress with—"

"Who said anything about a dress? We're going to the pub. The Central."

I cringed, but kept up the smile. "You wore a dress to the bar the other night."

"That was a once-off."

"Pfft. It's happening. Embrace it."

Despite her protests, Molly let me drag her up to my room. I dumped the suitcase I'd packed for Easter break off my desk onto the floor and pulled out my desk chair, instructing her to sit, then went to work in the wardrobe. She was a bit taller than me, and a tad bigger as well, especially around the bust. That would be tricky. Maybe she could keep the jeans after all ...

With dark hair and eyes the colour of well-watered grass she was striking. She just needed to drop the kiddie clothes and work those God-given curves. Maybe my Sportsgirl blouse would work. I grabbed the hanger and held the jade fabric up, closing one eye to focus on Molly's features hovering above the outfit. Yep, perfect. Eyes = gorgeous. "Try that one."

She took the hanger from me and peeled her baggy black T-shirt off, the love heart at its centre glittering under the fluorescent lighting as it fell on top of my purple suitcase.

"Dane going tonight?"

I turned to find some makeup in the cupboard and caught my reflection in the mirror, the loose curls I'd put in my own hair earlier bouncing. "Yeah …"

We hadn't exactly spoken about it, but he'd be there. He always was, flirting it up. A thought that made my stomach churn. Taking my cosmetic bag out of the cupboard, I pulled out my desk chair. "Sit."

Molly looked from the clutch in my hand to my face and raised a brow. Just as she opened her mouth, I intercepted with, "Now."

Sighing, she plopped herself into the tan swivel chair, slumping down so low her shoulders fell below the backrest.

"And be happy." I threw her a cheek-aching grin, then popped the bag on the desk and fished inside. She had a pretty complexion and didn't need a lot— just a little something to make those eyes pop even more.

"Tell me about Tori."

I set to work on her. "What do you mean?"

"You said that you're close, but I've never heard you mention her."

"Just because I don't talk about people doesn't mean they aren't important." *Kody, Mum, Dad.* Sometimes the truth was ugly. "Besides you and I have been friends for all of five minutes."

Molly's eyelids flicked open, and those pretty green orbs bore into my blue ones. "Spill."

"Close your eyes. I'm not done."

She gave me a hard look, then snapped those peepers closed. "We live in the same town—" *same house* "—have done since we were kids. She's a year older than me and was a grade above at school. Different schools, mind you, but we spent all our weekends hanging out. I was always closer to her than I was to my own sister. We were like twins." *Before that night.* "Not so much anymore, though. I mean, we're still mighty close, but with me here instead of there … I guess we don't get the time together we used to. Still, we chat all the time. I love the girl to pieces. It'll be good to see her tomorrow when I get home."

"And Dane?"

I finished up the green highlights on her eyes and placed the little tray on my desk, keeping my attention on the different eyeliners. God knew why it was so hard to actually look her in the eye while I was talking about this. "When I was sixteen, Tori brought the boy she'd been raving about for the past six months along to a party. They were both in grade eleven, and he'd moved to town and her school at the start of that year. That night they hooked up, and Dane became a permanent fixture in my Tori time for the next eighteen months, until he came here."

"And that's when they broke up?"

"More or less."

"The long-distance thing was too hard?"

"Maybe. Hold still."

I made her up with smoky eyes and applied a coat of mascara to her already long lashes, then stepped back to admire my work. "You can open up."

Molly blinked her eyes open, and her smoky green irises had popped to a bright emerald.

"Looking awesome, chicky."

She rolled the eyes I'd worked so hard on, and I scooped all my supplies back into my bag. "Let's get out of here. It's just about time to go."

I shoved my ID and a wad of cash in my back pocket then spun my room key off its tag and popped the cool metal into my bra, a trick I'd picked up from Kasi. Molly walked out into the hall and I followed, my gaze lingering on the purple suitcase as I shut up behind us.

"How long have you had a thing for him?"

The girl was nothing if not persistent. I traipsed down the stairs, wishing we'd had a drink before heading out. This conversation was getting painful, prying, pitiful even … which was fitting of the entire situation. One huge, pitiful mess.

"Since that very first party when you were sixteen?"

Only my whole life. I shrugged, and spotting an out across the courtyard, waved and shouted, "Hey Dono!"

He met my enthusiastic grin with its twin and held up a bottle of cider in greeting.

"Better down that real fast …" I tapped my wrist—not that I wore a watch. "Buses should be here already."

With a drinking Dono in tow, we made our way out to the parking lot where everyone had assembled. Oxley always put on a good crowd for social nights, but tonight the concrete lot was so full it seemed Olivia was the only one missing. Well, her and McFlirt. Not that I noticed. Noise surged through the people, the volume rising as everyone tried to be heard above the din. Just then one bus pulled around the corner, followed by a second, causing a cheer to erupt.

Everyone surged toward the opening door and piled on. When we finally reached the steps, Molly was in front. She clopped down the aisle and plonked into a seat smack bang in the middle of the bus.

"Savvy!" Kasi screeched from the back. In the centre of the boob patrol, she patted the spare seat beside her. Ordinarily I would've bolted down there and jumped in the thick of all the fun, but my gaze caught on Molly staring out the window, finger twirling around the end of her braid.

"Looking good, pocket rocket." A pinch to my butt accompanied the compliment delivered in a smooth voice. I looked down at a seat I'd just passed, into the cocky smile of Cade Matthews.

"Hands off." I flicked his shoulder then pushed on and dropped into the seat next to Molly. She gave me a small smile, but somehow seemed less herself than she had been up in my room. She tipped her head toward the opposite side of the bus, and there was McFlirt, looking this way. I pasted on a stretched grin and waved my fingertips. He never flinched.

"You know," Molly said, "if Tori loves you as much as you do her, then I'm sure she'd understand."

Pulling my attention back to my friend, I shrugged. "It's just not done."

"Have you spoken to her about him?"

I spun around to face the back of the bus, cocking my knee up onto the seat's backrest and yelled, "Kasi! How about we get this party started?"

Her squeal almost masked Molly's "you should."

Like a well oiled-machine, Kasi and I both burst into song. I raised my voice to shout, "B.I.N.G.O ..."

Before we'd even reached the 'and', the rest of the

bus had joined in. I laughed, I smiled—I threw everything I had into the stupid kiddie song. We'd been learning the tunes this week in class, and honestly it felt like I was five again. Sometimes a little bit of childishness made everything else seem less important.

Before the song was over, our bus pulled up out front of the bar. I kept my butt on the seat and shouted out till the very end while Molly wordlessly stared out the window and everyone else surged off.

I jabbed her in the side. "Let's get in there."

She shook her head and followed me down the aisle.

Inside the pub, music blared above the buzz of the crowd, stuffy warmth filled the air, and I set my sights on the bar. "You want a drink?" I shouted in Molly's ear. She nodded and we made our way to the counter.

I ordered us both vodka raspberries and spun around to find Molly chatting with Blaine Stratford. A forerunner of Dane and Christian's crowd, he looked at my friend as if he wanted to jump her right then and there in the bar. Smiling to myself, I sipped on my sweet drink and looked for someone to entertain me. Molly could use a little self-esteem building; I'd just leave her be for a bit. Of course the first soul my gaze found was Dane, brooding from a bar stool where he sat with the rest of his boys.

I tossed the straw out of my drink and downed the entire glass, set it on a table and started on the second one. I'd get Molly another later.

An older-style hotel, the Central was split into three rooms connected by wide-open doorways. I made a beeline for the one I knew held the dance floor, because that was where the party would be thumping so loud I could just join in without having to worry about prying friends or brooding surfer boys.

I edged through the crowd, the music thrumming louder with each step, until I reached the few stairs that led into the back room. With the lights dimmed, flashing strobes lit the area right before the DJ up front. The mood was swinging.

Kasi and the other girls from teaching class were rocking it up near the DJ. It took all of two seconds for her to see me and glide across, grabbing my hand and dragging me back to join them. These girls and I had been in the same classes for more than a year now and somehow we always gravitated together on the dance floor.

The music wasn't too bad, with plenty of dance mixes, the odd oldie, and top forty all mixed in with popular pub anthems. It wasn't until I'd been there for a while that I noticed the view through the wide arch that led back out of the main room. The square arch was like a frame, capturing the glory that was Dane Beaumont centre stage. Wearing a Stussy T-shirt that sat snugly across those perfectly formed pecs, he no longer had his brood on. Now he smiled across his beer at Christian, laughing at god only knew what. When he smiled like that ... all genuine and without the flirty show ... my heart turned to goo, and my hormones kicked in tenfold.

Maybe Molly was right.

Maybe Tori would understand.

Maybe my feelings for Dane just shouldn't take a backseat any longer.

CHAPTER THIRTEEN

Dane

The way Savvy moved on the dance floor had my body paying attention. Across the table, Christian banged on about some political issue that really didn't float my board. Cade had his night made with some fresher chick, and even though his beady eyes were glued to Savvy, his arm kept sneaking around his would-be conquest. Blaine was still MIA.

Gentle fingers brushed the back of my neck then settled on my shoulder, followed by a second hand to the other side. Clever digits kneaded the muscle, and a voice whispered in my ear, "Whatcha lookin' so serious about?"

Ella Parry.

"Serious? You've got the wrong guy." I picked up my schooner of James Squire and knocked it back.

From out on the dance floor, Savvy's eyes caught mine and I glanced away. She'd been avoiding me since we'd hooked up the other night, clearly regretting that we'd shagged. I shouldn't have cared, but after she'd tossed me out of her room, I'd felt all kinds of messed up. Girls didn't get under my skin like that. I didn't let them, not since I'd been screwed over by Victoria West. Yet this heaviness compressing my chest made it feel as if I was suffocating, and seeing Cade's efforts on the bus had turned my blood to lava.

"Mm-hmm." Ella continued kneading my tight muscles. "Serious."

Why Savvy chose that moment to glance my way again when she'd been focused on her friends all night I wasn't sure. But when our eyes locked a second time I didn't look away, because the way she stared at me was like she finally saw me for the first time since last Friday night. My stomach did some stupid damn thing where it felt like I'd just dropped onto an epic wave.

Hell, I had no goddamn control. It didn't help that Savvy raised her hands above her head and moved her body like a temptress, swaying, writhing, and dragging her palms down the sides of all those sexy curves. I picked up my drink and gulped a mouthful to wet my suddenly dry mouth.

The type of shiver that makes your teeth clench and thighs shiver followed the beer to my gut. Rippling through my chest and stomach, it didn't stop until it had drained all my blood south. A hot breath tickled my ear. "If you need some help loosening up, I'd be happy to oblige."

Savvy moved across the dance floor, her gaze still

locked on mine, and if loosening up was on offer then I was all down for that. I slammed my empty glass onto the table.

Savvy, the damn sexy torment, sashayed right up to me, then placed a hand on the sticky table and leaned in real close. "You could always come join me."

"Suppose I could." I raised a what-the-hell brow. This girl was more hot and cold than a faulty oil heater. I wasn't ready to have my heart drawn and quartered, and after the way the week had played out, Savvy was a sure-fire way to reach that outcome. Good thing term break started tomorrow. "If I felt like it."

The look that crossed her face cut into my good conscience as she removed her hand from my space and rocked back on her heels. "Your loss, McFlirt."

She disappeared toward the bar, and I leaned back into Ella's nimble fingers, kicking back the last of my beer.

The night wore on. Christian turned into a depressed drunk, moaning about his dumb-arse dumping Olivia. That was about the time Ella disappeared, only to be replaced by a brunette I knew from class and her blonde friend, who deposited herself next to Christian. Twirling a straw round her drink, the brunette babbled about something from uni while I stared into the other room. Savvy hadn't looked my way again, hadn't acknowledged my presence. She just trotted past the table, drink in hand, and resumed moving that body of hers as if she was putting on a show for every damn bloke in the place.

Screw it. What would a bit of fun cost, really?

Separating body from heart couldn't be that hard. I pushed off the stool and stalked through the thick crowd. Funny how the later it grew and the messier everyone got, the more people danced. Way more than in the early part of the night when they were only buzzed. Pressing through the crowded dance floor all the way to where the speakers were loudest, I found Savvy still running those tiny hands all over her sweet body like a one-woman cabaret. Heat flooded *my* body, and my hands itched to take the place of hers. This girl was damn beautiful, and she owned it. Couldn't get sexier than that.

I'd never wanted her more.

Coming up behind her, I set my hands on her hips and tugged her back into me so our bodies sat flush.

Thanks to the loud music, I felt more than heard her gasp. She stiffened for a moment, but when Kasi gave us the thumbs up Savvy resumed dancing, careful to keep enough distance between us so that we *just* weren't touching. A centimetre—less—had never felt so huge. My inner caveman growled at me to force that distance closed just to show every hot-blooded arsehole in the joint whose girl she was.

I brought my mouth right up to her pink-tipped ear. "I felt like it."

Savvy's shoulders dropped, her entire body loosening as she fell back into me, closing that god-awful space and hooking her hands behind her and around my neck.

I might have groaned at the impact of her arse hitting my crotch. Couldn't be sure, because every brain cell I had was concentrated on keeping this show fit for public consumption. Savvy ground that sweet piece of flesh against me as she moved to the beat, and I trailed my fingers along the sides of her body in the exact same way I'd watched her do earlier. Her friends danced around us, but it felt as if the rest of the Central ceased to be—it was just her and me, and the mad chemistry zipping between us.

I trailed my fingers over the dip of her waist to the swell of her hips then thighs, Savvy shivered beneath my touch. Without loosening her hold, she swung 'round to face me, her hands now linked behind my neck, our hips aligned. She rose onto tiptoes and feathered soft lips across my cheek. My pulse raced to a beat ten times faster than the dance music filling the room. I dropped my mouth onto hers, claiming what should be mine, claiming her like I should have done years ago.

Savvy moaned into my kiss. Her hands found my arse, holding me against her as she kissed me just as hard as I'd kissed her. Someone bumped into my shoulder, but whatever. I swept her mouth with my tongue, tasting the sting of whatever the hell she'd been drinking coupled with her own sweet flavour. My hand slid up her side again, my splayed fingers brushing the swell of her breast and something vibrated between us, against my thigh.

She pulled back, her cheeks flushed, her glazed eyes staring into mine. She caught her bottom lip between her teeth, and her eyes full of questions shut down with a snap. The bright blue turning cold and icy.

Whatever the hell had just happened, she was about to retreat, and fast.

I couldn't do this. Couldn't hook up with her again just to have her pretend it never happened once it was over. Savvy wasn't like all those other girls. I couldn't just walk away. I cared too much about her, had done since that night on the beach two years ago.

I dropped my hands and put some distance between us with a backwards step. "I can't."

"What?" Her expression morphed to angry.

I shook my head and retreated, leaving the dance floor. I stormed all the way through the front room and pushed open the fire exit, bursting into night air so cold it snapped the heat right out of me. Shoving my fists in my pockets, I pumped them open and closed, trying to dispel some of the pent-up tension. I didn't know what I'd been thinking, but it was a stupid idea. There was an obvious attraction between us, but that was all it was to her, and it was too late— I was already in way deeper.

"Dane!" Savvy called.

I crossed the deserted street, my sights set firmly on the empty taxi rank.

"Stop walking away, you arsehole."

I turned around slowly. "Arsehole? Really?"

"Yes! Arse. Hole." She stalked across the road and jabbed a finger in my chest.

"You're the one who offered up life altering-sex, then the second you were done, tossed me out. So if anyone's an arsehole here, it's you, Savannah."

She got right up in my face, her breath sweet with vodka and raspberry. "You're just dirty I beat you to it."

My mind drew a blank while my tongue worked to form words. "That's what you think of me? Of what I think of this ...?" I waved my hand between us. "Nice, Savvy. Real nice."

"I'm just another freaking notch on your desk, Dane, and we both know it." She was shouting now, yelling even, and my anger matched hers. I glared into those icy eyes.

Keeping my voice even, I said, "You didn't give us a chance to be anything more."

"Because you chose Tori."

She was so close I couldn't breathe, all over me like a hot rash, and there was no resisting anymore. Tori issues I could deal with.

I dropped my mouth onto hers, and kissing her like there was no tomorrow, I let all logic take a backseat to passion and anger. This was about Victoria, about a choice I'd made when I was sixteen and barely knew Savvy. I hadn't known she was full of passion and intelligence. Hadn't known that she was caring and kind and an all-round beautiful woman that it was impossible not to love. That she was a princess who deserved to be treated like she was special and unique and important. That despite the brave exterior, she just needed someone to care for her.

That I would fall in love with her.

With my hands cradling her face, I pulled back to look her in the eye. "I choose you, Savvy. Right now, I choose you, and that's enough."

She pried her phone out of those skin-tight jeans and fumbled with the tiny keypad. I took her other hand, and pulled her into the cab that had just pulled up. Sitting in the middle seat so I could tuck her under my arm, I told the driver, "Take us to Oxley."

CHAPTER FOURTEEN

Savvy

My chest burned warmer than a fresh pizza in stark contrast to my cool back, with the exception of a hot weight across the arch of my waist. My cheek pressed against the rock-hard electric blanket. I woke up slowly at first, then suddenly as I remembered where I was. I froze. Then digging my toes into the mattress, I pushed myself up to place a kiss on Dane's mouth.

He smiled against it. "Morning, princess."

"Morning, McFlirt."

He chuckled, and that sensation awoke all the tingles being so close to him always caused. Using the arm wrapped around me, he tugged me fully on top of him. The only thing between us was his Celtic necklace, resting against the dip of his throat. All that bare skin touching mine felt so heavenly, I moaned.

His fingers trailing along my side to my waist just amplified the deliciousness.

"Now isn't this so much nicer than kicking me out?" he asked.

"I can hardly kick you out of your own room now, can I?"

Long fingers dug into my waist and he kissed me, morning breath be damned. I must have looked a wreck with yesterday's makeup still on, and my hair all mussed from our long, long night. It didn't matter, because I soon forgot all about everything but the burn of Dane beneath me and how awesome it felt to wake up in his bed.

This guy didn't know it yet, but he owned me, from the tips of my curling toes to the lips he so expertly worked, and every part in between. I was all his to do with as he pleased. And that was exactly what he did right then with my body.

I could have stayed in bed with the six-foot hunk of defined muscle, but I had a bus to catch, and missing it would cause me more trouble than it was worth. I prised myself away from yet another round of life-altering sex with a life-altering man and pulled on last night's dress. Reaching to snatch up my black underwear from where it lay near my heels was a waste of time; Dane grabbed me around the waist and yanked me back into bed and his lap.

"Dane." I kissed his mouth. "I'll miss my bus."

"If you had of woken when I ... wait ..." His face screwed up. "You're riding the bus home?"

"Yes." I pried his fingers off my waist.

"What in the hell for? I drive back and forth every break. You could have been catching a ride with me."

"You never offered."

"I never realised you were on a bloody bus." I pushed at the glorious firmness that was his chest until he collapsed back on the bed. "Hell, Savvy. That's screwed up. I assumed Tori drove you."

Guilt stabbed my chest at the mention of my cousin's name. I retrieved my shoes from under the desk and slipped them on. "I can get the bus for half the price it would cost her to drive here and back."

"Get your shit together. We're leaving in an hour."

"From flirty to bossy in zero-point-seven seconds. I'm impressed."

He pushed his fingers through mine and used his hand to raise my palm to his lips. "And what about the bus ticket I already paid for? Tori's all set to pick me up at the other end."

"You're not catching the fucking bus."

I rose my eyebrows. "Really, Dane?"

"Really," he growled, spinning his legs over the side of the bed. He reached for his jeans and tugged them on, commando.

I opened the door and left his room. By the time I reached the entrance to the stairs, the door creaked opened again. "An hour."

The smile that spread across my face was completely unbidden as I gave him the finger and jogged down block B's stairs. How was I going to explain catching a ride with him to Tori?

****

The knock on my open door at eleven came as no surprise. I turned around from placing the last of my folded clothes into my open suitcase and found Dane's bulk crowding the doorway. I should have known he'd show up. Pushing past, he zipped up the case and hefted it off my bed. A three-hour car trip home with him would be a lot nicer than sticking my head in a book and hoping to god I wasn't stuck next to someone who stank. Plus, all that time alone with Dane ... there wasn't much point in fighting this.

"Geez, what've you got, half the library in there?"

"Library?" I raised a what-the-hell brow. "This is me we're talking about."

He rolled my bag out of the room, and I tugged my door closed and followed along, appreciating the fine sight that was Dane in jeans. He didn't wear them often as he was more of a boardshorts guy, but he really should, because that rear was almost as nice as his spectacular arms. Guess all the time spent pulling himself through waves paid off. Sighing, I slipped my laptop bag over my shoulder and jogged down the stairs. Dane waited at the bottom, and it looked as though Olivia was snared in his charm. She shot me a questioning look, but ignoring it, I slapped her arm. "How was last night?"

A tell-tale blush crept up her neck and into her cheeks. I let out a low whistle.

"No ... no ... it wasn't like that. We just ... we watched—"

"Watched each other?"

Dane chuckled and Liv squirmed. I shouldn't take joy in tormenting her. The fact I did most probably made me a terrible friend, but with Olivia it was so hard to resist.

"Make sure you have a great Easter, hon." I kissed her cheek.

Liv glanced at my suitcase in Dane's hand. "You too. Bye, Dane."

He gave her a quick nod and slid his Oakleys off the top of his head and over his eyes as we set off, traipsing through both courtyards and toward his black SUV. Dane clicked the keys and the hatch popped, as did the doors. He hoisted my bag into the back with ... was that a sock-covered surfboard?

"Dude, what in the heck do you do with a surfboard this far inland?"

"Mostly?" He peered at me over the rim of his Oakleys. "I leave it sitting in the car."

I climbed up into the passenger seat while he loped around to his side.

"And you can't leave it at home because ..."

"I'd miss it."

That was either really cute or really sad. I couldn't be sure which.

I settled down into the comfy seat, kicking my feet up underneath me. Despite fighting to stay awake so I could suck the most out of the three-hour car trip, my eyes grew heavy before we even reached the edge of town. Leaning my head against the window, I covered my yawn. From his position with one hand on the wheel, the other hanging out the window, Dane glanced across at me. "Grab a couple hours. It'll be full on when you get home."

I stifled another yawn. "I wouldn't be so tired if someone hadn't kept me awake all night."

"Yeah, I'm not sorry about that." He winked at me. "Life altering."

"Life altering," I agreed, slouching farther into the bucket seat.

Next thing I knew we were just outside of Coffs, slowing as the wide road opened onto the main highway and all the southbound traffic zoomed by. I rubbed at my tired eyes.

"Hey there," Dane said.

I shuffled around to get comfortable. "Sorry I flaked for so long. I'm terrible company."

"You're terrible nothing."

"You are such a sweet-talker."

"What?" His widened eyes flicked from watching the road ahead to questioning me. "What are your plans for the break? I could handle some more of that terrible company."

I glanced out the window at the houses passing by. The huge, mansion-like homes set close to the beach always made my heart hurt. "Not sure. I guess I'll be busy with Kody mostly, and I have a few assignments to do ... plus all the family stuff over Easter."

"Are you brushing me off, princess?" He pulled a too surprised look that would have fit a cartoon character.

"Your ego could use the let-down."

Dane slapped the steering wheel and fake-whooped. "You're a riot, girl."

All too soon, we turned into my street and the SUV dipped down into the driveway out front of the two-storey home with its pristine lawns and perfectly shaped shrubs. Tori's red Lancer sat on the street, and Aunt Rosy's van was in the centre of the driveway. That was when I remembered Dane and I probably shouldn't be hanging out. I owed my cousin some loyalty. At least until I could explain things to her.

Dane cut the engine and stepped out of the car. I slid out too and went around back to where he was unloading my luggage, and slipped it out of his hand.

"Thanks for the ride. It was so much nicer than catching the bus. I'll ... ah ... catch up with you later."

Frowning, he took my laptop bag from the backseat and slung it over his shoulder. "No more buses. You're coming back with me at end of break, too."

I held up both hands in surrender. "All right, you win."

Moving toward the house quietly, I pulled my suitcase up the ramp to the front door. Dane set my laptop bag down, and his mouth curled into that flirty smile I hated to love. My stomach did its usual thing, my heart followed suit and, dropping his stare from my eyes to my mouth, he stepped forward. I panicked, throwing us into a hug to escape any potential goodbye kisses that Tori might accidentally stumble out on. It wouldn't be the nicest way for my cousin to find out we had something going on.

He pressed a kiss to the top of my head anyway, and oh shit ... was that footsteps inside?

I pulled back just before the door swung open to reveal none other than Tori, looking at Dane with an unabashed open-mouthed stare. She never spared me a glance as she took in the surf-shirt jean-clad perfection that was showing her his McFlirt smile. That sat about as well as cement hitting the base of my stomach. He didn't break the grin. She didn't look away. It didn't seem like either of them would ever speak, so I pushed past Dane and hugged my cousin with a squeal. "Hey you!"

Her arms tightened around me. "Savvy. What are you doing here? What's *he* doing here? I thought the bus didn't get in until six."

"Surprise," I said, pulling back. "Dane gave me a ride."

He smiled again—or maybe it was still—and this

time those stunning green eyes rested on me. "Thanks for the terrible company, Sav. I'll catch you soon."

"My pleasure." I fake-smiled.

Dane frowned as he backed down the steps and onto the lawn. Then he turned to his car and climbed in with a lingering look I assumed was aimed at me. But with Tori standing beside me waving wildly, who could be sure?

CHAPTER FIFTEEN

Savvy

My stomach plummeted into my toes as she stood there, phone pressed to her ear and an expression that could only be described as horrific scarring her pixie-like face. She wouldn't look at me, just stared at the ocean. But that not-look from Tori was enough.

My legs gave way, buckling beneath me, and my knees hit the warm sand.

When something horrible has happened you just innately know, and right then I knew with a certainty that it was my family.

I have no idea how long the call lasted, but it felt like time stopped. Only my time though; everyone else partied on. The music continued, the fire kept lapping at the black night, and the waves ... they still slammed into the shore, but I froze there in the sand, my heart not beating, my lungs not drawing breath, my world not spinning.

"Savvy ..." Tori's hand slid under my elbow. "Savvy. We need to get home."

Her words were loud and clear, but my legs, they couldn't move. Didn't want to.

"Sav ..." Her wavering voice broke into a sob. Her cold hand snapped around my wrist and yanked, but still I couldn't move. "You have to get up!" she shouted.

I couldn't.

It was like my body wasn't mine.

Warm arms closed around me and scooped me up off the ground. The music seemed to have stopped, but my mind hadn't. Was it Kody? Mum? Dad? An accident on the basketball court ... a heart attack ... a mugging on the way to the game?

"What's wrong?"

"Is she all right?"

"Should we call an ambulance?"

All voices I could hear, but I couldn't utter a word. My tongue had stopped working.

"We've got to get home." Tori kept repeating that phrase over and over while Dane strode across the beach, my body cradled against him.

"Hey!" A cushion thumped me across the face. Tori had the footrest up on her dad's favourite recliner, lounging back. Clearly, she knew he wasn't home yet. My feet were up too, on my suitcase that hadn't even made it upstairs to the room we shared. "What's with you?"

"Nothing." I shoved the cushion behind me. Tori hadn't stopped talking since Dane drove away. Not that I was really listening, since paying attention was near impossible with the memory of last night fresh on my mind. Her eyes narrowed and her gaze wandered over my entire body, and I had the urge to hide behind Kody's baby grand sitting in the corner. "I'm just tired. Last night there was this party—"

"Ohmygod. You met a real man!"

"What?"

"You so did. Tell me more."

"I didn't tell you anything to begin with."

"Oh yes you did, dear cousin."

"It gets crazy on the night before break—"

Her raised eyebrow stopped me cold; we stared each other off for a few moments until finally Tori glanced away. I exhaled a long breath and leaned my head back against the soft cushion.

"I was surprised to see Dane. I didn't think you saw much of each other."

Holy shit ... I wasn't ready for this conversation.

"Our friends are dating, which has kind of thrown us into the same circle."

"Is that the Olivia chick?"

"Yep." I'd done a good job at keeping my college and home lives separate, but sometimes a little bit of info slipped through.

Taylor Swift burst from the direction of the black piano, and Tori jumped out of the chair and scrambled for her phone sitting on top of the shiny ebony. She picked up with a thumb jab to the screen and sounded cheery as she greeted whoever was on the other end of her call. Tori slipped out the side door and onto the balcony, so I pulled myself out of the chair and went in search of my sister. Aunt Rosy's van in the driveway should mean Kody was home from school. I climbed the stairs, careful to stick to the banister on the right side, leaving the left free.

Eerie quietness hung in the air; it was funny the little things you noticed after living away for a few months. I'd never realized how silent it was here until I'd learned what it was like to live with two hundred other students.

I turned to the right and knocked softly on the closest door. No answer. Easing it open, I peeked in, and right beside the bed stood Kody's empty chair. Seemed she'd fallen asleep curled on her side facing the door. My sister was usually keen to greet me, but maybe she'd gotten her days messed up. I pulled the door to. May as well bring those bags up.

Unpacking everything took the better part of an hour. It would have been done in a quarter of that time if Tori hadn't encroached on my wardrobe space in order to hang up an abundance of new dresses. After squishing my stuff into the crowded rack and dumping all my dirty clothes in the washing basket, I shoved the empty suitcase under my bed and headed back downstairs. My cousin was still pacing the balcony with her phone pressed to her ear, so I went to find my aunt. Not a difficult feat, since Rosy practically lived in the kitchen. Manicured hands dipped into a bowl of what looked to be ground beef, or maybe it was lamb—hard to tell. I pulled out a stool and plopped myself at the counter.

"Hi, honey." She wiped the meat off her fingers and rinsed them under running water. "I'd ask how school is, but ..." Shiny, straight hair dipped as she nodded toward the bowl. "I need to concentrate right now."

"Can I help?"

She wiped dripping hands on towel, a small frown creasing her forehead. "Hmm ..."

Aunt Rosy grabbed an onion and began peeling, dicing, adding to the mince mixture while I watched on. My dad's sister-in-law and I had never really been close, but I'd always found a certain comfort in being inside a kitchen. Even as a little girl I'd loved working alongside my mum, chatting up a storm about nothing and everything all at once. Rosy blended a few slices of bread and I figured rissoles were on tonight's menu. After a while, I pulled out my phone and flicked through my new messages. Dono was missing me already, Liv's flight had been delayed, but she'd caught the next one and now she was on the train home, and Molly was quiet. The smell of cooking meat hung heavily on the air, and I flicked over to check social media.

"Welcome home, Savannah." Uncle Trevor swept through the room, dropping a hello kiss on Aunt Rosy's cheek before he disappeared.

And that was her cue to begin dishing food onto plates. I carried them out to the table, setting them in our usual places; Uncle Trevor at the head, Aunt Rosy to his right, Tori to his left, with me by her side, and Kody directly across from me. The table arrangements were fixed in stone; heaven forbid anyone should upset them. Using the innate sixth sense I'd always wondered how she'd developed, Tori appeared and took her seat. By the time Uncle Trevor returned, we were all in place, save Kody.

Everyone joined hands for a quick word of grace then they all began eating, but I peered over my shoulder at the staircase. Where on earth was my sister?

"How's school, Savannah?" Aunt Rosy asked.

"Umm ..." I frowned, wondering why all hell

hadn't broken loose at Kody's tardiness. "It's good. Classes are interesting."

"Have you put any thought into the practical side of your studies? You have to take a block sometime this year, yes?"

"I need to start researching schools to find out which ones are open to student teachers."

Tori's fork scraped across the bottom of her plate and I cringed, but Uncle Trevor just ignored it, the same way he ignored Kody's absence, and shoved another forkful of mashed potato in his mouth.

"There are plenty of primary schools around here. Why, I heard that Mount View takes student teachers regularly."

"Is that so?" As much as I'd love to be close, doing work experience in a school where people knew me or knew of my family really didn't appeal. I glanced toward the empty staircase again and couldn't hold it in any longer. "Where's Kody?"

"Up in her room." Tori finally joined the conversation. "We'll take her up a tray later."

"What in the hell for?"

Aunt Rosy's fork stopped halfway to her mouth, and Uncle Trevor shot me one of his looks. "Language won't be tolerated at this table, Savannah."

"Sorry," I fired off like a well-oiled machine. "But why isn't my sister down here eating with everyone else?"

"Dear Savannah," Aunt Rosy started. "It's just the way she is lately."

"The way she is ..." I floundered, trying to make sense of why they'd let her wallow, if wallowing was in fact what was going on here.

I scooped my sister's plate off the table along with

her cutlery, and amidst a round of protests marched up the stairs, where I banged open her door without knocking. She was no longer on her bed but sitting in her chair, which was now by the window. She didn't turn away from her blank daze at my intrusion—didn't even flinch. I slid the plate onto her dresser.

"Your dinner is going cold, chickpea."

Maybe she hadn't heard.

"Kody …"

She could have blinked, but my sister didn't turn her head. Her fingers rested deathly still on the armrests of her metal chair, her bare toes tucked up on the footrest. I took a step forward.

"Kody, I'm home." Why hadn't they told me things were this bad? Gripping the handle, I spun her chair around so she was facing me. She stared through me, her sky blue eyes so like my own, clouded with an almost vacant glaze.

"What's going on? Talk to me."

Kody blinked once, and her hands resting in her lap flexed, but still no words.

"Dakota Jane West, answer me."

Her gaze finally flicked to mine. "I'm not hungry."

She seemed a little thinner in the face than usual. Just how many meals had she missed? "How's school?"

A blank look.

"Made any nice friends?"

"School is school. People are people. They're the same everywhere."

"That's not true … I'm not the same as Miles Cooper, now am I? If that hot boy was sitting here I'm sure you'd be thinking he was far more interesting than your boring sister."

Dropping the boy band hottie's name was a good move, but her mouth never twitched. I pushed her chair over to the desk and shifted her plate in front of her. "Eat up, chickpea. Cold potato sucks worse than Uncle Trevor's anal retentiveness."

Still no smile. This wasn't like my baby sister at all. Sure, she'd been down the last time I was home and plenty often since the accident, but this zombie-like girl wasn't her. After a long time of watching her staring at the rissoles, I left her alone with the food and retreated back to my own at the empty table downstairs. Everything had been cleared, except for my lonely plate, its pile of mash a half-smooshed tower of potato. I pulled out my chair and sat back down, eating the cold food that did in fact taste horrid. When I was done, I took my dirty stuff into the kitchen where Aunt Rosy worked alone, washing the pots and pans that weren't dishwasher friendly.

Her gloved-fingers scraped the caked meat from the base of the pan. "How did it go?"

I rinsed off my plate and shoved it into the dishwasher. "She was oddly sombre ..."

"She hasn't been downstairs much the past few weeks."

"What happened? What's changed since I was last here?"

"Nothing."

"It can't be nothing. Have you spoken to her doctor?"

Rosy's hand stilled, the cleaning brush hovering above the sudsy water. "Savannah, I'm the carer here, not you, and I've done everything that I can to help her, so stop questioning me like I'm an imbecile. She's just going through a rough patch. Depression is completely understandable, given all the circumstances. Her doctor is aware, and we're helping her the best way we can."

"Well, it's like she's not even there right now. She's been sad before, but never like this."

"The medication she's on—"

"Back up, medication?"

The brush dove back into the water, splashing up the tiles as Rosy scrubbed the pot. "Antidepressants, Savannah, prescribed by Dakota's doctor, and they seem to be working. She's stopped hating the world like she was before, but there are some side effects—"

"Like killing all emotion?"

The pot slammed into the drying rack. "I don't think that's the case."

"She's sitting up there, and she isn't sad. She isn't happy. She isn't anything but a zombie."

"She hated school. At least now she gets up in the mornings, she goes to school, and she seems to learn. This is just a short-term thing. She's getting better."

I slammed the dishwasher closed. That was not in any sense better. In fact, this whole thing reeked of worse, but Rosy had shut down the conversation by leaving the room, so I finished up and headed upstairs. When I got to our room it was occupied. Tori had her foot hiked up on the bed to paint her toenails a shade of purple that should be reserved for little old ladies' hair.

"How's the kid?" Tori said.

"Why didn't anyone call me?"

"You've got your own life, Savvy. Mum's on top of this."

I stormed over to the window and twisted the

blind open as if I could see the ocean, because old habits die hard. All that looked back at me was the house across the street and beyond that another house and another house.

"Your phone's been beeping like crazy."

My heart jumped right to the Dane conclusion, but I pushed that thought away. It was more than likely Olivia telling me her train had arrived in one piece. I fished around in my laptop bag, and my heart jumped at the name on the screen.

Dropping onto the side of my bed, I flicked the message open and saw a whole string of them, as well as a single text from Molly. Of course I read Dane's first.

This bed looks oddly empty without you in it, princess.

We should do something about that. Since the memory of that sweet arse holds nothing to the real deal.

Whatcha doing for Easter next weekend? I heard there's this thing down by the water, and maybe I could win you one of those huge-arse stuffed toys.

For real? I'd never picked him as the fair-going type. I smiled as I typed back.

I assumed hitting the beach together would be more your style.

"So …" Tori drawled, her knees pulled up under her chin and toes poised on the very edge of the bed. "… princess." My cousin waggled her blonde eyebrows, and my heart beat to the tune of oh-shit. "Who is this McFlirt?"

"Not a Pinocchio." I flicked open Molly's message.

Your disappearance last night must mean you two finally sorted yourselves out. If not, you suck for dumping me.

Oops. Dane had dragged me into the cab in such a state, I'd forgotten all about her.

I'm so sorry! I'm such a terrible friend.

She responded straight away.

The verdict? All sorted?

I sent back a smiling emoji, and she answered,

Then you're forgiven.

I tossed my phone on the bed and perched on the side, watching my cousin. Tori was beautiful in a way most girls envied. The tips of her dark-dyed hair framed her face as she dabbed at her drying toes. Shorter at the back than the front, the style framed her pretty face and bright eyes. She glanced up at me, and those topaz orbs crinkled a little.

"I miss you when you're not here."

"Me too." My stomach turned to concrete,

pushing my dinner back up my throat. I was more than a disloyal friend; I was a horrid human being.

"Heads up." The bottle of polish came at me, flying through the air, and I caught it on the full. "Kody will be all right. Switching schools just wasn't as easy as everyone hoped. It didn't fix all the issues she was having at East Coast."

I twisted the mini lilac bottle through my fingers. "I just want her to be well and happy, and this seems a long way from that."

Seeing her like this sucked. She deserved everything good in the world and because of me she'd missed out on so much. We both had.

CHAPTER SIXTEEN

Dane

Catching rays made studying on break more bearable. As did the knowledge that once I'd knocked out this assessment, which was due first week back, I was hitting the waves. The weather was cooling, but the locals had a little more stamina than those from out of town. We knew there were a few more weeks of days warm enough to suck the most out of the season and those who surfed didn't care about the weather. In fact, the surf was usually better in winter. I stretched my legs into the autumn sun falling across my spot on the rickety wraparound veranda and shot off a quick text to the girl I hadn't been able to get off my mind all weekend.

Going for a surf later if you feel like a roll in

the sand.

The churn of the lawnmower's engine changed to an idle for the second time in ten minutes. I glanced up in time to catch the old man running from the yard to a tree partially hidden by our hedge fence, where he spread his legs and took aim. The laugh I coughed out had him turning over his shoulder, but I ducked my head and ignored the man who used to fly fair up me for doing the same thing only a few years back. Flopping it out in public was only for little kids, he'd said. With one hand on his hip and the other holding his junk, he hunched over and held the pose.

This time I actually returned my attention to the books. Small Business Management wasn't a hard subject, so I should be able to bash out this assessment in no time. My phone pinged.

A roll in the sand? Come on, you can do better than that.

I see your game and raise you an intelligent discussion on the philosophy of a tree falling in the woods.

The mower spluttered back to work just as the screen door slapped against the peeling weatherboards with my mother's hurried exit. Her pint-sized terrier, Roar, shot out around her legs and I looked up, expecting her to shout that the kitchen was on fire, but instead she said, "Finish up the lawns for your father. There's ... ah ... I need his opinion on these new drapes."

I marked my page by turning it down and traipsed over the long grass to get to the patch where he was shooing the dog away from his work. I set my hand on the machine's handle. "Mum needs your help inside. I'll finish up."

After a long look, he conceded control of the mower and staggered inside, calling for Roar to come to heel.

I knocked the grass over in plenty of time to still make the beach before lunch. And from the waiting text, it looked like I was going solo.

> *I'm pretty busy today. Will see you soon though.*

Well damn.

It only took ten minutes to get from home to Five Mile. I pulled my board out of the back and peeled off the striped sock that protected it during all the weeks of non-use it'd seen while at Oxley. Suiting up took a few minutes, then I locked up and took off, relishing in the feel of the sand under my bare feet. I'd only managed to squeeze in one session between sorting out all the paperwork at the shop and keeping on the schoolwork. Dad wasn't exactly the best bookkeeper or up for anything outside of the realm of working wood.

As I crested the hill, small hands landed on either side of my waist, and I sucked in a surprised a breath. Tipping up my board to save it whacking her in the gut, I spun around with a smart-arsed remark on the tip of my tongue. It dried up the second my gaze set on a pair of brown eyes staring back at me rather than blue. Couldn't for the life of me remember the chick's name, even though we'd hooked up a couple of times after meeting at a party last year. Emily, Ella, Emma, Ericka, Ember ... nope, it wasn't there. I offered a smile in place of a hello.

She looked up at me through dark lashes. "I'd recognise this board anywhere. You home for the holidays?"

Her hands were still on my waist, the tops of her fingers brushing the bare skin above my wettie. The contact sent the wrong kind of shivers under my skin. Weird—a single touch from a beach babe usually made me look for more. I took a step back and kept going, walking backwards down the hill and to the beach. "Sure am."

She walked with me, and my gaze dropped to the bikini she filled out nicely.

"What are you doing later? Maybe we could—"

My heel clipped the timber step, but I kept retreating. "I'll be out there for a while. Gotta make the most of the waves before I head back to school."

She offered an understanding smile at my rebuff.

"See you later then."

"Later." I turned to face the ocean in time to step off the track and into the soft sand. It was well past time to hit the waves.

****

Whoever thought up fish being the mandatory meal on Good Friday more than likely owned a fresh seafood shack. Religion made for good marketing. The queue at Coasties Fresh Fish & Seafood wound its way through the shop and out the front door, which I had propped open with my foot, since our current spot in the line placed us as doormen.

"She wants all that for just the two of us?" I plucked Mum's list out of my father's hand. "Blue Swimmers, prawns, oysters, Balmain bugs and Atlantic salmon. Shit, is it Christmas?" It was enough to feed the entire street, not just the three of us. "We never get all this, not even on—"

"Keep her happy, Son. Makes my life easier."

"Stew …" Dad's head shot up at his name, and I glanced away from Mum's epic order in time to see one of the old man's mates, John. The two of them shook hands in the way only guys who went back a long way knew how, one hand clasped inside the other, and John's second sandwiching them together. "Been a while between fishing trips; how've you been keeping?"

"Not bad," Dad said.

Their handshake finally released, and John nodded in the direction of downtown. "I heard you set up shop with the driftwood furniture."

"Sure did. Just off the corner of Seaspray and Oaklen. You should call in some time."

The line shuffled forward, and I let the next person take over as door prop. John moved with us. "I've still got that garden seat you made … geez … seven years ago. She's as good as the day you finished her."

Dad smiled, pride plastered all over his face. "Glad to hear it. I'll make you another one to match when things slow down."

"Been busy then?"

Dad frowned. "Yeah, mate. I thought it'd slow down after summer, but not yet."

John's sharp gaze slid to me. "This young bloke

giving you a hand?"

"With the bloody paperwork," Dad said. "That shit is never-ending."

John reshuffled his load of seafood. "What've you got rocks in that head of yours, kid? With double the hands, you could be churning out twice the load. Time to learn the trade." He glanced at the cooler bag in his hand. "Anyway ... best get this snapper home before the missus sends a dozen messages. Nice seeing you, Stew." He nodded at me. "Dane."

Dad and I shuffled farther into the shop with the moving queue. The saltiness of fresh seafood hung in the cool air right next to the silence of the waiting queue, and the noise of cashiers calling for orders.

We were almost to the counter when a familiar voice thanking the cashier on the other side caught my attention. She spun around to leave, bulging white plastic bag in hand, and as she walked away from the rows of fresh fish she actually saw me.

"Sav ..." Shit, she looked good today. Her blonde mass of hair sat all up on her pretty head, held in place by a yellow ribbon. The bow matched the dress that hugged the perfect swell of her chest and that tiny waist. I ought to sweep her into the Outlander and head down to the beach, just the two of us.

She'd stopped when I said her name and her eyes, now I'd finally reached them, were roving over my body just as hungrily as mine were hers ... either that or I'd totally forgotten how to read her.

"Dane. I never got a chance to tell you how good it was to see you the other day."

Hell, I hadn't noticed Victoria was with her. Savvy's gaze flicked to my dad, who said, "Hello, Victoria. It's been a while."

"Eighteen months," she answered, right off the bat.

Savvy offered me one of her forced smiles and took the other girl by the arm. "Come on, Tori, we'd better get going."

She yanked a still-smiling Victoria toward the door, turning this from awkward to downright end-it-now. I'd never put much thought into the situation, but it was weird as all shit.

"I always did like that girl," Pa piped up before they'd left the building. "Pity she dumped your sorry arse."

I sighed, hoping like hell the curvy blonde I'd been dying to see didn't dump my arse, too. If what we had going on was dumpable.

He cocked a brow. "That look says it all, kid. You still got a thing for her?"

"What? No."

He glanced over my shoulder. "The other one, then?"

"Yeah."

"Next!"

We approached the counter.

"Half a dozen raw oysters ..." my old man started, not that I paid a lick of attention. My mind was in stasis, replaying the last two minutes. Standing there with her cousin, me hovering on the outside of their thicker-than-ever circle ... what a sharp reminder that Savvy was a West, and my heart had already taken a beating under that name. And now, from the way she kept avoiding every interaction with her I tried to make, it looked like I was setting myself up for round two. Still, it was worth trying at least once more. She was worth it.

We left the shop, three bags of food in hand, and after we'd both settled into the Outlander the old man cleared his throat. "John's got a point, Son. Not for the right reason though. Doubling the trade doesn't matter ... I could've sold that piece you made last summer ten times over. It's a shame to see such talent go to waste."

Holy shit, he was stuck on this.

"That shop will be yours one day, kid. You need to know what to do with it."

I barked out a laugh. "One day."

CHAPTER SEVENTEEN

Savvy

The cursor on the screen blinked in time with my breaths. On, off, on, off.

Dear Ms Butterfield,
I would like to request a position at East Coast Primary.

On, off, on, off.

It wasn't the body of the letter I was having trouble with, but rather the addressee. My finger slammed into the delete key and I started again.

Dear Mr Khan,
I would like to request a position at Ramont Infants School.

My phone pinged with a new message. *McFlirt.* I needed to finish these prac requests, not get sucked into another text-fest with Dane.

Dear Sir/Madam,

Screw it. I tapped the screen to life and read his message.

Fair's on this weekend.

The warmth of a presence at my back made me flinch.

"What's that?" Tori's breath brushed my ear.

"Prac placement letters."

"I meant the text. Are we hitting the fair?"

"Umm ..." I clicked my phone onto the black screen of none-of-your-business and shoved it away. "I need to get this sorted."

"Who was that anyway? I thought you didn't keep in touch with anyone from school. Wait ... wait ... was that Dane?"

"Tori, I really need to get this work done."

She flopped on the bed. "Cut me a break, cuz. Since he dropped you off the other day, I've been thinking .... Maybe he and I could make it work if—"

My phone beeped again and she stopped talking to raise a questioning brow.

It might be fun to get lost in the haunted house.

Shit. She still liked him. I tossed the list of possible

schools on top of the offending device and sighed. "I have no idea where I want to do prac."

Tori sighed. "Well, what do you want out of it?"

Being here close to Kody would be nice, but could I handle working amongst the same people who'd been my mum's colleagues? The knot in my stomach said no. Even spending five weeks straight in town wouldn't be fun. But Kody … the vision of my sister in her current slump was enough to trump my hesitation. For now.

"Just to pass."

Tori scooted to the edge of her bed. "Anyway, Gran's here for Easter dinner. You'd better come say hello before she sends up a search party."

As she left the room, I flipped closed the laptop and picked up my phone.

Tori wants to come

So?

I'm really busy, Dane. It's not gonna happen.

I hid the device under my pillow, then straightened my skirt before heading downstairs.

****

Quiet Renegade blared from the speakers of Dane's SUV, and I wasn't sure what it was about this band, but since they'd played at the bar they'd became the hottest thing on campus. We were half an hour into our trip back to Oxley, and the tension inside the car had built with each passing minute. Someone had to break it, or by the time we reached college we'd be suffocating under its weight. Only thing was, I had no idea what to say. *Sorry I brushed you off all Easter* didn't really cut it, nor did *look ... I think we made a mistake.* Because the truth was, even though we probably shouldn't have hooked up, I wouldn't want to undo that. The time we'd had together had changed things. Now when I looked at Dane, I didn't just want him— I wanted him forever and then some. Since we'd started hanging out again, I'd realised he was more than I'd ever thought. More kind, more caring, more of everything. He got me in a way no one else ever could. Definitely more sexy, the way he moved that hard body ...

"Good to see Kody?"

That one small sentence dragged my thoughts in an entirely different direction. I glanced away from his toned thigh, flexing against the fabric of his boardies as he worked the throttle. I'd had another argument with Aunt Rosy this morning just before Dane had arrived. Kody hadn't acted like herself during the whole two weeks I was there. She had barely even left her room, just allowed everyone to treat her like a fragile invalid. Something had to change.

"Yes and no."

"How's that?"

"She's not right ... They whacked her on some kind of meds because she was depressed, and now she coops herself up in her room and never leaves. She barely spoke to me the entire time I was home. I couldn't even coax a conversation out of her."

"That's not good."

I glanced out the side window. "Short of stealing

her away, I'm not sure how to deal with this one."

"Did you tell them it's messing with her?"

"No one wanted to listen. They're all happy she's not hating life anymore, but not living ... that's worse than hating."

Taking his eyes off the windy road for just a second, Dane held my gaze. "You can't win every battle for her, Sav. You need to worry about yourself too."

"If I don't worry about her, who will?"

He snuck a glance my way, his brow furrowed. "Why doesn't Olivia know about—"

"That night? I just can't, Dane." I twisted to look out the side window.

He took one hand off the steering wheel and set it on my thigh. The heat of his touch didn't burn through my jeans, sending my hormones into a mangled mess like usual. Instead, it warmed the place in my chest that felt so alone. Dane had a way that made me feel like more than just a victim. He made me feel like a person worth caring about. Like a person he cared about. How could I deny that?

In fact, he was the only person who knew the real me. I fished my phone out of the side pocket of my computer bag and flicked over the screen, sending a bubbly message to Olivia to slide back into my happy Oxley self.

Can't wait to see you today. I have super exciting news!

Now I had an hour to think up something worth sharing. It felt good to be headed back to college, away from all the memories, the pretence that everything was all right. That my life wasn't on some predestined course, which led to a future that excluded some of the most important people that had been in it.

"How about you?" I asked Dane. "How were your folks?"

"Good." He grinned at me sideways. "Always great to see them, but I missed you. What was with that?" His smile faltered. "Were you hiding me from Tori?"

"What? No! Why would I—it's not like I haven't told her." The lie pierced through me and that was the end of conversation.

Even though we didn't talk anymore Dane didn't move that hand the entire way home. Nor did I ask him to. Not until he had to set it back on the wheel to turn into campus. It felt better than nice to know someone cared. It felt warm and gooey, as if my blood had been switched for warm honey. I hadn't felt that way in an awfully long time, if ever.

****

After parting ways with Dane, I spent the next hour unpacking my room, then another hour in the courtyard chatting with Dono and a bunch of other people who happened to walk past. I filled in a little time stalking our hallway for Molly, who didn't appear, and checking out the airline arrivals to see what time Liv would get in, which, it turned out, was five-forty-five. It'd take her a good half hour to disembark, gather luggage and get a cab to Oxley, so I may as well have an early dinner before shooting up to her room to catch up on all the things. As for

Molly … she was anyone's guess. I had no idea how she even travelled or where she lived, short of *west*.

I plastered on my friendly smile and hit the dining hall, which was already abuzz with excitement. Two weeks apart, and everyone was keen to reconnect … I guess for some of us, Oxley felt more like home than anywhere else did, so being back was a relief.

That was until people noticed it was curry night. Horrid yellow slop faded the buzz pretty fast. I'd been a curry fan until I'd eaten what passed for the spicy dish that crawled out of this kitchen.

After collecting my meal, I headed for Kasi and the rest of my teaching crew.

"Savvy," she squealed her usual greeting. "How was break?"

I groaned as I sat down. "I spent it trying to sort out prac placement."

Everyone agreed prac was hard—where to go, public or private, which age group to request, kindergarten or grade six, and a bunch of other options to boot.

"Well, I'm going to hit up one of the primary schools here," Kasi said. "That way I can stay on campus and work through some of the major assignments with the library and lecturers on hand."

I tried to salvage some plain rice from the sea of curry on my plate. "Not a bad idea."

The conversation continued, but my attention wavered when Dane came in and stood in line with Blaine and Christian. After moving through the servery, the three of them joined a long table of guys. It wasn't like I'd expected him to sit with the girls and me.

I shovelled the last of the untainted rice into my

mouth. Then, excusing myself, I stacked away my dirty stuff and left.

Olivia's light shone out the window, silhouetting her moving shadow. Oh, that's right I said I'd tell her something exciting. Exciting. Excite—that was it. I'd tell her about sending off all those prac requests. Maybe not super exciting, but I was at a loss. I shot upstairs and dodged to the left to save from almost running into Cade Matthews. "Watch where you're going." I knocked on her door.

"Pocket rocket. You wanna go for a ride?" He planted a hand either side of his crotch and thrust it forward.

Thank god Liv opened the door.

"Grow up." I barrelled into her room to escape Cade following me, thrusting his pelvis with each step. I used my foot to slam the door in his childish face, then turned to my friend. "Livia. I had the best break. You'll never guess—"

Stalker Boy ... sprawled all over her bed like he belonged there. Well this was new.

He grinned at me. "Hi, Savannah."

"Logan ..." She said they weren't a thing, but it certainly didn't seem that way. I took a seat in her desk chair while Liv sat on the end of the bed just shy of his feet. Smiling, I shook my head. "I can't figure you two out."

"What's to figure out? We're friends. Just like me and you, or me and Molly. Nothing at all like you and Dane."

Yeah right. I shook my head. "Don't go there."

"How was your break?" she asked the day's standard question.

"Complicated." I so wasn't going to talk about it

with Dane's mate in the room. Actually, I wasn't going there, period.

"Oh, do tell."

Logan's phone rang and he picked up. "Yeah ... With Liv ... What ... Now?" He blew out a long breath. "On my way." He shifted Liv over so he could stand. "I gotta go."

"Oh." Yeah, that tone said it all. Nothing between them, my left foot. "Thanks for the lift."

As did the way she watched him until the closing door blocked her view. After her perve-fest was cut off, she turned to me with a cocked brow. "So, Dane?"

My phone started ringing too. "Geez McCheese." I glanced at the screen. *Kody.* That couldn't be right— not after the past few weeks. Mouthing *sorry* to my friend, I shot out into the hall for a little privacy and picked up.

"Hey you."

"Savvy ..." She sighed. "I miss you."

"I miss you too, chickpea."

"I'm sorry I was rude while you were home." Her voice still sounded flat. "Things have been ... they've been hard."

"I know, honey, and I'm so sorry you have to go through that."

There was a pause before finally, "Anyway, I love you."

"Love you, too."

The line went dead. Taking it away from my ear, I felt oddly confused. She hadn't wanted a bar of me or anyone else for weeks. Hadn't even come out to wish me goodbye today, so her calling now sat a little strangely.

I stuck my head through Liv's door. "I'll catch you tomorrow. I gotta deal with this."

Looking away from her computer screen, she glanced over her shoulder at me. "Night."

As I walked down the stairs, I scrolled through my contacts, looking for Tori's name. I could've called, but texting was easier with all the ears about.

*Just had the weirdest call from Kody.
Everything all right?*

I made it all the way up to my room before she responded.

Mum was chatting with her for ages after you left. Guess they had some kind of heart-to-heart. Why, what was weird?

It felt forced.

Maybe Mum made her call you.

Maybe.

CHAPTER EIGHTEEN

Savvy

The first week back moved slowly. That probably had something to do with my stomach being all knotted up about Dane, about Kody, and about the prac placement I had yet to secure. Tracing my finger around the edge of my phone where it sat on the picnic table, I glanced across at Molly. Her cheeks were rosy with the cooling air, and my friend leaned in, her expression all serious. "Did you talk to Tori while you were home?"

Well, crap. "Sort of ... You haven't told me how your break was."

"I haven't seen you for more than two minutes since I got back. You're a busy gal, Savvy."

"Never too busy for a friend."

"Ah, but when one has roughly two hundred

friends ..."

"Pfft. Spill."

She jigged her legs under the table so hard her whole body moved like a loaded jackhammer. I issued her a flat stare until she blurted, "Going home is always weird."

"Well, yeah."

"You too?"

I nodded, removing my hand from the phone and giving her my full attention.

"My hometown is really small, and I guess it's kind of struggling and has been since forever. So now they've set up this whole committee to brighten it up and draw in tourists or something. I swear the entire township has turned all 'save Bindarra Creek' crazy."

I tapped my foot against the ground. "Where the hell is Bindarra Creek?"

"See? Small." She shot me a shut-up look, and continued. "I guess I'm worried my parents might get sucked into it and lose money. Things have been hard for a long time, and they're way too gullible. They don't talk about it much, but I know they're close to going under."

By the way her whole body rocked back and forth, it seemed Molly was really worried. Looked like I wasn't the only one with issues. We all had our own stuff to deal with. "I'm sure they'll wake up to anything weird if they're even half as smart as you. You had to get those brains from somewhere, right?"

She smiled. "You're such a smooth talker; no wonder you and Dane work. Now, how'd that chat go?"

"Heads!"

The screamed warning couldn't have come at a

better time. I ducked and threw my arms up. Once I'd heard the ball whizz by, I glanced up, and Cade Matthews was grinning at me. "Savan-nah Boban-nah, ooh I'd like to bang-hah."

Ignoring the biggest pain in my arse this side of the Great Divide, I smiled at Molly. Her eyes dipped to the table and Cade launched himself across it, snatching my phone off the timber top.

He danced around, his finger sliding across the screen to wake up the device. "Ooh ... Facebook's unlocked. Savannah West ..." his mischievous eyes met mine, "... is in a relationship with—"

"Shit!"

I shot up off the chair and ran at him, my shoulder braced for impact. Cade cackled like a twelve-year-old and took off. This guy was insane, and I swear he brought out all the immature in me, but I chased him as fast as my untrained legs could run. No matter whose name he attached to that status, if he posted it, all hell would break loose. He was going to get it when I caught him.

He zigzagged across the courtyard, laughing like a hyena, but I wasn't fast enough. I couldn't get anywhere near him, damn it. That only made me all the more determined. I dodged to the left, cutting him off at the base of his path, but what I wasn't counting on was him swerving the other way, which I'd left wide open. He darted into Front Courtyard and screaming, I gave chase. "When I catch your sorry arse, Cade ..." I puffed around the words. "You're gonna regret it."

I sprinted down the few steps and into Front where he was lying on the grass in the middle of the quad, one arm cocked under his head, my phone held above his head as he typed. Arrogant shit. I dove at him, pummelling his pain-in-the-arse body with my fists, while he held the phone out of my reach behind him, all the while Cade laughed, one of those huge belly laughs. He rolled us over, pinning me beneath his ample weight with his knees either side of my waist. He placed the damn phone on my chest then dug long fingers into my sides, tickling the tender spot under my ribs and not stopping until all the mock anger slipped off my face, replaced by building laughter.

"You're such a turd, Cade." With a shove, I pushed him off me and sat up, frantically clicking into my Facebook. He pulled himself up beside me, resting his arms on his knees, and offered a cocky grin.

"And you're too fun, pocket rocket."

My chest fell with an exhale at the lack of a relationship status update. I drove an elbow into his side. "Yeah, well, you suck."

He waggled his eyebrows. "I'd love to show you how well in the privacy of my room."

Slamming my palm against his shoulder, I knocked him sideways onto the ground and all the jerk did was laugh his butt off. I pushed up onto my feet and my gaze caught on Dane, standing at the base of block B and glaring right this way. I could feel the anger seeping out of him even from here.

I couldn't help myself; he was a like a magnet drawing me over to where he stood, arms barricading his chest. We stood toe to toe in the midst of an epic stare-off. I heard Cade wolf whistle somewhere behind me, but I didn't give two hoots about his antics right now. Not when Dane was looking at me like he hated me and wanted to taste every inch of me all at the same time.

A muscle ticked near his jaw.

"God," I said. "Just yell at me and get it over with."

We stood there, glaring at each other.

"What's going on here, Savvy?" His tone was neutral, flat.

"Nothing! Nothing's going on, and that's just it," I yelled, and even though I knew we were drawing an audience I couldn't rein it in. Anger simmered below the surface, pounding right in my ears, and I had no idea why. "You can't stand there all brooding and ..." my hand flew through the air, "... you, every time I look sideways at Cade. You don't own me."

He shoved his face right up so our noses almost touched and kept his voice low. "It's not Cade who you want though, is it?"

I took a step back and so did he, shoving his fists in his jeans pockets.

"I can't read you, Savvy. You're so hot and cold I can't keep up, and I can't deal with it anymore, because I'm all in. I want you. I want you in my bed at night and even more in the mornings. I want you sitting with me at dinner. I want to talk to you until we're all talked out. I want to walk through college holding your hand so every last person in this place knows you're mine." He drew a deep breath. "I just want you, and I need to know if you're all in with me, 'cause if you're not then I'm out as of now."

My heart shattered. The pieces were so painful, my hand flew to my chest to hold them in. That he felt like that ... "I don't want anyone else either."

He dropped his head back against the wall. "Then

what the fuck is going on?"

"I guess I'm just all kinds of screwed up."

In one huge stride Dane was right there, his hands sliding up to cup my face, which he tilted toward his. Light played in his eyes, the earnest need boring right into my very soul. "Whatever it is, we can work through it. I've always been here for you, Sav."

Why'd he have to say a thing like that? Now my throat felt as if I'd swallowed a ping-pong ball. He dropped his forehead onto mine. "Stop fighting it, princess. Stop being scared."

"I'm not—"

His lips feathered over mine, and the sensation was overwhelming. My hands flew to his shirt and fisted in the material over his heart, using it to hold him in place while I kissed him like we weren't in the middle of the courtyard. If there was any question before about who I belonged to, now it was all out in the open. My heart was Dane's, it had been for a long time, and the fact he'd given his to me too was inconceivable. This boy that I'd loved forever was everything and then some.

My hands tightened in his shirt as my tongue danced with his, each of us devouring the other like we couldn't get close enough, deep enough. I wanted to crawl inside of him and set up camp.

"Get a room." It sounded like Cade yelling across the courtyard. "We don't need to see you two humping each other."

Dane broke away from me and flipped Cade the finger, which only made the younger guy laugh. The surfer's strong arm came around me, pulling me into his side, and he piloted me through the door of block B without protest. We hit the base of the stairwell, and he released me only to grab my hand instead. "I'm falling in love with you, princess."

No sooner were the words out of his mouth, than he towed me upstairs at full speed. I was pretty certain I was falling for him too, but the words wouldn't come out. I was too wrapped up in the fact that Dane Beaumont was falling for *me*. Sure I knew he cared about me and he was attracted to me, but the big *L* was a whole other ball game. All these years I'd thought I'd loved him from afar, but really I'd had no clue what love even was.

Our feet hit the landing, and using our joined hands, I yanked him toward me. Those strong arms scooped me up on his hips and I curled my legs around his waist, kissing him as if I'd lusted after him forever, which I had. We crashed into his door, and his hand dropped from cradling my rear end to fumble at the handle. Somehow he managed to get it open without breaking our kiss. Good luck or practice—at that point in time I didn't really care. Once we were inside, Dane kicked the door closed and I dragged my mouth away from his, peppering kisses along the rough stubble of his jaw. Dane tilted me back, his hands sliding out from under my rear to place me on his desk. With our hands free, we tore away from each other and began ripping off clothes. We were both on the same page, needing each other in every way.

****

Dane's fingers trailed over my hip and into the dip of my waist, blazing a trail along the zinging nerve-endings. I sighed, feeling more sated than I had since forever. This guy sure had a way of turning the world on its head and spinning it the way it should have been going all along. I could happily stay right here, wrapped up in his embrace forever. Leaving for four weeks of practical study sure would be hard, unless ...

"So ..." I rolled onto my back to meet Dane's steady green eyes. "Prac is coming up soon and I was planning on trying to line up a school on the coast, since I miss the beach when I'm here, but now I'm kind of thinking I might just miss you more. Maybe I should line up a placement here in Armidale."

His fingers continued their torturous path. "Sounds like a great idea to me." He kissed the spot right under my ear and I just about melted. Sure felt like it was possible. "Means I still get to see you every day."

"I'd like that."

He sucked the lobe of my ear into his mouth, and my eyes rolled back into my head. The sensation elicited a moan from me.

My phone rang, breaking the moment, and Dane groaned.

Showing him a forced smile, I dropped my hand down beside his bed, grabbed the device and picked up. "Hey."

"Cuz, this a good time?" She didn't give me time to respond before barrelling on. "Apparently they're taking Dakota off the meds and doubling her visits with Marree."

Dane's mouth moved over the sensitive skin of my neck and I sighed. "Sounds perfect."

"I thought you'd be pleased."

"Mm-hmm."

"You sound happy."

"I am. That's great news. Marree's a good therapist. She really gets our situation."

"No, it's more than that." She paused and Dane's lips briefly dusted over mine. "I bet I know," Tori said. "It's the mystery man you never did tell me about, isn't it? McFlirt?"

Dane's warm lips closed over my earlobe, and I sighed again. "Must be."

I should have felt guilty, but it was hard when everything about being with him felt so good.

"Well, spill the details then."

I froze, unable to think of a single thing to say that wasn't the truth she couldn't hear over the phone.

"I get it. You can't talk right now. Well, it's only two weeks until the big two-oh. Are you doing something fun?"

Dane's wandering hands made it damn hard to pay attention. The way his fingers moved—

"Cuz."

"Ahh … yeah?"

"Your birthday? What's happening?"

"No idea."

She sighed. "We'll chat later then."

"Sure …"

Dane kissed along my neck, across my throat, and my lips ached to lock with his again. I dropped the phone, which had gone dead anyway, and with my palms on either side of his face, I tugged him back up to meet my eager kiss.

CHAPTER NINETEEN

Dane

Traipsing down to the dining hall when breakfast first started was a chore, but hopefully it'd be worth the early morning to see Savvy smile. It'd taken some thought to come up with the perfect birthday present and this was just the way to start it. Tray in hand, I walked out of the servery and where the hall had been empty before, two people had walked in. The only one crazy enough to hit breakfast at six-thirty on a Saturday was Olivia Dean, and no doubt she'd dragged along the other chick her and Savvy were friends with. When they spotted me crossing the wooden floorboards, Liv smiled and the brunette clapped. "I love it!"

I tipped my chin toward the plate in my hand. "Not too cheesy?"

She shook her head. "It's perfect."

"Hey ..." I shifted my attention to Olivia "... what have you got planned for tonight?"

"Not a lot."

"I need you to help me out. You know who all Savvy's friends are?"

"I like the way you think." Smiley grinned. "We're on it. You thinking big?"

"Just the people who matter, maybe the Central?"

Olivia gave me a weak nod. "Sounds like Savvy's sort of fun, right Molly? I haven't managed to catch her all week. What's she up to today?"

"Nothing," the other girl—Molly—answered, then narrowed her eyes at the tray in my hand. "Or so she thinks."

I smiled at them both and tossed in a wink for good measure. "See you tonight, ladies."

"We're on it!" Molly threw over her shoulder as we walked away from one another.

Both courtyards were dead empty as I wandered through, and everything was quietly still when I reached the middle floor of Block L. All the sane people were still asleep. I raised my knuckles to Savvy's door and gave it a light tap then, with the lighter in my pocket, set the thick candle aflame.

Minutes went by in silence. I shouldn't have been surprised she didn't answer. She slept like the dead. I knocked again, a little harder, and a muffled groan that could've passed for "who is it?" came from inside.

A third knock issued what I was after: her head, poking out the door. Without a single glance at my cargo, she tugged the thing all the way open, pulled me inside and slammed it closed, then collapsed on her bed, barely opening her eyes. I flicked on the light and said eyes disappeared completely when she wrenched the covers all the way over her head. I set the plate down, toed off my Cons and scooted in with her. In less than a second, she'd flung an arm over my stomach, curled a leg over my thighs and nestled her cheek on my chest. The closeness sent my pulse into overdrive and she wriggled, her leg rubbing against my hip and her soft cheek brushing my pec as if she couldn't seem to get comfortable. Pity we both had too many clothes on.

"Happy birthday, princess." It was going to be impossible to get moving if she kept wriggling against me like that. I kissed the top of her blonde head. "Time to wake up."

She pressed herself against me again, and damn it. I had awesome plans and crumbling self-control but seriously limited time, so I slid out from under her and Savvy moaned. "But it's my birthday ..."

"Exactly, and that means things to do, people to see."

"I'd be happier doing you."

I chuckled. "Plenty of time for that later. Right now we've gotta hit the road."

That got her attention. Rubbing puffy eyes, Savvy pulled herself upright and blinked at me. "Say what?"

"Get that pretty little arse out of bed and get dressed. It's time for breakfast." I nodded toward the tray I'd set on her desk. Her gaze followed my less-than-subtle indication, and the smile that lit up her whole face made the early morning worthwhile.

"Birthday pancakes. A whole stack with a little candle on top and all ..." She swallowed her thick voice. "Are you going all soppy on me, Dane

179

Beaumont?"

She climbed out of bed and I rolled the desk chair up, catching her in its seat, then pushed her over to her breakfast. "Where are we going?"

"Where do you want to go?" I asked.

"Back to bed?"

I pressed a kiss to the soft skin of her shoulder. "We'll get back there later tonight." I winked. "And when we do, you won't be leaving until morning."

A sexy grin spread across her sweet face, and I couldn't resist dropping a kiss on her full lips. When I pulled back, Savvy was still smiling. She picked up the fork and paused, her eyes shining as she looked at the breakfast as if it were an injured puppy.

"Hey." I hooked a hand over her shoulder, but Savvy shook whatever had come over her off and tucked into her breakfast.

I checked out the weather on my phone while she ate. Looked like we were in for an all right day, despite the late autumn air. She scraped the last skerrick around her plate, sopping up all the syrup, then climbed to her feet and flung open the wardrobe. "So, what are doing today?"

"It's a surprise."

"Bushwalking?"

I raised a brow. "In those skyscrapers you call shoes?"

"Vineyard touring?"

I pretended to sip out of a cup, pinkie finger extended. "Now that is more your cup of tea, Ms West, but no."

She tapped a foot against the carpet, trying her best to hide a smile. "Well, I don't know. I hate surprises."

"If you could choose any one thing to do today, what would it be?"

"You know ..." Her eyes rolled up to the right. "I love ... oh my god ... are you taking me to the beach?"

"Not if you don't hurry up and get dressed."

She squealed and shot across the room, planted a solid kiss smack on my lips and returned to flinging clothes out of the closet and onto her bed. I chuckled, and she waved a hand in my direction. "Go find something else to do for half an hour."

"Half an hour? Baby, you've got ten minutes." I gave her arse a tap on my way out of the room. Ten minutes would be long enough to grab another coffee for the road.

The lone beam of morning rays landing on the dark bricks of block K was the perfect spot to sun myself with a coffee in hand. A good half an hour later, Savvy finally appeared, looking gorgeous in a pair of jeans and an open jacket that revealed a shirt tight enough to show off her ample assets. I caught her hand and slid my fingers through hers, pulling her in. Her lips parted the moment I sought entry, and my other hand slid along her spine as Savvy leaned into me, the pressure of her soft chest making my pulse pound.

She pulled away. "I thought we were in a hurry."

I kicked up one side of my mouth. "That was a taste of what's coming later."

Curtains opened, and sleepy faces trudged downstairs—all signs of the college slowly coming to life as we made our way out to the car. I held open the door and Savvy climbed up into the Outlander, letting out a tiny giggle when her foot slipped on the running board. Savvy was all smiles this morning, as she should be.

Leaving the country behind, we headed east toward to the coast. Our hometown was the closest coastal area to college, so that was where we were off to. It must have been sometime around eight-thirty when her phone beeped. She glanced at the screen and tapped back a message right away. "Birthday wishes?" I asked.

"Yeah, just the family."

"Did you tell 'em we'll be in town?"

"I'd rather spend today at the beach."

I glanced across, surprised at the sudden slump in her mood. "Is this about Tori seeing us together? I would have thought family time—"

Her phone beeped again and she sighed. "A message from Aunt Rosy, and no. I don't really want to see them today."

I peeked across, and the message looked short. Did these people not call her or at least send a message longer than two words to wish her a happy birthday?

Savvy scooted down in the seat, settling her legs out, and she leaned her shoulder against the window so she was half turned my way. It'd been quiet for a while when she said, "Do you ever think it's strange, the way things have turned out?"

"That's philosophical for before nine."

She shifted her gaze out the window. "I guess sometimes life just lands in an entirely different place than what we imagined."

I nodded, even though I couldn't relate. Sure, I lived a couple hundred clicks away from the coast, a place I'd never envisioned myself leaving, but other than that my life was pretty much on path. Hers sure had turned upside down the night of the accident though, and that had to be damn hard to swallow. Then again, here we both were, together...

She peeked at me from the under long lashes, then focused on the scenery again. "In some ways it's a better place, but others ways are just ..."

I reached out and closed my fingers around the hand fidgeting on her thigh. "My life's much better than it was a few a months ago. There's this great chick who I've finally convinced to put up with my shit." I squeezed her hand, and Savvy raised my knuckles to her lips.

I had to release her to swing the Outlander into the dirt track that led as close to the beach as we could get. It wasn't Five Mile, but then I wasn't after the best swell. Besides, Shelley's had always been her favourite. Savvy straightened up, her stare set on the sandy shore as she froze. Her head dipped, paying attention to the shoes she slowly slipped off her feet. I killed the engine and climbed out into a gust of chilled air then walked around the car, opening her door. Unclipping her belt, Savvy spun and set a foot on the ground, then stopped. Her back straight, her shoulders square, and if it weren't for the audible breath she took she could have been a statue.

Shit. I hadn't even stopped and thought about where I'd brought her.

I pressed a comforting hand against her shoulder. "If you're more comfortable at Five Mile—"

"No." Swatting my hand away, she shot out of the car and took off, her bare feet leaving tracks in the sandy dirt. I locked up and followed her onto the grass that overlooked Shelley's Beach. Considering the biting early June wind, there were a surprising number of people about. Savvy passed me a grin wider than the lifeguard flags that usually rippled in the breeze and sprinted off, seemingly unbothered by the fact we were at the same beach as we'd been on that fateful night. I hung back, slowly making my way over the grass and down onto the sand where Savvy dug her toes in and out of the white grains.

"Best birthday ever." She grinned at me and took off again, running toward the water, like a little kid. I could tell the moment the water washed over her feet by the squeal that broke through the morning air. Savvy turned around, clearly looking for me, so I toed off my Cons, rolled up my jeans and joined her.

"Where's your board?" she asked, toes wriggling in the cool, wet sand.

"Not here. Today's all about you."

She looked confused for all of two seconds, then the grin returned. Of course the fox kicked up a foot full of briny water, which flicked up the length of my jeans. She laughed about it, too. With both my hands around her tiny waist, I pulled her up short, and Savvy blinked at me out of wide eyes then stepped up onto my toes. The cold water washed over my feet again and she tensed as it lapped at our ankles. She kissed the point of my chin and that was the real start of this game. I turned us around, her feet still anchored on mine as I walked us out of the chilly foam and onto the firm sand. As soon as we hit the spot where it was no longer wet, but not yet soft, I dropped her onto the beach and climbed over her, my knees nestled either side of her thighs. Savvy looked up at me all innocence, sunshine, and something that warmed my whole chest. Her windswept hair, framed by the sand and coupled with wind-chilled cheeks, made her more beautiful than ever. I dropped my mouth onto hers and kissed her like I should have this morning in her bed. I kissed her like I intended to do dirty things to her right there on the wintry beach. In our heady rush to get closer, somehow we wound up the other way round, with her straddling me and the sun warming us both while the past lapped at the shore, forgotten.

****

An hour on the beach, a feed of fish and chips, and a ten-minute drive later, we pulled into the tiny parking lot out back of Driftwood Creations. Technically this day was all about Savvy, but I couldn't come to town and drive right by my folks.

Her fingers twirled around themselves as she stared at the back of the shop as if it were a live viper. I reached across, stroking the back of her hand. "If you're too uncomfortable—"

"It's all right," she said, then climbed out of the Outlander. She sure got props for guts. Savvy would do anything with a smile that most people couldn't see through. I slung an arm around her shoulders and steered her toward the back door, whispering in her ear. "If nothing else, it gives me a break from your boring company."

A thud marked her palm connecting with my gut, and I chuckled. "Honestly, princess, it's no big deal."

Her arm coiled around my waist, and I felt a tug that had to be her lithe fingers hooking into my back pocket. With a raised brow, I shot her a reassuring look, and the smile she passed back was enough to make anyone fall for her. She had nothing to worry about. Everyone adored her; they always had. To think she'd been right in front of me all those years and now, that amazing smile, this wonderful woman was all mine.

I pushed against the wooden door and it didn't budge. Old man must've shut it to keep the cool air out. "Looks like we've gotta go round the front."

Savvy made a noise of agreement. The parking lot was almost empty, but that didn't mean a lot. Just from studying the books I knew that even with tourist season at a low, Saturday mornings could still get a bit hectic. People liked to park on the street and walk its length, looking through the shops. Sure enough, the footpath was packed. I steered Savvy toward the shop, but before we even reached our destination it was obvious there was no point. The *closed* sign hung behind the glass pane of the front door.

"Does he normally shut at lunchtime on Saturday?" Savvy frowned.

"Weekends are the biggest trade. It shouldn't be closed." I peered inside, but the shop was well and truly closed and had been for days by the look of the lack of lights on the Coke fridge. The only time they stopped glowing was if the thing had been shut off at the power. Warm drinks wouldn't sell, so the only reason Dad would do that was if he wasn't planning on opening.

Once we climbed back in the Outlander, I picked up my phone and dialled home. My mother answered on the fifth ring, breathless.

"Hey Ma, what are you up to today?"

"Sweetheart, it's nice to hear from you."

"Are you busy?"

"No, sweetie, we can talk. Is this about the girl

you've been seeing?"

I glanced across at Savvy, who was watching me as if I might bolt on her. "Ah, not today, Ma. What are you up to?"

Silence bled down the line as I kicked the Outlander's engine over.

"Are you in the car, Dane? You know how dangerous it is to be on the phone while you're driving. So many accidents are caused by careless lack of attention. In fact, it's illegal. Did you know that?"

"I—"

"I'm going to hang up now and keep you safe. Love you, honey."

The clunk of her setting the phone back on its base filled the line before I had a chance to ask about the shop. I tapped my foot on the clutch.

"We could call in on them," Savvy said.

"Yeah …" I pulled out onto the road.

Fifteen minutes later, we turned into the driveway of my parents' single-storey brick veneer home. It was small and out-dated, but the sight of this house always made me feel good in a way no other building could. I hopped out and swung around the passenger side to help Savvy down, but she'd already slid to the ground by the time I reached her, so I settled for closing her door.

The front entry to the house was closed too, which set my heart on a strange beat. My parents were generally so relaxed with security that all these locked doors weren't right. Raising my knuckles to the timber, I did something I'd never done before— knocked on the door of my parents' home. Although a sharp yap started almost immediately, no one answered.

"Everything all right?" Savvy asked.

I fumbled with my keys until I found the one that was ridged on both sides, then slid it into the lock and turned. Leaning my weight against the door, I pushed and just about fell over as it opened to reveal Ma on the other side, Roar tucked under her arm.

"Dane, honey," she said, still clasping the handle. "We didn't know you were coming."

"That why the shop's shut?"

Her gaze slid to my right, and *shit*. "Mum, this is Savvy. Savvy, Deanne Beaumont."

It seemed my mother remembered her manners, too. She set the fluff ball down, stepped back and waved us in. "It's so nice to meet you, Savvy." She embraced my girl, and my heart swelled for a moment. "Come in. You must be thirsty after the drive. Let me get you a cold drink. Or a tea. Would you prefer something hot?"

"We've been in town for a while. Just on our way back out," I said. "I was gonna call by the shop, but it was shut up. Where's Pa?"

Roar wove between my feet as we followed Mum into the kitchen, where she busied herself filling the electric kettle. "He's not well today."

Mum kept her back to us as she went about making tea. "What brings you kids to town? Are you staying tonight? I'll make up the spare—"

"Ma," I interrupted her unusual spew of words. "We're just here for a few hours. Thought we'd call in before we head back to college."

"I see." She sounded disappointed.

The kettle whistled and she snatched it off the element. "That's a shame. Your father would have liked to see you."

"He's not here?"

"Not today." Steam billowed as she poured the water into a pot.

"Then where is he?"

"Come Savvy, dear, let's get better acquainted. I've heard so much about you."

"Ma, where is he?"

"He's away, Dane." She flattened the conversation with a glare and Savvy shot me a wide-eyed look and followed my mother out onto the back porch.

My old girl was acting weirder than a rip between the flags. Something was wrong with my family. Had my dad left my mum?

CHAPTER TWENTY

Savvy

"Thanks for today," I told Dane, as we drove into Oxley's parking lot. "I had a really nice time."

He shut off the engine and turned in his seat to face me. "My mum loved you."

"Of course she did." I half grinned. "Really though, thank you."

"It was my pleasure." He placed a gentle hand on my cheek and pulled us closer despite the gearstick and console between our seats, then brushed a gentle kiss against my waiting mouth. I slipped a hand into his hair and Dane deepened the kiss, his tongue sliding over mine, and both our lips moving with more force. He'd been brooding for most of the trip home, so I'd been concerned about his promises for later that I'd been looking forward to all day. If our hungry kisses were anything to go by we could both practically smell the alone time.

Dane's stomach let out a loud growl, despite the epic feast his mother had called afternoon tea. Sitting in the sun, her and I had enjoyed a cup of honest to goodness tea. I don't think I'd ever had actual tea leaves before, but it was official. I was never using bags again. Dane had disappeared for a while, but wound up joining us for sandwiches, scones and homemade cookies.

His tummy grumbled again, and I smiled against his kiss. "Guess it must be dinnertime."

"Mmm." He nipped my bottom lip. "I know what I want."

I gave him a taste with a sweep of my tongue over his. Playing right into my move, he kissed me until I could no longer tell if it was light or dark, even though the sun had sunk below the horizon somewhere along Waterfall Way. Every part of me swam with that heady sensation that he was so good at creating. My head floated, chest felt lighter than air, and I swear if I wasn't still strapped in I would have soared away. My entire body was swooning and I didn't give a damn ... until a knock on the window pulled us apart. I struggled to catch my next breath thanks to the heat coursing through my body.

Dane groaned and opened his door to a chuckling Cade. That guy had a knack of showing up everywhere. Cade peered around Dane to meet my eyes. "Give a guy a break and get it on somewhere I'm not likely to walk by. You're breaking my heart, pocket rocket." He held his hand over said heart.

Dane grumbled, and Cade laughed.

I exited the black SUV only to be scooped off the

ground by the burly footy player. Cade twirled us around and smacked a loud kiss on my cheek. "Happy birthday." He hooked a thumb toward Dane who'd come around the car and had his arms crossed over his chest in the most aggressive way a surly surfer could. "If this bloke doesn't treat you right, you come see me," Cade said.

I whacked him on the arm and struggled to get out of his grip. "Stop tormenting Dane."

Cade roared with laughter and set me back on my feet. "Sure thing, rocket girl. Now tell me, what's this I hear about a party, and where's my invite?"

"A party?" I frowned.

"Yeah. Aren't we hitting one of the bars?"

I shook my head.

"You, me, a bottle of tequila?"

We were?

"Fuck's sake." Dane groaned, and I spun around to face him.

I tugged his hand out from under his crossed arm and twisted my fingers through his long digits. "Something happening tonight?"

"Oh shit." Cade slapped his own forehead.

I grinned up at Dane. "You didn't … not after everything else today."

He placed a kiss on my knuckles and started us walking toward Oxley's main gates. "You only turn twenty once."

"Aww." Cade wiped a finger under his dark eyes. "That's so sweet."

"Piss off, already," Dane growled.

"I'm sorry about blowing the surprise, mate." Cade held out a hand to Dane, which he shook. As we walked through the gates and into Oxley, Dane's phone rang, and he glanced at the screen. "We're going out at nine. I'll meet you in the courtyard for dinner beforehand."

I nodded and he hit accept on the call, passing me a small smile as he walked away and greeted whoever was on the other end of the line.

****

"Change of plans." I leaned between the front seats to speak to Logan, who had Liv's fingers trapped in his between the seats. "We're going to the Queen. It's got a smaller dance floor, but it's quieter than the Central, so we can sit in one of the little nooks and chat."

"No worries." Liv's new man flicked the indicator on and, driving one handed, turned toward the eastern side of town.

I nestled back next to Molly, running a steady eye over my masterpiece. The Bardot dress I'd talked her into wearing made her boobs look great. Its shade really set off her shiny black hair, and even the Doc Martens looked all right with her white socks folded down to create the same two-tone look as the rest of the ensemble. The hoop earrings and chunky white necklace were the pièce de résistance. I gave her the thumbs up. "You look stunning."

She tipped the corner of her mouth in return.

I set a smile in place and looked out my window at the warm glow of family homes drifting by. I'd give anything for another birthday lounging around the family room, watching my pick of movie with those who I loved best of all.

Birthdays were hard.

But today I'd almost forgotten … almost had a normal day.

I twisted my gold bangle around my wrist and wished Dane could have fit in this tiny car, too. Instead he'd taken the bus with everyone else, so we could both enjoy a drink. Right now, I wasn't sure it was worth the sacrifice. I ached to curl myself around him and forget all about the past.

Logan's ancient car shuddered to a stop in the parking lot, and we all piled out. The lovebirds exchanged a too-sweet look as he came around to join us on the passenger side. It was past time to put my game face on, so I grabbed Molly's hand and skipped inside, my toes bouncing off the tarred road. "It's time to par-tay."

Liv gave us a both a head shake and moved closer to the sensible guy I doubted even knew how to have fun. I had to give him some credit though; the blond-haired ex-collegian had her smiling in a way I hadn't seen since well before the Christian mess went down.

The music was already flowing as we entered the Queen, albeit a little softly. That should change later on. I hit the bar straight away, eager to get the party started and forget all about those happy families enjoying their cosy family time. I hadn't even heard from my sister today.

The place was empty enough that I could waltz right up to the bar and put an order in without waiting. After receiving the three vodka lemonades, I paid the bartender and returned to the long table Liv had nabbed for us.

Molly arrived next with a tray full of shot glasses that she set right beside the drinks I'd gotten. She flopped into the chair next to Olivia, her slumped pose totally undoing the femininity of her gorgeous outfit. "Happy birthday!" she shouted across the table, sliding a shot glass across to me.

Now we were talking. "What is that?"

"It's your birthday celebration." Molly skated another drink along the table, this one to Olivia.

"No way," my conservative friend said. "I'm not doing any shots. Especially not something … is that green?"

Molly laughed. "You'll love it."

The look on Liv's face said it all. She wasn't going to play.

"Come on," I pleaded. "It's my birthday, and all I want is to drink and dance with my best friend." And maybe get hot and naked later on with my boyfriend.

Shit. Was that what Dane and I were doing? *Boyfriend* was a title that carried serious meaning. My phone vibrated in my tight pocket, but ignoring it, I lifted my shot for a sniff. "Smells like liquorice."

Liv pushed the tiny glass away as if the green liquid might burn her, but Molly nudged the shot right back where it had been and raised a brow, beckoning for my best friend to loosen up. Liv forced an almighty sigh and picked up the glass, clinking it against mine and Molly's with a less than cheery, "Happy birthday."

The green liquid burned like hell on the way down. The fire landed in my gut and spread through my veins. Nasty stuff. Liv looked as if she'd swallowed boiling water, so I slid a vodka chaser her way.

"You guys are wusses." Molly laughed. "That stuff is awesome."

"If you like setting your throat on fire." I took a sip of my own vodka and lemonade.

Just then Logan returned, setting another drink in front of Liv. I suppressed a smile that the girl renowned for nursing a single drink all night would soon be on her third. She squinted at me. "Are you guys trying to get me drunk?"

Molly spluttered her black drink across the table. "Loosen up, Olivia. It's not every day Savvy says goodbye to her teens."

"Yeah," I said. "Twenty's ancient. I'm like … almost an adult. Before you know it, I'll be all old and wrinkled."

"Pfft, you'll never be old." Liv leaned back into the arm Logan had thrown over the back of her chair.

Noise burst through the front doors, and my eyes immediately sought out Dane, who was laughing with Cade. Kasi and a few of the teaching crew trailed along behind them. Even Dono and Becca were there. My heart warmed at the sight of all my friends, but mostly at the guy who'd pulled this all together and given me a truly fantastic day. He was too great.

Everyone crowded in around me, so I had to wait a full hour and at least a dozen birthday drinks before I could get close enough to whisper in Dane's ear. "This is fun, but you'd better keep that promise you made about later."

He looked up at me from where he lounged back in the armchair, his gaze roving my skinny jeans with appreciation. "I intend to. Just don't get too messy."

"I'm not drunk." I could feel myself swaying as I lied. The lies, they rolled so easily off my tongue that some days it made me feel ill. I glanced back up the table toward my favourite fake friends. Not that they were fake—that was all me. The happy carefree girl they all knew hid so much. Underneath all that I was torn apart, gaping at the heart where two people-shaped holes still bled. But playing this persona was better than receiving the pity. The blame.

Careful to keep my steps even, I returned to my seat, and Molly had ordered another round. This one was a black liquor that I suspected was probably liquorice flavoured, just like the last lot. Her and Olivia argued back and forth for a bit before I picked up my glass and said, "What the hell. I'll only turn twenty once."

I knocked back the shot.

Molly clapped.

"Livia." I tried to raise my brow, but it didn't want to play.

"Don't call me Livia."

"O-livia then."

"O-livia," Molly repeated, and we made it into a chant.

"Leave it be," Logan warned. "Liv's had enough." My friend almost fell off her chair trying to hug her newfound sobriety protector, and for some reason that was the funniest thing that had happened all night, 'cause neither Liv or me could stop laughing.

"Party pooper," Molly said, around a grin.

The DJ finally got to work; music faded in, and that was the only cue I needed. It was well past time to move this party to the floor. "Dance?"

Liv jumped up and grabbed my hand across the table, singing, "I love this song!"

"Duck," I warned, but Molly didn't manage in time. Our hands tangled around her and came apart. Hilarious.

Maybe we'd all had a little too much to drink, but I didn't care. Everything was so much easier when it felt like more vodka flowed through my veins than blood.

We managed to fill the small dance floor. But much to my disappointment, Dane kept his sweet rear on his seat, talking to the other guys. Dono was the only one who made it out; even Cade didn't bust a single move. Didn't matter. I partied it up with my girls in a way we hadn't done since the night of the Quiet Renegade concert. I kept trying to catch Dane's attention, but whatever he and Logan were talking about had him too engrossed. Instead, I concentrated on having a great night and dancing out all the alcohol that flowed through my system so I'd be sweet for later.

At one point, I looked across at Liv, and she was all up and cosy with Christian. His arms were around her waist as she shimmied her perky rear against his groin. I blinked, thinking my drunk goggles must have been blurrier than I'd thought, but after a second take it most definitely wasn't the guy she'd been dating. It was the ex who'd screwed her over.

She turned around and stepped back, her shoulders a rigid line as she poked him in the chest and started shouting. Something tickled my thigh, and I rubbed the hard phone my skinny jeans pressed against my leg.

Olivia and Christian kept at it, and Logan appeared, only to slide across the floor when Christian punched him fair in the face. I needed to do something to help, but my foggy brain couldn't process what was happening quickly enough.

"Logan!" Dane shouted, and that was enough to snap me out of my stupor. I grabbed Liv from behind and pulled her out of the fray. With all those huge fists flying she was likely to cop a stray one.

Dane stepped in between the two brawling guys, holding them apart with his palms flat against each of their shoulders, but the imbeciles kept at it, trying to hit each other around him. My heart lurched into my throat as Christian's fist connected with Dane's ear. I held onto Olivia even tighter. If I didn't, she was sure to rush in. Dane managed to get a hold of Logan's shirt and tore him away from the other bloke. Then Olivia broke free, and she flew at Christian with her whole body slamming into him. Dane grabbed my escaped charge and bodily hoisted her up under his arm.

"Logan," Dane growled. "With me. Now!"

"Bastard needs—"

"Right now, damn it." The three of them disappeared into the crowd, while I watched on open-mouthed, then spun around to face the arsehole who'd just ruined everyone's night.

"What the hell, Christian?"

He didn't meet my gaze. He was probably ashamed of the fact security was shoving him away from the scene of the fight and about to kick him to the curb, quite the embarrassment for a prissy upstart like himself.

Dane didn't come back.

My phone buzzed in my pocket, and this time I had enough sense to realise what it was, so I fished the device out and was a little surprised to see Kody's face on my screen at this time of the night. I picked up right away.

"Dakota."

If she spoke, I couldn't hear her over the loud music. I blinked away the spots the strobe light had left in my vision and went in search of somewhere with less noise. "Just hold on, I need to find a quiet spot."

I ducked around the other side of the bar, but it wasn't much better. I eyed off the toilets for a second but thought better of it, then my sights set on the door where Dane and co. had disappeared. "Almost there," I said to my sister, hoping she was still hanging on. I pushed through the heavy wooden door and stepped out into the freezing night air. In the midst of winter, this town was like the polar opposite of the fiery pits of hell. Maybe more like a hellish ice castle. How anyone could ever stay warm outside was beyond me. Even the alcohol wasn't helping tonight. "Kody, you still there?"

A soft sob came from the other end of the line.

"Chickpea, what's up?"

"It was your birthday …" she sniffled, "and I didn't even remember."

"Hey." I wanted to hug her. "It's okay. It's just another stupid day. No biggie."

"Yeah, but birthdays are hard. Sheesh, everything is hard, Savvy." She sniffed.

"I know, but we've gotta do the best we can with what we've got."

Silence echoed from her end. One, two, several long heartbeats, then she said, "Did you at least have an all right day?"

"Yeah, actually, I did."

"Cake?"

"Better. Pancakes."

She choked on another sob, then sighed. "Like Mum used to make for birthday breakfasts?"

The double doors to the Royal blew open to reveal

Kasi and Cade. My eyes welled involuntarily at the memories Kody's words evoked, but I held it together as I looked at my friends.

"There's my girl," Cade boomed.

"I'll let you get back to the party." Kody sighed.

"No, it's—"

Cade slapped a wet kiss on my cheek. "Come on, birthday girl. There's fun to be had. Forget about that pansy for now, he ditched you, and ..." Cade waggled his brows, leaning in to place his booming voice near my phone, "I'm here and he's not."

"Who's that?" Kody asked.

"No one." I shot Cade a pointed glare. "Thanks for calling, Kody. I love you."

"Love you too." She sighed once more. "Sav ..."

Cade pulled on my hand, and Kasi pushed me along from behind.

"Yeah."

"Do you think it ever gets any easier? Do people stop looking at you like they know just how broken you are inside?"

I glanced at my friends, Kasi's huge grin and Cade's proud smirk, no doubt thinking he was pissing Dane right off. "Yeah, chickpea. It does."

The sigh she emitted this time was softer, almost wistful. "Night, Savvy."

"Night." I hit *end call* and Cade's hand darted out to grab my phone, which he shoved in his back pocket. "No phone calls during party time."

"Come on, give it back."

Cade grinned, but it lacked the usual mischievous quirk. "I won't touch it, pocket rocket, promise."

Kasi dragged me back inside. Being immersed in the world of family was making things so much harder for Kody. She didn't need meds; she needed to get away, and start a new life that wasn't overshadowed by the one we'd lost. Aunt Rosy meant well, but the contrast in her ways to those we were raised with were a constant reminder Kody didn't need. Still ... my sister sounded more with it than she had the last time we'd spoke. Thank god she'd come off those meds.

It took a moment for my eyes to adjust to the dimmer lighting once we were inside. Kasi soon disappeared, leaving me alone with Cade, who had mischief plastered all over his handsome face. It slipped right off for a moment as his gaze settled over my shoulder, only to return tenfold. But Cade didn't have time to act on whatever plan he had brewing because strong arms slipped around me, and a husky voice I knew well whispered in my ear. "Having fun?"

I spun around to face Dane, and in lieu of an answer set my lips to the pulse throbbing in his neck. Huge hands slid down my back and over my butt. The denim was way too thick ... "Maybe going home would be more fun."

"That's my girl." Dane's tongue followed the trail of kisses he placed along the side of my neck, and it was so deliciously excruciating that I tipped my head to the side to allow him better access. Someone cleared their throat, but we both ignored the noise that no doubt came from Cade while Dane moved his ministrations from my neck to my jawline and finally stopped at my lips, which he claimed with his own.

"Drinks!" Kasi shouted, and I reluctantly broke our kiss, setting my forehead against Dane's. "It's been such a long time since I had an awesome birthday."

His gaze, grassy orbs of melting sadness with pity dancing at the edges was something I never wanted to see in eyes I loved so much. I loathed pity.

I pulled away and slapped him on his perfectly toned rear. "Spanks."

Dane pinched my butt in return.

"Let's dance."

I dragged his face down to meet mine once again.

CHAPTER TWENTY ONE

Savvy

With my hand gripping the silver railing so tight my knuckles popped, I took a deep breath to steel myself.

"Take your time getting ready." Tori clutched a bunch of white roses to her chest. Pity the smell of antiseptic drowned out the sweet perfume the florist had talked up.

Time was useless. I could have stood there all day and still not been ready. Meanwhile, she was inside, in pain. She needed me. I was all she had. Releasing my death grip on the railing, I took the few long strides to the double doors that led to the paediatric ward and pushed through. My heart slammed into my throat as if it were trying to escape my body, but I would be strong. I had to be strong for my baby sister.

Tori's arm looped through mine and gently, she guided me to room nineteen. Another deep breath did nothing to kill the pulse trapped in my neck, nor the stinging in my eyes.

"Hey Dakota," Tori said cheerily as we stepped into the hospital room.

My sister didn't respond. With tubes sticking out of her and screens beeping every few seconds she looked half-machine, and those were the least disturbing traits. Some kind of rubber brace was wrapped around her head and had been secured to yet another machine that seemed to stretch her neck. Huge metal arms held one leg suspended above the bed. And above the brace her tiny face was all red and black and swollen.

Tori caught my arm as my knees gave away for the second time in two days.

My eyes shot open. My heart raced as I inhaled ... *a dream*. It felt as though I'd stepped back in time, but sun tinged green by my curtains proved I was at Oxley, Almost three years after that horrible night. I sought out the clock on my wall, and for reasons unbeknownst to me I was wide awake at seven a.m. We must have had a late night, since the last I'd seen of the time it had been smack on midnight, and technically no longer my birthday. Or so Cade had shouted in my ear. Dane ushered me upstairs to bed when we got back to Oxley, but refused to spend the night, despite my protests. He'd said something about letting drunken girls sleep it off.

After an hour of tossing and turning, I gave up on the hope of more sleep and rolled myself out of bed and into the shower, where I washed off that skanky morning-after-a-big-night smell. Then I went in search of the man who owed me one promise, broken or not. Hauling my heavy bones all the way up to his top-floor room was a feat that ended up not being worth the effort. If he was there, he must have been passed out, because no amount of knocking on the thick timber made it budge. All the noise did was echo through my hyper-sensitive skull, and the blame for that surely laid in the crazy shots Molly had inflicted on the three of us.

Since she was pretty much a non-drinker, Liv probably wasn't coping well either. We had, after all, knocked back at least three of those hellfire shots before she left. I hauled my lazy self back down the stairs, across both courtyards, and up the staircase that led to my friend's room, stopping short when my foot landed in the hallway. The sight that befell me wasn't one that I'd expected. Logan sat with his back against the door. His head hung in his hands, his hair covering his eyes, and to put it bluntly, the guy looked like death turned over.

"What's going on, Stalker Boy?" I asked, dropping the pet name Liv often called him.

Logan looked up, his blue eyes shining with sincerity. "I wish I knew."

"Shove over," I told him, and once he did, I bashed on the door. Him sitting out here lamenting whatever woe had befallen their young relationship didn't make a lot of sense. Last night, things had seemed pretty serious. They'd both looked so happy. Well … until Christian had caused a huge scene.

She didn't answer the door, so I squatted beside Logan, who'd returned to staring at his no-brand shoes. It took a moment to grab his attention, but when he pushed his blond mop back and met my gaze, I told him, "Give her some time. Whatever it is, she'll come around."

He grunted.

I wasn't about to force my friend to open up if she didn't want to see this shaggy-haired hottie. He'd either have to sit it out, or suck it up and wait for her to be ready. I was pretty optimistic. The way she was when she was with him was different ... *special*. Whatever was going on, they'd come out the other side without any scars, that was for certain. I gave him a pat on the shoulder and said, "Good luck."

He offered me a wan smile, and I turned and walked away. Maybe I'd just go back to bed and sleep for a few more hours. My head pounded, and there was an insistent burning behind my eyes. I rubbed at them as I stepped down the last few stairs and emerged into the courtyard.

A shrill squeal almost shattered my already ringing ears. "There she is!"

My gaze shot across the way, seeking out the sound's source, and landed on a wheelchair parked in a sunny corner of Back Courtyard. My stomach didn't know whether to drop or jump for joy at the last two people I'd ever wanted to see in the middle of Oxley College. Kody pointed at me and from behind the handles of her chair, Tori pushed my sister over the bumpy grass at full speed.

It was great to see them, but what on earth were they doing here, three hours from home and without warning when they'd never, ever, visited me in the whole year and a half I'd lived at Oxley?

"Savvy," Kody said, now they were closer. She held both arms out toward me as if she intended to jump right out of the metal chair that confined her.

"Kody ..." I glanced from my sister to my cousin. "What are you doing here?"

"Happy birthday," they both yelled.

I wanted to be happy to see them, but there were too many other factors to worry about. Besides, they'd both sent birthday wishes just yesterday, so this was a little odd. "You drove all the way here to tell me happy birthday?"

"Yep." Tori sported a proud-as-punch grin. "Surprise."

My heart gave a little squeeze.

"You're not happy to see us …" Ever the perceptive one, Kody clasped her hands in her lap.

"Of course I'm happy to see you. I'm just, well, surprised, is all." I glanced around the empty courtyard. "Let's head out and find somewhere nice to have a breakfast celebration, yeah?"

"Ooh, that sounds fun," Tori cooed, but Kody wasn't so easily distracted. Instead she looked up at all the windows facing into the courtyard. "Which one's yours, Sav? I wanna see where you live."

My tummy dropped for the second time in as many minutes at the wish that just wasn't possible, since this building was older than the hills and sported no lifts. I pointed toward Block L's second floor, at my window whose curtains were still drawn tight. "Just there. Second on the right."

I rubbed a hand over the small of my back where the muscle ached—I probably twisted it on the dance floor—then took the handle of Kody's chair and spun her around. "I'm starved. What do you girls feel like?"

"I'm easy." Tori broke into an almighty smile, only it wasn't directed at me, it was directed at whoever was behind me.

A warm hand settled on my hip as Dane leaned toward me, his eyes full of intention. I dodged the kiss he was about to deliver in the nick of time. Fumbling to correct my less-than-stellar move, he said to Tori, "I wouldn't say that."

My cousin groaned, and from what I understood Dane was right. She had been anything but easy during their time as a couple. "You loved every second," she said, and the way she cocked her head to the side and slipped into flirt mode was like a knife twisting in my stomach.

She seemed to have missed our near moment. Dane's hand fell from my waist and he stepped back, placing a ton of cold distance between us. He cocked a brow my way, totally ignoring my cousin's blatant ogling of his gorgeous muscles. Those sleeveless tops should be banned when he was out in public ... if I angled myself just right, I could catch a glimpse of the hard curves that made up his glorious pecs.

"How are you feeling this morning, princess?"

Yawning, I dragged my gaze away. "Mostly just tired."

Tori glanced from me to him, her eyes narrowing. "Big night? Is that why I couldn't get you this morning?"

"Couldn't get me?"

"On the phone."

"Huh ..." I couldn't remember it even ringing. My fingers slipped into my pocket without thought, but only brushed against empty denim. I hadn't looked at it all morning, in fact since ... *Cade*. Damn him.

"Are we gonna eat or not?" I didn't wait for her answer, just started pushing Kody toward the gate that led out of Oxley. It was well over time my past wasn't in my present, lest the pity police show up and start issuing permanent statements. My sister harrumphed and took control of the wheels herself, spinning the chair back to face me. "What's with you, Savvy? We just came to visit."

I cast a nervous glance toward where Dane and Tori still stood, talking about god only knew what. "Nothing," I ground out. "I'm really happy to see you guys and just don't want to share the few hours we've got together with anyone else."

Kody braided her fingers. "That so?"

"Who's this?"

I jumped at the sound of Molly's cheery voice, and tried the best I could to put on a happy face when the two worlds I'd worked so hard to keep separate were in the midst of a mid-orbit collision. My heart felt as if it was about to implode; it beat so darn nervously.

Kody stuck her hand out. "I'm Savvy's sister, Dakota."

"I've heard a lot about you." Dear Molly didn't miss a trick, even though I was sure she'd never heard me drop Kody's name. She even kept the surprise off her face. My ears pricked up as the conversation behind us grew closer.

"You should come along with us …" I felt myself blanch at Tori's invitation that was no doubt directed at Dane.

Molly looked from me to him and across to Tori, and I could practically see the puzzle pieces falling into place in her mind. Her eyes narrowed a little, and when they came back to mine there was an unspoken question between us. I was totally busted for not talking to Tori, and now I was paying the price. Molly held out a stack of white envelopes I hadn't noticed in her hand for me to take. "Friday's mail. I figured you were too wrapped up in celebrating to collect it."

"Thanks," I said, taking the pile from my friend.

Molly said something to Kody, but it was impossible to keep their words in focus with Dane and Tori and another voice rumbling in the background. I glanced over my shoulder and Cade was standing next to my cousin, his usual sleazy gaze sliding over her curves. His attention didn't slip by her either. Tori moved a little closer to Dane.

"You should get going. All the best places will be full by noon." Molly said, bless her. She turned her attention the other way. "Have you boys had brunch yet?"

"I was just asking—"

She interrupted Tori with a wide a smile. "I'm sure you drove all this way to spend time with Savvy, not us, so we'll leave you girls to it. Have fun."

Dane's gaze sought out mine, full of an understanding that scared the hell out me. He nodded once, hard. "Catch you later."

I offered up a smile that I really didn't feel.

"Nice seeing you." Tori gave a little wave and practically bounced as she turned around while they walked away.

It took all of two minutes for me to get them both out of there and into the parking lot where I spotted Aunt Rosy's van sitting proud as limes amongst all the clapped-out student cars. I wheeled Kody up beside the passenger door which I'd opened, and she manoeuvred herself inside. After folding down her chair and stowing it in the back of the van, I climbed in the backseat.

"Where are we headed?" Tori asked.

"Umm ..." That was a good question. "Just drive into town. There are a whole bunch of cool little cafes around. We'll find something."

Her gaze connected with mine through the rear-view mirror, and a flood of warmth enveloped me. It really was good to see her, and even better to see Kody looking so normal.

"Visiting is a cool birthday present," I said.

"It was a last-minute idea." Tori pulled out of the parking lot, and I settled back in my seat, staring at the contrast between Kody's golden locks and Tori's midnight black style-cut. In contrast to her natural blonde waves, so like my own, she'd gone for the bold look around the same time her and Dane split. Even though I knew she was the one to blame, she'd sure suffered a broken heart. I let my eyes slide closed with the heaviness that suddenly consumed me. I didn't want to be the bitch here, but Dane had my heartstrings wrapped around his fingers in a Celtic knot, and there was no way those babies were ever coming undone. I needed to toughen up and really talk to Tori about him, but what if she saw me being with him as a betrayal? No matter how wrong loving my cousin's ex was, everything about Dane and I was right.

Whilst I was lost in thought, Tori found the mall and parked underneath it. She already had Kody's chair out and my sister in it before I snapped out of my reverie and noticed. I climbed out of the van and stood beside my sister. "How're you feeling, chickpea?"

"Better now I've seen you. Your friend seems nice."

We moved away from the car. I didn't take control of her chair, but rather walked beside my sister, allowing her the dignity she so often demanded. "Yeah. Molly's really great."

"And what's with Dane?" Tori asked from my other side. "You two seem pretty tight."

I swallowed the huge lump that had sprung into my throat, but didn't have time to give an answer before she barrelled on. "It's been so great seeing him again ... makes me remember how good we were. I'd love to start something up with him again."

Love. I just about swallowed on my own saliva. The damn knife was back in my gut again, not twisting this time but stabbing, stabbing, stabbing.

"Is he single?"

My tongue had swollen to three times its size, which meant there was no way any words could seep out around it. My brain had even frozen in place. I couldn't issue so much as a nod.

Tori seemed oblivious to my reaction, charging on with her observations. "He was always super sweet, but man, he got hot. I mean, he's always been a babe ... but those arms. Have you ever noticed how toned they are now?"

I fell back behind Kody's chair and set my palms around the handles so tight my nails bit into the soft flesh. Yeah, I knew it all right. I also knew Dane was so much more than a hot body.

"Breakfast," Kody piped up. "What about that place over there?" As we emerged from the top of the escalator, she pointed toward a cafe in the middle of the mall. It looked pretty nice ... not top notch, but kind of quaint in a country way.

"I don't eat out often, but it looks nice." Breathing in and out was a feat when my lungs felt as if they were made of molten lead. Victoria had been the one to cheat on Dane; surely she couldn't think he'd take her back. Want her back ... I knew he wouldn't, but this ... this complicated things even further.

My sister took control of her wheels, lurching

away from me, and my strides lengthened to catch up, putting as much distance between myself and that awful conversation as possible. Kody was in the cafe, a waiter striding up to seat her when I arrived.

"Table for three," Kody said, and the woman zipped a rapid glance around the tables then gestured to her left. She pushed a hand into the pocket of her apron, retrieving a notepad.

"If you don't mind squeezing up a bit, I've got a free table just here. Sorry about the dishes. I'll get someone out to clean it up for you right away." She shoved the order pad back in her pocket without using it and glanced around the cafe again. She yanked one of the chairs away and shoved it in the corner, making way for Kody. The poor woman looked a little harried.

"Thanks." I offered the waitress a friendly smile, but she never saw it as she rushed off to collect a bunch of waiting coffees sitting on the counter. The place wasn't that packed, but the staff sure looked pumped.

Within a few minutes, a tall slender girl bustled up and cleared the empty plates. "Sorry about this," she said. "We're a bit understaffed today."

After she'd wiped down the table and handed us each a menu, Tori spun sideways to face me. She put her plastic menu down, propped her elbows against the table and made a tepee with her fingers. "Tell me about your new man. I was hoping to meet him."

Kody watched me intently from her side of the table, and I wiggled my fingers into my suddenly too tight collar. "What makes you think there's a guy? Just because I said …"

Tori twisted her fingers in the air between us.

"Because I know you."

Shaking her head, Kody let out a bitter laugh. "I need to find the bathroom."

I pushed up off my chair, but my sister waved at me to sit down. "I'm a big girl."

She backed out of the way and made it to the door. "They're near Kmart," I called.

My sister waved at me to indicate she'd heard. My tummy flipped and flopped inside me, but I kept my eyes forward and picked an easy topic of conversation.

"She seems more like herself."

"When I got home last night, she was still up. She'd been upset about you; I could tell. This whole trip was her idea, and I tell you, Sav, I haven't seen her this excited in a long time. I should've brought her to see you long ago."

"The meds?"

"She's not off them completely. Honestly, I think she does need them, just not the iron-strong dose she was on."

I nodded. "I guess that's good."

The waitress returned with a bottle of water she set on the table, followed by three glasses. Picking the bottle up, I poured us each a glassful.

"It's only a few weeks and you'll be home again for winter break, then you've got prac which is another month at home ... it does her good to have you around."

I hummed my agreement, even though I'd applied to schools here and would stay in college if one of those panned out.

"Now, about this real man you've been seeing."

My fingers trembled around the glass, and I had

no idea why this was so hard, but I just couldn't do it. That probably made me a coward and completely undeserving of whatever was happening between Dane and I, but as I looked into my cousin's violet eyes, fear grabbed me by the heart. I was scared of losing her, scared of losing Dane, scared of losing everything good in life. It had happened once before through my careless actions, and it was sure to happen again if I didn't handle this delicate situation carefully.

Somehow I fumbled my way through breakfast, feeling like I was going to throw up the entire time. Tori bubbled away in excited conversation, and Kody watched me carefully with eyes that always read the truth.

We made it back to Oxley not long after noon. I leaned between the front seats of the van and kissed Kody on the cheek then Tori. "Thanks for coming to visit. It was really great to see you both."

I jumped out of the car, slamming the door a little too hard in my haste. Another door squeaked open, but I threw out, "Safe travels. I love you both."

I wasn't fast enough, though. Tori was already out of the car, her brows drawn in a what-is-this-crap look as she glared at me, waiting for an explanation.

"Savvy," Cade boomed from god only knew where. His feet fell heavily on the concrete of the parking lot as he pulled up right beside me and draped an arm over my shoulder. He smacked one of his awful kisses on my cheek, grinning the whole while.

Bloody hell. I couldn't catch a break.

My phone materialised in his hand, and Cade passed it over. "Thought you might be looking for this."

Understanding flared in Tori's gaze and a grin broke out across her face. Good god, she didn't think ...

"So you're the new man?"

Cade didn't move his arm, just exuded his typical charm. "New to who?"

"Don't play dumb with me." She chuckled.

"I think you've mistaken me with—"

I curled into Cade's side, wrapping my arm around his waist, and of course the flirt lapped it up. His other arm curled over my tummy to pull me right up against him. My heart hammered a beat of betrayal, at my lies or at my letting him manhandle me when it was Dane's arms I ached to have in his place, I wasn't sure. Maybe all of the above.

Ever the opportunist, Cade squeezed me tight and leaned back so my feet lifted off the ground and my chest pressed against him. I squealed with the unexpected contact and had to throw my arms around his neck to hold on.

His lips came awfully close to touching mine, and as much as this little scene would get Tori off my back, I hated it. I gave Tori a huge smile, and satisfied, my cousin hopped in the car, only to lean back out the window, my mail in her outstretched hand.

Cade leaned forward and took it. She smiled at him. "Maybe we'll see you during winter break."

"Maybe." He gave my butt a squeeze. Jerk.

I waved as they pulled away with Kody glaring like she knew all my secrets.

No sooner had the van rounded the corner and disappeared from view than Cade peeled himself away from me and thwacked my shoulder with the wad of envelopes. "What the hell was that all about, pocket rocket?"

I sighed. "Nothing I want to talk about."

At least not with him.

CHAPTER TWENTY TWO

Dane

Why I even had the books open was a bloody mystery. I'd spent the past hour alternating between turning my music off and on, opening and closing the door and the window, then covering up the time on my digital clock. Nothing seemed to make a damn difference to my concentration. It was shot. It was stuck a few hours ago in Back Courtyard when it was obvious Savvy hadn't told Victoria about what we had going. What that said for the way she felt about us wasn't good. This thing didn't hold the same value to her as it did to me. It was a damn shame, because my heart was all in, and it seemed the reservations I'd had about being torn up by another West girl were well founded. Especially now, as I watched her walk across the courtyard below with Cade bloody

Matthews. She swatted his arm, and they both laughed. I wasn't jealous of the rugby winger, not when I knew that he didn't know her. She didn't let anyone—other than me, perhaps—in, but watching how easily they flirted made me wish things between us were simpler.

My phone hummed against my desk, and keeping my girl in my line of sight, I picked up, knowing who was calling.

"Hey Ma."

"Dane." The way she said my name made it sound like a blessing.

"What is it?"

"Nothing, sweetie. It's just nice to hear your voice. How are you?"

"You saw me just yesterday. Nothing's changed." I picked up a pen, and let the nib glide over the blank page. "Right now I'm studying."

"That's my boy. And how's your young lady?"

Logan joined the group downstairs and my friend looked like I felt—as if his heart had been tossed in a churning rip. His long hair stuck out every which way, and his manicured scruff was more messed than usual. Savvy patted him on the shoulder and Logan glanced toward Back Courtyard, fisting his hands in his pockets as he did so. Last night mustn't have gone down well. Maybe Olivia wasn't the type of chick that dug a guy throwing fists on her behalf.

"She's complicated," I answered my mother.

"The best loves are never easy, honey. Oftentimes you've got to fight to make the other person see how much you care, and that fight sometimes never ends, even after you've been together for years."

I wasn't sure what to say to that, so I grunted a,

"The old man about?"

"Ahh ... let me see ..."

I hadn't spoken to him the past few calls. I didn't set eyes on him yesterday either. "Here he is." I heard a rustle as she passed the phone off.

"Son, sorry I missed your visit. That business trip was unexpected." His voice sounded thin. "Your mother's been talking up this young lady you brought home. Sounds like a keeper, so you better make sure you treat her right."

I watched the exchange in the courtyard below. Savvy was acting happy, but I could see the tenseness in her stance, the way she moved a little slower than normal when Cade pounced on her with eager fingers.

"I'll treat her right," I said. And *right* would start with sorting out whatever the hell had happened when Victoria showed up. "I gotta go. Catch you later, Pa."

"Take care of yourself, Son."

I shut off the call and slipped out of my room. When I emerged into the courtyard, Cade took one look at me and backed away from my girl, who had a handful of mail. Logan was nowhere to be seen, but the footy-head gave me a look I didn't care to process. The sympathy in his eyes could nick the hell off. He slunk away, and Savvy tried to do the same, but I stepped around in front of her. No way was she leaving before we had this out. She looked up at me with those swirling blue eyes, the colour in them almost consumed by darkness. The space between us was agonising, but I made sure to keep it steady while I waited for her to speak first.

Her small fist closed tighter around the white

envelopes. She blinked up at me, sucking in her bottom lip. "I couldn't do it."

"Couldn't do what?"

Her slight frame shook with a rattly inhale, and she bit down on the lip harder. The plump flesh reddened, so full and soft ... using my own teeth to tug that lip into my mouth would be so damn satisfying. Slipping my tongue along—

I needed to get a grip. This girl got me so riled up it was near impossible to think straight. *Tori, hell yes, Victoria* ... Savvy's cousin was the elephant in the room she had to stop pretending didn't exist. If she couldn't, then there was no point in fighting, no matter how much I loved her. You couldn't fight for something that wasn't real, and to her I was just another part of the act.

"Couldn't stop the damn charade?" I asked. "Couldn't tell Tori the truth? Or was it just that you couldn't care?"

"I care." She raised her voice, waving the papers in my face. "That's the whole problem here, Dane. I care too much. I care about hurting Tori. I care about hurting you, but most of all, I care about stuffing everything up."

Clenching my jaw, I growled just loud enough for her alone to hear, "Then stop acting and take *us* seriously."

Her mouth opened, then closed, then opened again, like a fish gasping for water.

It took every ounce of my willpower to ignore the intense sexual pull between us and turn around instead of pushing her up against the wall and sealing my mouth over hers. I spun, about to stalk away, but turned back at the last minute. "Olivia doesn't know about Kody or your parents. Tori doesn't know about me. Molly doesn't know shit, and me ... what don't I know about, Savvy? Huh ... what?"

Her eyes shone, her mouth worked, and she screwed up the paper in her tiny hand, but I was far from finished.

"Everything is pretend with you. Things aren't going to feel right, and life's not going to get better until you stop the damn act. I love you, Savannah, but I don't want to be a part of your fake life. I want the real deal."

Her eyes welled with unshed tears, but I couldn't back down from this. There'd been enough lies, and it was time they stopped. Savvy needed to get better, and it seemed that us being together wasn't helping. It was just complicating her present with more of the past, and a complication was not what I wanted her to feel when she was with me.

I backed up, my heart pounding, my nerves tighter than a brand new wood plane, and I did the only thing that I could to stop from dragging her into my arms and my bed. I jogged out of the courtyard, and I didn't slow until I was in the Outlander and Oxley was well behind me. Until there was so much distance between us that the only way to get more was to hoon along the road out of town without stopping to look in the rear view mirror.

When I finally made it back to Oxley, my feet raw from pressing against the metal without shoes, she was nowhere to be seen, and that was probably for the best because my body ached to be with hers, and I wasn't convinced it wouldn't betray me.

CHAPTER TWENTY THREE

Savvy

Dear Ms West,

We regret to inform you that we are unable to offer you a placement during the upcoming term. Unfortunately, our student-teacher intake is already at capacity. We wish you the best of luck with your studies.

Kind regards
This school, that school, every primary school in Armidale.

The white envelopes all said the same thing. It was probably for the best anyway. Avoiding someone who lived in the same dorm was near impossible.

Everywhere I turned Dane was there, and seeing him just made my heart hurt. He wasn't the right guy for me, and I needed to move on. I needed to concentrate on Kody, and that meant keeping the peace with my cousin.

I picked up my phone and dialled my sister's number. It rang. And rang. And rang until finally the call went to voicemail.

"Hey, chickpea. I just wanted to hear your voice, but I guess you're busy ... or something. It looks like I'll be undertaking my practical experience back home at one of the local schools, so you'll have my gorgeous face around for two weeks of break, then three weeks of prac."

I glanced at the pile of letters. So much for more time with Dane. I hadn't spoken to him since our argument in the courtyard. There wasn't anything more to say. I shouldn't have let myself fall when I knew an 'us' was impossible. What a stupid thing to hope for. I swallowed the lump in my throat and swallowed again until it was gone. I wasn't weak. I could deal with this.

"Okay, well, call me back."

I pressed *end call* and dropped my phone onto the desk.

Dane was right. I had bled some epic lies and it was wrong. But if something made you feel normal, how could it not be right? It wasn't like I'd lied to hurt people; I'd lied to protect myself from deep emotions I'd felt far too often. And it wasn't even a lie really, more an omission of facts. No one had ever actually asked, *Savvy are your parents dead?* So I'd never actually said *no, they're not.* Just like no one had ever asked *is your sister disabled*, so I'd never had to say *it's my fault.*

CHAPTER TWENTY FOUR

Dane

Technically school didn't finish for another three days, but since I had a good academic standing, I'd skipped town early. I couldn't take another day of tiptoeing around, acting like Savvy's choice not to tell Victoria wasn't eating me up. Ducking my head when I saw her on campus or turning the other way if we crossed paths just wasn't cutting it. The past few weeks had been torturous. The constant ache in my chest, the loneliness that lasted all day even when other people were around … it made my insides feel as if they'd been laid open. If I'd thought being stomped on by Victoria was bad, then this … what was happening with Savvy … it was like a killer wave had dumped me into rock-hard sand. A good dose of ocean air was just what I needed to get my head straight.

The old man and I had been working hard all morning in an attempt to clear out some of the backlog of orders he seemed to have accrued. I sucked in a deep breath of the salty air as I strode down the street toward the Seabreeze Cafe. Diners spilled onto the street, filling the tables, even though the lunch rush should be well over. Tourist season didn't seem to apply to this part of town.

The biggest issue with this many people about meant there was sure to be someone around I knew. Not in the mood for chitchat, I kept my eyes on the counter. The chick behind the coffee machine offered up a friendly smile while I placed my order and moved back, waiting for it to be ready. That was about the same time as I heard what I'd been dreading.

"Dane Beaumont ..." The delivering voice caused my stomach to clench. "You just keep popping up everywhere I am lately."

"Maybe you're the one turning up where I am, Tori."

The huge smile she offered me seemed genuine. Guessed that meant Savvy hadn't spoken to her, not that there was any point now. The five-foot-nothing pixie slid her Ray Ban sunnies from her nose, up onto the top of her short hairdo. Victoria West had always been a babe, but right now it was her eyes that undid me, so much like her cousin's sapphire pools.

"You're on my turf here, Dane. Aren't you supposed to be a few hundred kilometres away?"

"Term break." I looked toward the counter; that coffee chick needed to hurry up. Flirty exchanges weren't on today's agenda. I had a shit-ton of work to get done if Dad and I were going to catch up anytime soon.

"But Savvy doesn't get home until Friday ..."

"If you don't have plans tomorrow night ..." Tori continued, but I'd drifted into my own thoughts. Thoughts about how different, how gorgeous Savvy was when compared to her party-hard cousin. After spending so much time with Savvy, it made me wonder why I'd hooked up with the other West girl instead when Savvy and I had such a strong connection. Even back then, Savvy was the one I'd sit in the sand chatting to all night, though her cousin was the one who'd wind up in my arms. Tori had been insistent, and I'd been pretty driven by big tits and a willing smile. Shallow, without a doubt. Sixteen, absolutely.

"Are we done here?"

That voice snapped me back. Much like her daughter, Rosy West wore her hair short, only hers was that fake blonde older women preferred rather than pitch black like Tori's. Like her hair colour, Rosy's eyes were also the dead opposite to Savvy's cousin; they were cold and judging. The older West woman watched the exchange play out between Tori and I with a firm mouth and a tight fist on her designer handbag. Her daughter seemed oblivious as she rattled off the details of a band that was going to be in town this weekend. It was an obvious invitation to hook up that I intended to ignore. Tori didn't float my board like she once had; her hair was the wrong colour, her voice the wrong tone, and her eyes didn't have the right warmth. And she sure as shit didn't have what it took to keep me up all night with just words.

Victoria wasn't the West that I wanted to wake up next to every morning.

"One cappuccino, a macchiato, and three ham and cheese toasties."

Saved by the waitress.

I stepped forward and collected my order, only to turn around to a smiling Tori. She stepped into my space. "Maybe Saturday—"

I repositioned the brown paper bags in the centre of the cup tray then stepped around her. "Later, Tori."

The girl still grinned in that I'm-here-for-the-taking way. The only way to deal with that shit was to ignore the hell out of it. One of Savvy's fake smiles touched my lips as I edged past her cousin and made like hell for the door. I was almost home free when cold fingers closed around my wrist.

"Stay away from my daughter."

I glared into Rosy's cold stare, wondering if the same rules applied to her niece.

"Victoria's grown into a fine woman. We don't need your kind of influence in our lives."

Typical. Her daughter was never the one to blame, even though the pot I'd been carrying that time was hers, not mine. "Oh don't worry," I deadpanned. "I plan on staying well away."

I tugged my arm free from her grip, and seething, made my way back to Driftwood Creations. That woman was one I'd crossed a long time ago, and it seemed it didn't matter that I was no longer into the crap I'd pulled during high school, or that Tori had her own mind and had made her own choices. The past was the past, and it was far behind me. Still, Rosy's opinion of me churned my gut the wrong way.

I pushed through Driftwood Creations' front door to the jingle of the old-school bell overhead. A lady, dressed much like Rosy West, in all designer gear, looked over her shoulder from where she stood at the counter. Her gaze dropped to the tray in my hand, then returned to meet mine. "Some service would be nice."

I bit down the retort in order to keep the customer happy and issued another friendly smile I didn't feel. "How can I help you?"

"I paid the required half price for an item that was supposed to be delivered two weeks ago. Despite calling repeatedly, oftentimes to no answer, I might add, I'm yet to receive the loveseat I ordered." She slapped an order receipt on the counter, jabbing a finger at the delivery date. "I was assured this would be ready by the tenth, yet here we are on the nineteenth and still nothing."

Making sure to hold eye contact, I told her, "I'm terribly sorry we're running late. I can assure you that piece will be ready as soon as possible. Let me check on an estimated date."

"As soon as possible isn't good enough. I need it yesterday."

I held up my hands. "Since yesterday's impossible, let me see when we can have it."

I slipped out the back door into the workshop, where the old man was hunched over the same coffee table he'd been working on all morning. "Loveseat for Monroe, what's the ETD?"

He glanced up, his eyes a little hazy as he blinked and pushed the safety goggles onto his forehead. "Haven't started it."

"Shit, Dad. It was due almost two weeks ago."

He grimaced. "I'm doing my best here."

Grinding my molars together, I returned to the shop's front. "It's going to be another week. We'll take twenty per cent off the price for your inconvenience."

The woman's face turned as red as her painted lips. "That's not good enough. My daughter is getting married on Saturday. Next Saturday, and that seat was to be used for the ceremony. What are we supposed to do now? The entire beach ceremony is centred around that piece."

Well shit. Her poor bag looked like it was being strangled. Good thing there wasn't a rat-sized dog in there, like I'd seen some women carrying. I pushed out the tight muscles along the back of my neck. "Look, I can't make any promises, but we'll see what we can do. Call back this time tomorrow for an update."

Her mouth set in a firm line. "The news better be that I'll have my seat in three day's time."

I watched her leave the shop, not moving until the highbrow broad was out of sight, then I slipped out back. "Where are the specs for that loveseat?"

The old man waved a hand toward the counter lining the side wall where a ragtag pile of papers was scattered. He didn't look up from his work, and in the light shining through the high-set window, his colour was a little off.

"You all right?"

"Fine." He set his tools down and stood up slowly, but not all the way. A groan slipped out of him and he stopped, half crunched over, and clutched his lower back. I flew across the room but wasn't fast enough to catch my old man before he went down.

I dropped to the floor beside him and patted his cheek to get a response, but he was out cold. Stone cold. Warmth hit my knees, and I noticed the wet patch on his pants. Whatever the hell was wrong, this wasn't good. He'd always fit the bill of perfect health. Stomach bugs didn't cause people to pass out, piss themselves … to look the way he did right now.

"Pa." I gave his shoulders a small shake, and his eyes fluttered open only to roll back so all I could see was white.

I shot up off the floor and ran out front to dial 000. The bloody call centre kept me on the line for longer than I wanted to be there. I told the lady on the other end to send the ambulance already and raced back out to my father. Still lying on the floor in a pool of his own piss, the sight of the old man sent me into a tailspin. Whatever the hell was wrong, it wasn't good. I dropped onto my knees again, and this time his weathered eyes met my gaze.

"Help's coming," I told him.

My heart beat the shit out of my ribs, and it felt like I watched my father fade in and out forever, but it must have only been a few minutes before the sound of sirens drew close. The paramedics rushed in, and that was when I remembered Mum. I fished my phone out of my pocket—why hadn't I thought of using it earlier—and dialled her number. She didn't get a single word in before I murmured, "The ambulance is taking Pa to hospital. He's not well."

"Oh no…" She gasped. "Put one of paramedics on the phone."

"Ma … they're taking care of him."

"Just do it, Dane. Quickly."

I approached a female ambo. "My mother wants a

few words."

The brunette squinted in confusion, but took the phone from my outstretched hand. I turned my attention back to the floor where her two co-workers were lifting my old man onto a stretcher. He had a white blanket draped over him and an oxygen mask covering his face. Once he was settled, they hefted the stretcher up and popped down its wheels.

My heart beat a wicked rhythm while I watched them wheel away the man who'd been my rock forever. We'd always been tight. I guess being an only kid made for plenty of time with just him and me—hours working wood, kicking a ball, playing on the beach. He'd been there through it all without hesitation or judgment, even the arrest. He hadn't judged me, just dealt with the cops and told me I was loved.

A soft touch on my shoulder pulled me around to face the pretty brunette. She handed back my phone with a grim expression. "We've got him stabilized, and we'll be taking him to Memorial. Do you need a ride, or can you follow behind?"

"I'll come with."

She gave a quick nod, and I put the phone to my ear, but the line was dead. Ma must have jumped in the car already. I swallowed the huge-arse burn in my throat and locked up real quick, jumping up into the back of the ambulance just as they were settling him in for the ride.

CHAPTER TWENTY FIVE

Savvy

To be honest, the thought of working at a school back in Coffs where everyone knew my story wasn't the only thing keeping me awake at night. What Dane had said played on my mind constantly. Even back home, the soft sound of Tori sleeping across the room wasn't enough to soothe my fitful mind. Nights were late, mornings were early, and there wasn't a lot of sleep in between. That was how I wound up walking Five Mile at seven a.m. on the first Saturday of winter break, my numb fingers pulled inside my sleeves to try and get them warm. The crash of the waves on the shore was somewhat peaceful, and the sun rising on the horizon a solid reminder than I was just a tiny cog in the mechanics of a much greater world.

I walked the entire five miles that morning, my feet leaving solid prints in the hard sand near the shore, and my nose bitterly cold from the biting wind. And while I walked, I thought about all that I'd lost. All that had come about because I'd been a reckless teenager, and all that had changed during the past few weeks.

"She needs you. Get in the back, Tori."

I dragged my knees up onto the seat, twisting my arms around them, and curled myself against the window.

"We need to go home."

"I know, babe. Climb in and look after Savvy."

Tori flopped against me, her arms covering my own as the Lancer surged to life.

Life.

How fragile it could be.

I didn't close my eyes, nor did I sleep, but somehow, between one thought and the next, I was alone in the car and the door I'd been leaning against opened. Strong arms caught me and hauled me against a hard chest, but I was lost to the moment. I was still lost in a moment that had happened three hours ago.

"I don't feel too well. I'm just going to stay home."

"Sure, sweetie. Have a warm bath and slip into bed. You'll feel better for it tomorrow."

Bile coated the inside of my mouth ... I'd lied and snuck out the second they'd left. A sob tore out of my aching throat, and Dane's arms tightened, drew me so close there wasn't a hair's breadth between us.

Four weeks. That was how long I'd been avoiding Dane, how long he'd been avoiding me, and how long our friends had been treating us as if we ought to be covered in bubble wrap. But it didn't matter that his absence had left a tight ache in my chest, that the few times I'd seen him from a distance my throat had clogged up, or even that every second of every day it physically hurt that I couldn't touch him or even just call him up to say hi, because he'd made it abundantly clear how he felt; I was a liar, and he hated that. Sometimes I did, too.

With my tummy churning for reasons far from the fact I hadn't yet eaten today, I slumped onto the dry sand not far from the track and just watched the waves. There were a few keen board riders out there, dropping in on the choppy surf. Even though the water was pretty churned up, the odd huge wave was clear as glass. I sat and watched for a long while. The way they rode the waves in was quite magnificent— the way they used their bodies to sway the movement of the boards... It was a sport I'd never tried, but growing up around the beach I had always loved watching people surf.

Huddled in my big trench coat with the morning sun warming my face, I didn't notice the guy jogging out of the surf until he was right upon me, wearing a neck-to-ankle-to-wrist black wetsuit that hugged every dip and plane of his body in all the right ways. The sight of Dane made my mouth arid. With a red, black and white surfboard under one arm, he strode up the beach and shook the water out of his hair, which hung just shy of his eyes in all its curling damp glory. The only indication he saw me was a slight falter in his step.

I braced myself for him to turn the other way or walk right on past, but Dane didn't. He approached my little slice of beach and jammed his board into the sand. I tilted my head up toward him and fought to hold control of my crazy hormones at the sight of all that hard muscle up close, even if it was covered up. Dane looked at me for a long minute, his eyes stormier than the wind-whipped current.

I spoke first. "Hey."

He tilted his chin and seemed to hesitate, moving forward then stepping back. I hated this awkwardness between us. Hated it as much as I sometimes hated the stupid choices I'd made in the past. I didn't get up from my seat in the sand as I craned my neck. The lump in my throat felt bigger than ever as I pushed out, "How was the surf?"

Dane's firm shoulders shrugged, and he flicked wet hair out of his eyes. "Being in the water is never bad."

We stared at each other for another long minute, until finally I pulled my gaze back to the water crashing against the shore. I wasn't sure what it was about the sound, but I'd always found the ocean soothing.

"What are you doing here?"

I flinched at the cutting tone in his voice. "Shelley's isn't exactly my favourite beach. Too many memories."

He shifted his weight to lean against the board, and boy, he looked tired. His eyes were rimmed with so much redness that it couldn't have been caused by the salt water alone. His cheeks were a little hollow, and he hadn't bothered to shave the speckled blonde and orange shadow covering his cheeks and jaw. I hoped he hadn't lost sleep because of me.

"What are *we* doing, Savvy?"

I closed my eyes. How could I tell him that I cared

about us when I couldn't stop the lies? I still hadn't broached the subject of us with Tori. Even though he and I were over the guilt continued hanging over me, but I just wasn't sure I could cope with losing someone else, and I was scared silly that she'd walk right out of my life. But then, by not 'fessing up in the first place I'd lost Dane, and that tore my heart right out of my chest.

I glanced out at the stormy ocean. "I don't know ..." The waves crashing against the hard-packed sand beat a steady rhythm while we sat there until I took a deep breath and dove in. "I was supposed to go to Dakota's basketball game that night, but I was a brat who wouldn't spare three hours out of her time. There was this beach party happening at the same time, and this boy was going to be there. Even though he was taken, passing up an opportunity to see him ..." I swallowed the ache in my throat. "I didn't even ask. Knew they'd say no; they always did. Instead I pretended I was sick ..."

Dane took a step forward and lowered himself onto the patch of sand by my side.

"I'd already sent a message to Tori asking her to pick me up. I didn't tell her I wasn't supposed to go, just jumped in her car when she pulled up in the driveway without a second thought. That night I had the best time, the boy ..." I glanced at Dane out of the corner of my eye, "... was happy to see me. He watched me over the top of her head as she kissed him and the three of us laughed and sang and drank. We'd always had a good bond, the three of us, and I relished every moment we shared. Yeah, I was jealous of Tori, but I kept all those feelings buried, because I had a solid friendship with each of them."

I paused, my throat aching with the memories, raw at putting it all out there. I stared at the waves, the water pounding into the sand, and I tucked a flyaway strand of hair back behind my ear, bracing myself against what hurt the most.

"I knew I had to get home before them. What I didn't count on was Kody's game being cancelled due to the other team not showing. I'm not sure how the rest of the night played out; I only know there were a bunch of missed calls from my mum on my phone when I got home, and that night ... well, you were with me when Tori got the call. They must have been searching for me when the truck hit."

Dane's arm came around me, pulling me against his side, and I hung my head, resting it on my knees. The tears came slowly at first, then like a dam bursting, all at once. It was quite possibly the ugliest cry I'd ever had, let alone in front of another person. In a way it felt like all the hurt of the past three years had built to a head and erupted out of me in that moment.

Dane held me, his hand gently rubbing along my arm until my outpour stopped. He never spoke, never told me he was sorry, never said any of the typical things people say to try and make you feel better about losing the people who matter most. He just sat there with me like a rock in the stormy ocean while the biting wind whipped around us.

"They had to have been out looking for me."

Dane squeezed me tighter against him, and once again didn't let go. This morning sure hadn't taken the direction I'd expected it to when I'd left home to try quieten my fitful thoughts. I hadn't come to seek him out, hadn't even realised this was the beach where he surfed. I straightened up and swiped my thumbs under my eyes. Between the wind and the tears, I probably looked a hot mess.

"Anyway … I didn't come here to make you feel bad for me."

He shook his head. "We were always friends, Savvy. That hasn't changed and never will."

He needed to understand. "Not telling people I'm an … orphan … is easier than facing the pity and the constant reminders."

I'd trained myself not to look at people when I thought that pity would be present, but Dane was different. His gaze set on the ocean before us, and his forehead rested in his hand. He didn't say he was sorry, or that he understood—he didn't need to.

Pushing up off the sand, I watched him do the same. The thought of walking away from him hurt everything inside of me, but I couldn't very well throw myself into his arms when nothing had changed. I bit down on my lip to stop from lurching forward.

His eyes churned like the water behind him, but Dane didn't make a move to leave, just watched me while I watched him. His left hand slowly raised and took my elbow, which he used to tug me into a hug. As Dane's arms closed around me, my heart gave a slow, sad flutter, and I let myself slump into his embrace. We stood there while the wind blew around us, while the waves smashed into the shore.

"We'll always be friends," he repeated, his lips brushing the side of my head.

But how could I be friends with this guy from whom I'd always wanted more? Extracting myself from his steady hold, I said, "I guess I'd better get going."

Dane tipped his chin. "If you need a ride back to Oxley ..."

I offered up a smile I didn't feel. "I've got prac right after break. I won't be going back until midterm."

Turned out scoring a placement here was much easier than landing one in the same town as college. Everyone must have had the same great idea about staying close to campus.

That tiny muscle in his jaw ticked as he gave a single nod. I'd never experienced such a drawn-out, painful goodbye, so I ended it right then by turning and walking up the beach without saying the actual words.

I might have lusted after Dane since I was sixteen, but loving him now after everything that had happened ... because I had wanted him when he wasn't even mine to have ... felt somehow twisted. My parents had been my world, just like Kody and I had been theirs, and I'd thrown that all away for a few hours with this boy. Now I couldn't even spare him that.

CHAPTER TWENTY SIX

Dane

Running into Savvy at the beach had screwed with my head. More than anything, I wanted to wrap her up and take away all the hurt, but I didn't know where we stood. If she'd decided not telling Victoria and not moving forward was for the best. That was why I never told her about Pa. After his first night in hospital, when both my parents were cagey as all hell, but tight-lipped, I'd spent the rest of the week slogging away at the shop to get the loveseat finished on time. Visiting hours were a wasted effort; neither of them told me shit, so I spent the rest of my time in the surf. Now he was home, the truth was finally out. About bloody time, too. I stared at my father across our polished wood dining room table, a whirlpool of emotions churning through my gut. Grief: check.

247

Hurt: check. Anger: check.

"We didn't want you to worry." My mother's hand smoothed over Roar's head with far too much pressure, but the dog didn't care. Tucked under her arm, he panted, tongue lolling, as if he were the centre of everyone's world.

With my back against the kitchen bench, I clenched my palms on the laminate counter either side of me. "I can handle knowing the truth."

"Yes, but we're your parents, and your father didn't want—"

"My father has a tumour the size of a small country inside his prostate and you thought it was best to protect me from that truth? When the hell were you going to tell me? When it was too late?"

Tears rolled down my mother's face and I felt bad, but shit. I could have been there with her weeks ago to help shoulder the pain, shelter her a little, but no, they'd frozen me out of the loop entirely.

"Son, it's not like that." My father shifted in his wooden chair. He looked a little better than he had in hospital. He was still kind of grey, but at least he was lucid and seemed pain-free. That didn't stop the hurt spearing through my chest though.

"It's not like surgery is an option, Pa. Not like you could cut it out and not tell me. Hell, even if you could, that's still screwed."

Setting the scruffy dog down, my mother reached across the table my father had made years ago and clasped his clenched fist, but it was all bullshit I couldn't take anymore. I shoved off the counter, scooped my keys and phone up and left them both sitting there, sharing the pain they'd shut me out of.

I jumped in the Outlander and took off. Solitude

was what I needed, some space to process this shit and this time, throwing myself into finishing some stupid loveseat wouldn't cut it. I needed to be farther away.

A few clicks out of town my phone rang, but I kept my eyes on the road.

I drove and drove until it seemed stupid, then I turned around and came back the other way. My phone rang again and I snatched it up, sending the call from my mother straight to voicemail.

Somehow I found myself in the George of Wales. It wasn't the best drinking hole in town, but one I often frequented during break. I perched myself at the bar, tuning out the music and the other patrons and downing beer after scotch. A chaser for every spirit. So long as they kept coming, there'd be no complaints from me.

Sometime around the bottom of a glass, perhaps the fifth or sixth—maybe even the tenth, I wasn't bloody sure—the bartender cocked two sets of pretty eyebrows, and I blinked to bring her back into focus then held up an index finger. "Another."

She took away the empty glass. "I think you've had enough, hot stuff."

Surely squinting would bring the two heads she seemed to be rocking back into one. A girl that pretty shouldn't be disfigured by beer goggles.

"Just one," I said.

Two heads shook.

"Are you harassing this poor girl, Dane? Shame."

My stool swivelled and tipped to the side, my hand shooting out to catch the counter. Close call. Victoria West stood before me, her fingers twisting hair that should have been too short to twirl, and a lopsided smile painted on her pretty face. I groaned.

"That impressed to see me, huh?"

"Not the West I want."

"Oh, really?"

I pulled my chair back to face the bar, but the damn thing moved too fast and my arse slipped off the vinyl. With an unsteady hand on the counter, I hauled myself back up and onto the seat moments before my arse hit the floor.

"You friends with this guy?" the pretty bartender asked.

Scooping up my schooner, I raised it to my mouth. Damn thing was bone dry.

Savvy said something back to the barkeep, and with a smile, I looked her way, only it wasn't Savvy, it was Tori. What the hell? I could've sworn those pretty eyes were the ones I'd been missing for weeks. Ah, but I had seen her just the other day ... and more torn up than she ever should be.

The five-foot midget hooked an arm around me. "You're going to have to help me here, Dane."

I slid down off the stool. My weight toppled to the left, and we both stumbled for a second before Victoria righted us. Sure as shit I couldn't have managed to get us upright on my own. My balance was all out of whack. I grinned, even though being this close to the wrong West felt all kinds of screwed up. Some distance, that was what I needed. One sidestep away wasn't enough, so I took two more. I had no idea what she had planned, but no way in hell was I taking her home. When I thought about being with a chick, no one but Savvy would do. She was the beginning and the end and everything in between.

Tori pushed through the front doors and out into

the night air, then dragged me around the corner of the pub where she leaned against the brick wall. I took another step back.

"What the hell?"

Ignoring me, she fished a metal case from her handbag and flicked the top open to reveal a single rolled smoke. Ah, now this I understood. She lit up and the sweet scent of pot filled the air. She dragged in a lungful then offered the thing to me for a hit.

A perfect ring of smoke left her mouth. "So who is the right West?"

I shook my head. "Nope."

"Nope on the joint or nope on finally coming clean about you and Savannah?"

"Nope."

I wasn't gonna tell her shit, just like I wasn't gonna light up when I'd stayed away from the green stuff since her and I had gotten done for possession a few years ago.

"Can't say I'm surprised." She puffed out another smoke ring. "You and her always had something we didn't."

I closed a single eye to better understand what she was saying. Didn't work. Did make it easier to see her though. Whatever Tori was talking about, I'd had enough … the ground was spinning, the stars were shooting through the sky, and my stomach lurched. I stumbled away from where she leaned against the wall toward my Outlander that had somehow wound up in the parking lot of the Central. Wait … Tori was at the Central?

"Not a good idea." My arm was tugged in the opposite direction. I frowned at the pint-sized pain in my arse. Her hand on my back wasn't gentle, nor was the way she pushed me along.

"What gives?"

"Shut up and get in." She kept shoving me until we reached the taxi rank, where she opened the back door to the nearest cab. I turned to ask her what the hell was going on. I wasn't going home. Wasn't ready to face my lying parents or their fucked up news.

She slapped a hand on my shoulder and bore down with all of her weight. Next minute, I found myself inside the cab, Tori's lean frame hovering over me as if she were ready to get it on. I shrunk back against the seat. Wrong girl. Not sexy Savvy. Not suave Savvy. Not my Savannah West.

A click echoed through the car and with the squeak of knees on the vinyl seat Tori extracted herself from my space, telling the driver an address that sounded mighty familiar. Home? Pity it wasn't the home she shared with her cousin. I sighed out a lungful of heavy air, and just before Tori shut the door, I told her, "Everyone lies. Everything is one ugly fucking lie."

CHAPTER TWENTY SEVEN

Savvy

I lurched forward as the bus pulled away from East Coast Primary School. Halfway through my first week of prac, I was forced to take the bus with all the kids since Tori was in classes across town and Aunt Rosy needed the van. Tori had been acting strange anyway, in a 'secret smile' kind of way. Like she knew something I didn't.

Kids screeched around me, an orange hit the window, and I covered my free ear with my hand to better hear Molly on the other end of my phone.

"What did you say?"

"How's prac going?" she shouted, as if that would help me hear her against all the noise around me.

"Yeah, it's great."

I lurched forward then back in my seat as the bus

picked up speed.

"How are the kids? The teachers? What's it like being in an actual classroom?" Molly's tone was way upbeat. Something good must have been in the air back at Oxley, because Olivia had sounded just as cheery when I'd spoken to her the day before last.

"It's all great." As we moved up into third gear, the shops and parked cars fled past. I didn't stare at the trendy shop that I knew belonged to Dane's folks. Didn't look in the window wistfully or notice that the closed sign was flipped around. Nope, I was too busy not looking to actually notice any of that. Besides, my brain was fried from hanging with little people all week.

"Doesn't sound great ..." Molly's tone had turned serious.

"It is."

"You can't fool me. I'm guessing you're not enjoying it."

I sighed. "It's not that I'm not enjoying it per se ..."

"Spit it out then."

"You sound like an old lady." Molly huffed on the other end, but I barrelled on. "It's not what I expected, that's all. Do you know how many tissues a single grade-one class goes through in a day? How many snotty little fingers came out of noses then touch my Sass & Bide jeans to get my attention?"

Molly snorted.

"It's not funny. Those kids are walking germ factories. And don't even get me started on the shoelaces. I haven't been studying all these years to wipe noses and tie laces. And lunchboxes. Oh my god, you've got no idea. No one can open cling wrap, and those juice boxes with the straws? Forget it."

Now she was laughing so much I held serious concerns for her bladder.

"It's not all bad though. They're so innocent and unjaded by the world around them that everything is exciting, and the way their little faces light up when they understand a core concept … just wonderful. Then there's the surprise hugs; they're pretty great." I sighed. "What's news from Oxley?"

It took a few moments for Molly to pull herself together enough to form a coherent answer, but when the laughter finally died down she was left puffing for breath. "Cade's trying to shag anyone who glances his way. Olivia and Logan are all loved up. I quit netball, and Oxley feels too quiet without you. Plus did you realize you're going to miss the formal ball next weekend?"

"No!"

"Yes."

"That's so unfair. Kick Olivia's butt. Social committee should have worked around prac when there are so many teaching students in residence. I guess I could come back …" but I wasn't ready to see Dane flirting it up with the boob patrol. He had called us *friends*, nothing more.

"Oh yeah, Liv quit social committee."

The view out the side window had changed from shops to houses a while back, and we'd been slowly creeping toward the brick-and-tile cookie-cutter homes I rode past every day. I juggled my phone to rest between my ear and shoulder and scooped up my bag with one hand, using the other to keep balance.

"What about you?" I stumbled down the aisle.

"Looking forward to spring break."

This time I laughed. "Winter break only just ended."

"Ah, but there's this—"

The phone slipped from the grip of my cheek and hit the dirty floor. I swore as the bus pulled to a stop, and I had to grab the handrail to stop from falling on my butt. My phone wasn't so lucky. It slid along the aisle a million miles a second and slammed into the front of the bus as the wheels stopped, propelling me forward. I swore again, apologised to the lady I'd slammed into, and chased after my phone. When I retrieved it from the stairs leading down to the door, it had a cracked screen. Another expletive slipped out and I exited the stupid bus, stepping onto the curb. The vehicle rolled away, and I examined the series of cracks starting in the corner of my poor phone. They had spread like veins along the entire left side. Bloody hell.

I tucked it into my pocket and glanced up at our house at the end of the street. Aunt Rosy's black van sat proudly in the drive, the hatch up and front door open where my aunt was helping Kody out. I picked up the pace, keen to see my sister.

Kody caught sight of me just as I reached the driveway. With a hand indicating to stop, she must have told Aunt Rosy that she'd wait for me because my aunt moved inside and Kody wheeled herself around to face me.

"How was school, chickpea?"

The smile that touched her lips was genuine, albeit a little hesitant. "Okay."

"Just okay?" I gave her shoulder a bump. "On a scale of one to sucks-a-lot, how would it rank?"

"Probably sucks-somewhat."

I raised a brow. "That's pretty good, wouldn't you say?"

She shrugged. "Ms Morrit compromised on my songs, and I've met a few people who don't play the I'm-sorry-for-you card."

Kody grabbed the arms of her chair for support as I turned her backward to bump it up the stairs and inside. "In a few years I'll be finished college, you'll be finished school, and we can just take off someplace where no one knows our story."

"Sounds awesome."

My phone buzzed in my bag, and I thanked all things sweet that it still worked. Now we were inside, Kody took control of the wheels and rolled herself over to the baby grand. It was one of the few things from our old life that was still around. Mum and Dad had bought it for my sister when she'd passed the fourth grade of piano at only eight years old. Being good parents, they encouraged her to play the best she could, and shit, she could play. Kody rolled right up to the black instrument and hooked a long stick up to her elbow so she could work the pedals, then she flicked open the hatch to expose the shiny keys. My sister was one of those lucky people blessed with being good at everything. Music came naturally, school was easy, and she'd been a great sportsman, plus back then she was always a popular kid. Things were a little different now, but at her core she was still the same kid who had been the apple of everyone's eye.

The buzz of my phone vibrated through my bag and I fished it out, grimacing at the shattered screen. Two green bubbles indicated received texts, but the words were too hard to make out. I couldn't even tell who they were from.

I paused by the base of the staircase, my hand on the rail that lifted Kody's chair up to the second floor while I listened to the sweet melody of classical music. Kody sure was an exceptional musician; she poured so much into the way her fingers hit the keys. I was glad the adaption to her beloved piano allowed her to hold onto her love of music. It was something that seemed to keep her grounded.

Aunt Rosy's hand brushed across my shoulder, and we both stood there for a few minutes just listening. When the melody softened and finally faded out, my aunt sighed. "How was school today?"

"Glorified babysitting for a bunch of little monsters who all seem to have the same lurgies."

She shook her head with a smile. "It's the first grade. That's what it's like for the little ones in winter. Did you craft?"

"Finger painting." I pointed to a smear of blue on my red Sportsgirl shirt.

"Oh Savannah, what did you expect? You've wanted to be a teacher since you were a little girl."

"I thought it would be more about teaching and less about crowd control." What I didn't say was that when I was younger I had wanted to be a teacher because I'd wanted to be like my mum, and now I was older I was clinging to a dream that the two of us had created together. In many ways it made me feel like she knew me as the adult I'd become, not the selfish teenager she last knew.

Aunt Rosy walked past me on her way to the kitchen. "It's only day three. I'm sure it'll be better toward the end of the week."

I shrugged. "Maybe."

Nimble fingers tugged at my hair, pulling the strands back into an intricate braid. It didn't matter how old I grew, there was something comforting about my mother's tender hands working my mass of hair into something pretty. I closed my eyes, enjoying the moment.

"Did you sort out those elective choices for next year?"

"Handed them in yesterday."

"I'm sure you made the right decision, honey."

"I guess. I just … I know what I want out of life, and none of those subjects take me there."

"A solid foundation in all subjects will take you exactly where you need to be for teaching."

"Chemistry and Advanced English won't help me teach primary school."

"It sure will. Today, my grade four class talked about alliteration, onomatopoeia, and similes."

"Sally sells seashells by the seashore, until a wave womps into the sand like a huge fist and washes her away."

The thick braid fell against my back and I felt her hand rest on my shoulder.

"You'll be a great teacher someday. Now, go get changed. We're leaving in half an hour."

"About Kody's game … I'm not feeling so well."

CHAPTER TWENTY EIGHT

Dane

With a sky full of storm clouds, Wednesday afternoon was damn miserable. I should've headed back to Oxley a week and a half ago, but Driftwood Creations had too much of a backlog, and it wasn't like I'd be expecting any help with clearing it. As it was, I hadn't caught us up entirely, but I couldn't miss any more classes. At least the piece for Mrs Munroe was done and dusted. I glanced up at the sky as I pulled the shop door closed. The likelihood of the clouds opening before I hit Waterfall Way were high.

Huge globs of water splattered against my back as I slid home the deadbolt. I could hang out in the shop, catch up a little more. Could go home for a feed too, but honestly, the thought of seeing my folks after the news they'd imparted this morning; that the cancer was stage three ... if I went now I might miss the downpour, and then if I waited, maybe it wouldn't get better until tomorrow. Murphy's law said whatever course of action I took would lead to the worst possible outcome.

Worst outcomes could be faced head on when nobody lied.

Screw it. Long strides got me to the Outlander in just the nick of time. The second I slid into the seat, the rain fell by the bucket load. Murphy's bloody law could take a hike. I pulled my phone from my pocket and shoved it in to charge, then turned over the engine. I'd filled up with fuel on my way to the shop this morning and had a bag in the backseat ready to go. Leaving here at five should put me back at Oxley at a decent time.

It didn't take long to get through town and reach the eastern end Waterfall Way. The windy road that led away from the coast and up the mountain range was usually pretty quiet, and today was no different. I pumped up the music and shuffled in my seat to get comfortable. The rain pelted against the windshield so hard I had to kick the wipers up a notch.

I flicked the headlights on for good measure. It was starting to get dark, even though it wasn't late. Must have been the overcast sky—the pelting rain. I ramped up the heat and rubbed my brow. My bloody head had been pounding all day.

Cancer was a bitch. There was no arguing with the facts. Just thinking about the aggressive nature of the beast was enough to rile me up. There was no cure, and nine times out of ten the treatment wasn't effective in the long run. Rotten surf, aggressive drunks, bad grades I could fight against, but this ...

Heat flared through my chest, up my neck. My head pounded.

How could they not even fucking tell me the whole story?

Headlights cresting the corner just about blinded me. All I could see were white spots, almost stifling in their brightness.

The Outlander jerked sideways when something clipped the front corner, spinning my car round and round.

Black swamped the white spots.

And *CRASH!*

CHAPTER TWENTY NINE

Dane

Pain.

Shooting through my shoulders, along my arms ... my chest.

So much pain.

My eyes struggled to open.

Yelling. From somewhere. Couldn't quite be sure.

Everything spun through the night. Felt like movement.

A bright light, shining through the darkness.

Eyes. Couldn't open. So bright.

Chest pinching.

"Are you all right in there?"

"In where?" The words barely croaked out.

"We're going to get you out. Just hold on."

Hold onto what? My head; it pounded.

****

Flashing lights filled the night. Blue. Red. Blue. Red. Blue. Red

I sat on the edge of a tailgate, blinking like I'd just woken from a realistic dream. Too realistic. My chest stung like a bitch, and my entire face pounded.

"Can you tell me your name?" The voice came from my right, where a dude dressed in a blue jumpsuit pulled a blanket around my shoulders.

"Dane."

"Full name?"

"Dane Beaumont."

"Do you know what day it is, Dane?"

"Wednesday."

I looked up at the dude, whose fingers pressed into my neck, moving to my forehead. "Is there anyone we can call?"

"Ah, yeah. My phone ..."

"We've got it."

He moved away, and my gaze slid across the road to where a black car had wrapped itself around a tree. *Shit.*

Nausea hit at the familiar back hatch, license plate, and twisted surfboard sock sticking out the back. I'd totalled the Outlander. I jumped up, the blanket rattling as it slid off my shoulders.

A firm hand forced me back onto the tailgate.

"You need to stay calm, Dane. Everything is okay."

Like hell it was okay.

"Hays. Call Logan."

****

A whole day in bed eased the pounding headache I'd scored from the crash. Olivia had insisted I needed round-the-clock care, so here I was twenty-four hours later, still sitting on Logan's couch. Being monitored. I twisted open the cap of my second beer for the evening. The ambos had cleared me of a concussion; Liv needed to loosen up.

The front door of Logan's apartment slapped against the wall revealing Jordan Hays, with a leggy redhead trailing behind him. The chick couldn't be more than sixteen, but then, Jordan wasn't exactly much older. He pushed dark hair out of his eyes and slid an unfocused gaze my way.

"Daaaaane." He threw an open palm into the air, but no way in hell was I moving. I only had one working arm and this couch was too bloody comfy. All my muscles ached. Instead, I raised my bottle of James Squire in greeting. "Jordan."

The kid grinned all lopsided as the girl slid a bold hand under his shirt and onto his stomach, leaning close to talk in his ear. Logan emerged from the kitchen with a frown in place, and I watched their standoff play out over the lip of my beer. It didn't take long before Logan lost his shit, probably 'cause the kid reeked of pot. Logan's expression darkened as he took in the state of his brother. The younger Hays was almost seventeen, and I was sure my mate had played around alcohol and girls at the same age, but Logan went ape shit when it came to his little bro cutting loose.

After a bunch of cussing, Logan acting like a paranoid mother, and some hurled abuse, Jordan turned and staggered right back out the door, chick in tow, leaving Logan dragging his hands through his wavy hair. My friend threw himself onto the couch beside me, and I passed off my beer. With a hand on the dewy bottle, Logan pushed it back my way.

"Little shit needs to realise his life is worth more than drunken nights and loose girls."

This was about the sister they'd lost, no doubt about it. I wasn't in the know when it came to all the details, but I was pretty sure drugs and alcohol had been involved. Whatever the cause, Kayla's death had made Logan tighter than a nun on Sunday.

I took a swig from my bottle. "You were no better a few years back."

"Well, he can do it someplace else," Logan grumbled.

I shook my head. "You don't mean that."

Logan tapped his fingers on the arm of the chair and we both sat there, him glaring at the footy game on the TV, me only half paying attention. But then something changed. Logan jumped up off the chair, punching the air and cheering. A try. But no, the couch dipped as Logan slumped into it, cursing. "That was bloody in. Give it to them."

Looked like it was going to replay.

My phone rang, and I fished it out of my pocket. *Mum.* My heart pounded in my throat at her name illuminating the screen. I hadn't told her about last night. I picked up, even though I wasn't really up for the call. Honestly, I felt a little sloppy.

"Hi Ma."

"Dane, sweetheart. How's college?"

Always with the niceties ... "Ma, what's up?"

"Nothing's up. I just wanted to hear your voice."

She sounded kind of down. I probably should have spent some quality time with her while I was home on term break. But I was too mad. "We visited the oncologist today and he said your father is doing well. He's putting him on a new treatment which hopefully won't knock him about like the last one."

A slow-mo play of the try revealed that the touchdown on the TV had in fact been legit. Logan harrumphed beside me. I raised my beer into the air and cheered. Silence echoed from the other end of the phone. "Uh-huh."

"He made it into the shop today. He didn't stay all day, mind you, but he got that piece finished he had been working on."

Pity Driftwood Creations was going downhill, even though Dad worked his sick arse off to keep it afloat when he should've been in bed. "Yeah, I'll be back in to work on some of the backlog next weekend."

If I felt like it.

"We'll see you then?"

I groaned.

She sighed.

"I'll try and call in."

She sighed again. "We'd really love to see—"

"I said I'd try."

"Okay then, well … goodnight."

"Night, Ma." I slid the phone across the coffee table, but the push was so hard it slipped right off the other side and thunked on the carpet. I slumped back in the lounge, cringing at the sting that caused in my chest. Drawing back the last mouthful of beer, I swore under my breath. Logan kicked his feet up on the table and crossed his arms, glaring at the screen.

"Shouldn't be so rude to your Mother, man."

I got up and grabbed another beer then slumped back in the chair. Footy was a welcome distraction that we both slipped into. The truth was, I was still pissed about my folk's lies. The old man was probably on limited days, and they'd only just told me. God only knew what else they hadn't told me. The cancer could be hereditary for all I knew. They'd told me jack shit.

Not long later, the door blew open again, and Logan's head swivelled, his expression stormy, but it wasn't his wayward brother that burst in with a gust of frigid wind. This time my mate's auburn-haired beauty blew in the door, her cheeks rosy with the biting air. Her whole face lit up when she grinned, but the joy slipped off her lips mighty quick as she took in her boyfriend's surliness.

"What's up with you two? When I left it was all cheery *let's watch the game*. What happened; someone die?"

Logan jumped up off the couch, his head shaking back and forth.

"What?" Olivia said.

My mate shut her up with a kiss that made my heart ache for Savvy, but it wasn't like Liv had to can it for my benefit. "No one's died yet." I placed my empty on the floor next to the couch. "I can't believe she didn't tell me." Logan pulled away from his girl, and I told her, "The folks finally decided to tell me Dad's got stage-three cancer."

Her eyes closed for a moment, and Logan pulled her into his side then let her go to look me in the eye. "They didn't tell you he was sick. So what? You knowing before there was a prognosis wouldn't have changed a damn thing, and in your final year of study, what was the point in letting you stew it out? They were coming from a good place, man."

I couldn't meet his eye. Logan sure had hurt enough a few years back. He'd had a shitty upbringing too.

"You've got great parents, so drop the bitterness. If you don't, you'll regret it later."

I pushed off the couch, stumbling forward, but managed to right my balance before face-planting the chunky coffee table. Olivia's judgy gaze followed me all the way to the fridge as I reefed the door open so quick it crashed against the counter.

He was right. Later might be too late. It still didn't dull the fact they'd lied.

CHAPTER THIRTY

Savvy

I slung my messenger bag over my shoulder and said goodbye to Mrs Hamilton, the teacher who'd taken me in. With truckloads of patience and a love for little faces, the portly older woman was well suited to the job. She'd been lovely to work with, but boy was I looking forward to getting back to studying via books. Next week, I wouldn't be with her ... she was shipping me off to a year six classroom which she said I'd find totally different. The change was pretty exciting. Older kids wouldn't need as much supervision, so I'd be able to spend more time teaching. Maybe things were looking up.

When I reached the tall fence that marked the front of East Coast Public School, the blast of a car horn cut through the afterschool chatter. The flood of kids and parents exiting the place had died off to a slow trickle, so Tori's Lancer was easy to spot.

I crossed the road via the crossing lady to where my cousin leaned against the side of her white car with her arms crossed. It was all very reminiscent of a bad rom-com, only instead of a heartthrob I'd scored a grim-looking chick. Some punk-rock band thrummed through the speakers, and even though the weather had cooled, my cousin still rocked her Havianas under the hem of her jeans. She looked me up then down, squinting when her gaze returned to mine. "You look terrible."

"You would too if you'd spent the day wrangling craft glue, crepe paper, balloons and twenty-two over-excited six-year-olds."

I climbed in the car a moment before she ducked inside. "What are you doing here?"

"Can't I swing by to pick you up without a reason? You won't be here this time next week."

"I'll miss you, t—"

The obnoxious blare of my phone interrupted. "Too," I finished, before swiping my finger over the screen to pick up the incoming call from god only knew who. Cracked screens sucked.

"Hello."

Tori pulled away from the curb, squeezing into the traffic that always seemed to congest the roads around the school. I swore no one let their kids walk these days.

"Savvy." Liv sounded a little flat. "I've texted you a few times while waiting all day for school to let out so I could call. When are you back?"

"I've got another week yet." *Silence* ... "What is it?"

"Look ... I don't know what went down between you and Dane, but if there's any way you can wrangle coming home early ..."

My heart thumped two times too fast. "What's wrong?"

"He wrecked his car and—"

"Ohmygod." My heart jumped into my throat.

"No, no, he's mostly okay. It's his dad. He's really sick, and Dane's not coping."

"Shit. Mostly okay?"

"He's a bit beaten up. Massive gash on his left arm, but he'll be okay. It's his Dad that's the real concern. Dane isn't handling himself."

Dane was really close to both of his parents. He wouldn't be handling it well, and despite all the bad air between us, I had to go. I knew what this was like; he'd be hurting worse than hell. No one understood that pain, and that was the worst thing. They all just wanted to tell you how sorry they were.

"Sav …"

Liv said my name again, and I snapped back to the phone call. "I'm coming."

"Thank goodness. We hung with him last night, but he won't even answer Logan's calls anymore. We're worried."

I nodded, even though she couldn't see me. "I'm coming."

We pulled up in the drive, and I shut off the call and jumped out of the car, running inside. If his dad was really sick, then why was Dane still at Oxley? Hopefully it meant the sickness wasn't dire, but then he'd be coping better, right? Still, nothing changed the fact that he was hurting, and that made my heart ache. Pushing past Aunt Rosy, I raced upstairs and started throwing clothes in my suitcase. By the time I'd squished all my cosmetics and shoes inside too, I'd realised I would need a way to get there. I zipped up the bag and turned, but didn't even need to step out of the room to find someone to beg for a ride. Once again the image of relaxation, with a shoulder against the doorframe, Tori watched me whiz around like a woman possessed. Rosy stood behind her, her back near the other side of the hall.

"What's wrong?" My cousin held my stare, and this was it. I had to tell her.

"Dane's not in a good way. I've got to get back to Oxley."

She crossed her arms over her chest and despite the tense mood, a small smile touched her lips. The same one she'd been playing with for a week. "You ... oh, really?"

The bag hung from my fingers like a dead weight, somewhat like my heart, which felt as if it were lynched from my fingertips, too. I took a deep breath. "I love him, and I need to be there."

"Savannah—" Tori stepped inside the room, slamming the door between her mother and us. Her smile became full-blown. "Savvy, I don't care that you guys have something going on. All you had to do was tell me, and I would have backed off."

I raised a brow, more out of surprise than anything else.

She kept smiling. "He was an important part of my life, but I let him go because really, I don't think he was ever mine in the first place. I was always jealous of the easy friendship you two had."

"But ..." It didn't make a lot of sense. They'd been so into each other. "... he was devastated when you broke up."

"He was never in love with me, Sav. No matter how much I wanted him to be. It was always obvious that you were the one he loved. He just didn't recognise it. That's why I had to let him go ... set them free and all that."

It was like a huge weight just slipped off my chest and pooled around my feet. "I'm so sorry, Tori."

"Rubbish ..." She waved a hand my way. "There's nothing to be sorry for. Now, tell me everything."

I blew out a relieved breath. "Okay, but I need a favour. How do you feel about me telling you while we drive?"

"Let's go then." Tori opened the door to an empty hallway.

I didn't need to be told twice. Grabbing my bag off the bed, I raced down the stairs and headlong into my aunt. She eyed me in that way she had which made my knees want to buckle, but I didn't have time for this today. I pushed around her pencil-pleat business suit, but her icy grip on my wrist stopped me cold. "Savannah, a word."

I tossed my bag to Tori and waited for her mother to say whatever was so urgent it drew her from the kitchen. Aunt Rosy pulled herself up to full height, which was a little above my five-three. "I hope there is nothing between you and that Beaumont boy. He's not the type we want hanging around now, is he?"

"Excuse me?"

"He has a criminal record, Savannah, and I will not have that kind of influence around any of you girls."

"Is that so?"

She raised a thin brow. "If you continue to see him, you will not see Dakota."

I stood up straighter, matching her glare. "I am a grown woman and you cannot dictate who I do or don't see, nor can you stop me from seeing my sister.

I'm tired of living a lie, and there's no way you're going to force me back into that corner."

I turned around and walked right out her door.

****

The trip to college was anything but easy. Telling Tori that I'd not only being seeing her ex for the past few months, but hidden my feelings for Dane from her for years hurt my cousin in a way I'd never thought it would. Her hurt didn't stem from my broken relationship with the surfer, but rather from the fact I'd kept it secret. I'd thought keeping it to myself, forcing it to not be a thing would be better for her, but as we drove up to the New England tablelands watching the sun sink below the mountains, it became apparent that in doing so, I'd hurt her just as badly as I'd hurt myself by suppressing those feelings for years. We'd always been tight, and my secrets seemed to make Tori feel as if I wasn't as invested in our friendship as she was.

Dane wasn't my only confession. I told her all about Oxley, and how I'd managed to keep my life there separate from the heartache that was my real deal. I told her that my other best friend, Olivia, knew nothing of the fact my parents had died in that car crash or that Kody was disabled, yet we were close.

Although the entire conversation made me feel dirty, I felt somehow free. As if all my sins had fallen away to reveal the raw me that hid beneath them. Not once did Tori judge me, but sadness rolled off her and filled the inside of the tiny car. It made me feel horrid.

From there we went onto easier topics, like how

much kindergarten wasn't for me. Tori agreed that grades five and six would suit me better, since I enjoyed kids who were a little older and the curriculum was more History, English, Science, and less learning how to read and write.

By the time we reached Oxley, it was nearing full dark and I was worried about just how bad his injuries were. Liv might have been downplaying. Tori dropped me in the parking lot and disappeared to find a motel, saying she'd keep in touch. I jumped out and marched right inside. The courtyard was scattered with people coming and going to the dining hall. I didn't slow, didn't stop when I heard my name, just threw out a few waves and *I'll catch you laters* as I made a beeline for block B.

The climb up the stairs was the slowest, longest few minutes there ever were. I just about shoulder-barged the gossiping freshmen out of my way to get to the middle floor without so much fuss. It would have been better if I had, for they turned off on the same floor I wanted and blocked the middle of the hall, chattering. I'd had enough. I squeezed through their little circle and reached Dane's closed door.

First sign of not coping = locking oneself away from the world.

I rapped on the door for all I was worth, but there was no joy. He didn't open up. The girls down the hall stopped talking long enough to stare, and I remembered his little trick. Giving the bottom right corner a solid kick, I stumbled off balance and grabbed hold of the doorframe to save myself just as the door flew open. It shot back at me just as fast, but I jammed a foot between it and the jamb, then edged my way inside.

Second sign of not coping = looking like the spawn of a hobo hobbit cross. Maybe a little Gollum thrown in for good measure.

The hair that covered Dane's chin was so long and unruly it blended right in with the blond mess covering his head. It looked like he'd decided forming natural dreadlocks, matched with sweat pants and no shirt, was the way to go.

He was slumped in the chair at his desk with a huge bottle of whiskey in his hand.

Third sign of not coping = eyes like glazed pottery.

I took a moment to reach those eyes, due to the mess that was his face. One of those plastic strips held together an angry cut right above his left eye. Yet, it held nothing on his battered chest. I got caught up on the defined contours of his chest for all the wrong reasons. The usually glorious muscles were the colour of a bruised strawberry. His naked chest was all bruised black and red, and a white bandage covered his left arm from elbow to wrist.

I moved across the room faster than I drew my next breath. "What happened?"

Dane raised the ridiculously-sized bottle to his lips and kicked his head back to swallow, then clunked the liquor onto the desk. His gaze didn't meet mine, didn't so much as sway from its vacant stare.

Fourth sign of not coping = acting like you're alone when you're not.

Screw the fifth sign. I gave him a solid shove in the shoulder, since his chest looked like an overused punching bag.

The back of his chair hit the desk with a *thunk* and slowly, his hazy green eyes rose to meet mine. They narrowed as if he were trying to focus.

"What the hell, Dane?"

Worse than reacting, he stared right through me. I gave him another shove to crack him out of it, and his hand snapped around my wrist. This time that shifty gaze did focus on me, and his expression was full of so much pain my heart hurt. He must have seen the anger slip off my face for his handsome features twisted into a sneer. "What are you doing here?"

"Kicking you in the butt so hard you won't know if you land in last week or next year."

Using the firm grip on my wrist, he tugged me off balance and into his lap. Between one breath and the next, his whiskey-flavoured lips smashed against mine and I almost … *almost* gave. Sure, he was hurting, but using me wasn't going to make it better. I pulled back and he let go. His arms hung limp and dangled beside the swivel chair, and my heart broke a little more. I took his face between my palms and kissed his lips feather-light, then pulled him into a gentle hug. I didn't say I was sorry, didn't say I understood, because those were just empty words that every other person had probably already said. Instead, I held him against me as he broke down. And there was nothing unmanly about it. His chest heaved against my breasts as silent sobs wracked his body. The wetness of his tears touched my cheek, and I just knew his heart tried to beat a normal tune when nothing could quite be normal ever again.

This guy who'd always been strong was so broken that the only thing I could do was hold him and hope that somehow that helped.

He seemed so drained that I coaxed him to lie down and finally, he fell asleep in my arms, and I slid out of his bed, closing the door behind me.

CHAPTER THIRTY ONE

Dane

The best dreams always happened when I was drunk. Maybe it was the deliria, or perhaps it was just an over stimulated mind. Either way, it felt like Savvy's arms were curled around me when I woke. If it wasn't for the empty whiskey bottle on my desk, I'm not sure I would have believed my eyes that she wasn't there. Some dreams just felt too real.

After a speedy shower, I threw back on yesterday's sweat pants and a fresh shirt.

The chime of an incoming text drew me out of my own head. Logan's name filled the screen.

You coming?

I didn't bother flicking a text back, just shoved the

phone in the pocket of my sweat pants and locked up. Being ten on a Saturday morning meant the place was deserted as I trudged through the courtyards and out back. Most people usually spent weekend mornings catching extra zees or at sport. Today, I was doing neither. On reaching the parking lot, I opened the door of the beat-up Corolla and got in. The pressure of the belt across my bruised chest stung like a bitch, but readjusting it to rest under my left pec eased the pain. I didn't miss the way Logan sized me up from the corner of his eye, nor did I miss the way his fingers tapped anxiously against the wheel.

He started the engine without making any stupid statements about my smelling like a brewery, which was a relief. I wasn't sure I could handle having the obvious pointed out today.

We rode in silence until we reached the turn that led to the industrial estate on the outskirts of town. We pulled into a lot full of banged up cars, surrounded by nine-foot-high security fences, and my chest felt heavy, even though it was only a damn car. I hadn't been in much of a state to check out the damage the other night. The ambos had insisted I keep calm and hadn't even let me grab my board from the back before the wreck was towed.

Logan exited the Corolla and I followed his lead, making for the front entrance of a huge work shed set in the fence like a gate. Charging ahead, I pushed through the glass door to the toll of a chiming bell, and the grease monkey working the desk looked up.

I approached the counter. "Just want to check on the 2005 Outlander that came in on Thursday night."

The man ran a critical eye over my face, the exposed bruises on my arms and finally the mess that was my right hand, then let out a long whistle. "Damn. I dunno how you walked away from that wreck with barely a scratch."

I had no answer to that, so mutely watched him retrieve a set of keys from under the counter and flick around a sign on the front door, locking it after us. Logan and I exchanged a look as the rake-thin man hobbled around the side of the building and out into the middle of all the smashed up cars. We wound our way through the metal graveyard until finally he stopped in front of a heap of mangled black metal that could not be my Outlander. The entire front end was cactus. It looked like a pole had rammed into the passenger side, while the driver's side was banged up too, only not so bad.

"Dare say they'll write it off."

I blew out a breath and circled the junk heap that was my car. The hatch was up in a way that looked like it would never close again. The striped sock that belonged to my surfboard stuck out the end, stretching taut over the fibreglass board which protruded in a jagged mess from somewhere around the centre of the soft cover. The board was screwed. I couldn't even salvage the protective sock.

I swore and kicked the rear bumper.

"How long does this shit take?" I asked the skinny dude. "I gotta get back on the road."

"Ah, depends on your insurer. A few weeks, at a guess."

I kicked the rear end again, and Logan cleared his throat. "Take the Corolla. We need it tonight, but you can have it after that."

I walked around the side of my car and peered in the window at the spot where I'd sat less than forty-eight hours ago. My throat closed in at the tiny bubble of open space that was the driver's seat. I hadn't realised just how close I'd come to facing St Peter's pearly gates. And now that I'd been close, there was no way I was letting life go without a fight.

****

Logan had missed his lady's hockey game to take me to the wreckers, so it was only fair I sat through his brother's footy match before heading back to Oxley. Not that I really followed the game; my head wasn't it. Keeping his eyes on the field, Logan said, "I don't want him to go down the same destructive path she did."

"Not gonna happen." I leaned to the side to relieve a little pressure from my sore leg. "He might let loose every now and again, but that kid's got you watching his back. He's showing keen potential on the field, and you said he's got a good group of mates, a job even. There's no way he's sliding off the rails."

Logan's jaw clenched. "He needs to forgive himself for the past and move forward."

I bit back the laugh that tried to break free, and instead rested my arm on my thigh. "In time, I'm sure he will."

Tucked in my jeans pocket, my phone vibrated against my thigh.

Hey.

I stared at the unfamiliar text for a full minute before my thumb slid over the screen, replying.

Hi.

A response came in right away.

It's Savvy. My phone's broken, so I borrowed Tori's. How are you?

Nothing for weeks, and now small talk, and from her cousin's phone. I wouldn't jump to the conclusion she'd put us first. I couldn't assume. It wasn't worth the head-on-with-a-semi feeling.

Fine.

You sure?

How's Victoria? Been chatting?

Arsehole move, but it got us right to the crux. The silence that strung out spoke for itself. God only knew what she wanted. I watched the rugby game play out, watched Logan jump up and cheer as if we were at the State of Origin and the Blues had scored a winning try. I watched the screen on my phone until it lit up again with Victoria's name.

This friendship thing goes two ways.

I had no idea what that was supposed to mean. Maybe she was calling me out on being rude.

With the game over, Logan started moving and I followed along, not really thinking, not seeing, just not anything. By the time we rolled into Oxley's parking lot, it was mid afternoon.

"I'm not going, mate." I told Logan for the fifteenth time, but he wouldn't take no for a bloody answer.

"It'll be fun. I'm going for Liv."

"Sucks to be you."

Logan's mouth kicked up. "Sucks to be you too, because she's got it in her head that you need tonight. Something about loosening up for a few hours."

"Loosening up?" He couldn't be serious.

"Yeah ..." He eyed me up, and damn, I was thinking the same thing. I was already too loose after last night's bender. I didn't need any more. "Either you come along quietly or she drags you, which probably includes forcing you into dancing and all that other crap. Up to you, mate."

I cracked open the door and set a foot on the ground.

"Tomorrow, the Corolla's all yours if you want to see your folks."

I reached back in the car and slapped his shoulder. "Appreciate it."

"If you want some company, give me a yell."

"Thanks, Loges."

"Three hours until this thing kicks off. I'll see you there."

Shaking my head, I pushed open the door all the way and stepped out of his car. Oxley's formal ball wasn't that great. I'd gone the last two years, and it was just a bunch of college kids playing dress up while they partied, same as at any other function.

Savvy's laugh cut across the courtyard, and I took a double take. When I'd woken this morning and she wasn't there, I was pretty damn sure I'd hallucinated her showing up last night, but maybe I hadn't. Surrounded by her usual entourage, she looked happy. Her blonde hair hanging over one shoulder shined in the afternoon sun as she tossed her head back and laughed at something Dono had said. She had on one of those tiny dresses with a layer of skin-tight material underneath that covered all her long limbs in black. And those boots … also black and sexy as hell, they came all the way to her perfect thighs. Blood raced under my skin, and cutting across the grass to scoop her over my shoulder was so tempting it took everything I had to hold back. To remind myself that I wouldn't be another one of her secrets.

I turned into Front Courtyard without saying hello. Good thing she didn't catch my eye; I wasn't certain I was strong enough to back away with those sapphire beauties staring into my heart. Ignoring the caveman urge that was shouting at me to get over myself and haul her into bed already, I stamped up the stairs that led to my room.

CHAPTER THIRTY TWO

Savvy

Dane wasn't about, or at least wasn't answering his door, and when I broke in his room was empty, so I'd kept a low profile all day, spending most of it with Tori. Just back from town, we were chatting when Becca waved me over from her sunny corner of the courtyard. Stretched out on a beach towel with her long legs catching the rays, she looked cosy. She shaded wide eyes with a slender hand. "You're back early."

"It's just a quick visit. I've got to be at prac come Monday."

She nodded, her gaze flicking up to Tori who stood confidently, eyeing up my sunbathing friend. My cousin thrust a hand toward the girl on the ground. "I'm Tori."

"You're going to love the shirt I picked up for—" Dono broke off into an excited squeal as his attention shifted my way, and his arms flew around me in a shoulder-crunching hug that was over almost before it began. He pushed me back so he could run an appraising eye over my hands, hair and face, no doubt looking for signs of preparation. "Savvy, my girl, you made it back for ball. What colour are you wearing? We can't clash."

Seemed everyone around Oxley had been busy getting ready for tonight; the buzz of excitement sure was thick. But for the first time since forever, I wasn't pumped for the ball. In fact ...

"I'm not going."

Dono's mouth fell open. "You are not missing the highlight of the social year. There's no way you'd do that ... never."

I offered him a put-on smile.

"Not acceptable." He pulled one of those attitude-filled hand moves that said 'no way'. Honestly, this year the ball didn't even rate on my priority list. Tori cleared her throat, and she was right; we had things to set in place.

After prying myself away, I turned to Tori. "We needed to find Liv and Molly."

She frowned.

"They're my—"

"Savannah Louise West, get yourself up here." It turned out our search was over before it began. It took a second to spot Molly hanging out of Olivia's window.

"Molly Meredith McLean, stop spilling my middle name!"

"Not even close to right." Her laugh echoed through the courtyard, bouncing off the brickwork loud and clear.

Tori gave me a strange look, but ignoring it, I surged up the stairs and into block K. It felt like I'd been gone forever and hadn't seen my girls in a month. I guess it had almost been that long with winter break and prac. When I reached the landing and peeked down the hall, Molly had already emerged from Liv's room and ran full pelt down the hall. She threw herself at me and I stumbled back, almost squashing poor Tori under my heeled boots.

"You came all the way back just for the ball? I knew you wouldn't miss it." Molly extracted herself from my grasp, and it looked like her and Liv were working on hairstyles. Molly's dark locks were all twisted up in some kind of an intricate up-do that left wispy strands brushing her round face. I fluffed a particularly curly lock with my finger. "This look suits you."

She blushed and ducked her head. "Take the compliment," I told my timid friend. "Embrace it."

She smiled at me through upturned lashes and spun around, striding down the hall to where Olivia's door stood open. Tori lingered near the opposite end of the hall, looking like she didn't belong. I offered her an encouraging smile, that I probably needed more than she did and entered my friend's room.

It looked like a cosmetics explosion had erupted on Liv's desk, and maybe it'd reached her arm too, because the inside of her wrists resembled an artist's easel. She smiled when she saw me, and I pulled her into a hug.

"How is he?" she whispered.

"Thanks for calling me." I squeezed my arms around her tighter. "Now, let's get this colour sorted. Where's your dress?"

Liv pulled away and grinned. "I picked up a gorgeous Witchery number, but I can't for the life of me match the colour. There are so many different shades of red!"

She pointed toward a silk dress hanging from her curtain rail. With a mid-length fall and an off-the-shoulder cut, she'd be absolutely stunning. The deep burnt red wouldn't clash with her auburn hair—instead it would make her reddish brown eyes really pop, while complimenting her scarlet waves.

Molly cleared her throat from behind me.

"Where are my manners?" I'd almost forgotten the reason we were here. I moved back toward the door so I could see both of my friends at once, even though this conversation would be directed more toward Olivia.

She frowned as she noticed the girl behind me for the first time. "This is my cousin Victoria—"

Said cousin stepped forward. "Call me Tori."

True to her socialist upbringing, Liv swept in with an extended hand and a friendly smile. "It's so nice to finally meet you."

"Likewise." Tori took the offered hand and granted Molly a small smile, which the quieter of my friends returned.

"There are some things I need to tell you." Olivia turned her emerald gaze on me and Tori studied the ground. "Big things ..."

Liv's frown morphed to full blown, and I prayed to whoever was listening that my secrets wouldn't hurt our friendship. Honestly, it would have served me right if they did. Olivia was such a beautiful person, and I was a downright liar.

I took a big breath that did nothing to calm my anxious nerves. Finding the right place to begin wasn't easy. "I didn't mean to lie to you ... to anyone really. At first it wasn't a lie; it just wasn't divulging certain info, then when the topic came up it was easy to just let you assume and now ... somehow, two years later it's turned into an outright lie, and I'm sorry. I'm so sorry, Liv." I glanced toward my other friend. "You too, Molly. I'm sorry I never told either of you the truth."

They both looked a little confused; a frown scrunched up Molly's forehead, and Liv rocked back and forth on her heels as if she were nervous, but neither took their eyes off me.

My knees ached to give way, yet I stood stiffly. "Tori and Dane were a year above me at school. Same as you, Molly, and I used to hang with them a lot. Toward the end of grade eleven, I was feeling pretty crappy about them both going off to college. But ... that's beside the point. On November third of that year, Tori and I met Dane at a beach party. One I wasn't supposed to be at. I was supposed to be at my sister, Dakota's, basketball game with the rest of the family, and because I wasn't ..." My throat felt as if it was trying to cave in on itself, and the warmth of Tori's hand settled on the curve of my spine. "My family was involved in a crash." I took a shaky breath and ploughed on. "Neither Mum nor Dad made it, and Dakota was left a paraplegic."

Molly gasped. Liv fell back onto the desk, her butt hitting the timber with a *thunk*, and as hard as it was to keep eye contact when this story I'd kept to myself for so long was burning on the way out, I managed. Liv's ever-kind eyes teared up and I swayed, but Tori's support held me firm.

"I'm sorry I let you believe what I did. Kody lives with my aunt and uncle, Tori's parents, just like I did before I came here."

Molly was the first to recover. She bent a knee and fell back against the closed wardrobe door, her arms sneaking across her tummy. "Wow."

A tornado of red flew at me, and I wasn't sure if bracing for the impact of a slap was the right thing to do, but Olivia's short arms snapped around me and she sob-hiccupped into my hair for a good five minutes before she finally spoke through a croaking voice. "I'm the one who's sorry. I'm so sorry you went through that, and I'm sorry—"

"Don't ..." I pushed my friend back to make solid eye contact. "There's nothing to be sorry for, and I loathe that word."

Liv sucked in her bottom lip.

"Forgive me?"

She looked as pale as the departed, yet she agreed. "Of course. I'm always here for you."

"Ditto." Molly pushed off the wardrobe. "We're real friends, Savvy. You can trust us to be there."

Liv pulled her arms around me even tighter than before, and Molly rushed in to join us. Excluding my cousin, these girls truly were the best friends I'd ever had.

****

Tori had perched herself on my desk, watching the show downstairs with a Vodka Cruiser in hand while

I paced back and forth across my tiny room. Exactly three steps—that was how much space there was between the bed and wardrobe. Five—that was the number from the door to the desk, which sat under the window. Not that big at all. Half the size of the room we shared back home.

"I think it's time." My cousin shot back the last of her drink. "There're plenty of people around, and I'm pretty sure I just saw Olivia wave us down. God, her boyfriend is gorgeous, but what's with the cap?"

"He's wearing the grandpa hat with a suit?"

"Yup, and looking edible." Tori gave a queenly cupped-hand wave out the window. "Definitely a cue from Miss Liv. Time to roll, cuz."

My stomach clenched, and I wiped sweaty hands on my jeans. "Right."

I strode the five steps to the door and tugged it open with far too much force, then marched along the hall and down the stairs.

Everyone had assembled in the courtyard for pre-dinner drinks and fancy nibbles, so me striding through the throng of finely dressed collegians in my jeans and favourite Havianas sure turned some heads.

I jumped up on the wooden picnic table and cupped my hands around my mouth before I had time to chicken out, shouting, "Oxley!"

A roar went up, and I sought out my target in the crowd then glanced away once I knew he was there. My throat squeezed around my next words, but I forced them out without wasting time. "My name is Savannah West, and for the past two years I've been lying to everyone I care about."

Silence fell over the courtyard, all two hundred–odd people focused on me. My stomach churned.

"I am an orphan. A sister. A liar ...

"But mostly a coward."

I paused, even though I had everyone's full attention. The entire courtyard had fallen quiet, and all eyes were pointed my way.

Liv and Molly both offered encouraging smiles from where they stood near the back of the courtyard. Cade had his head tipped to the side, as if he were eagerly awaiting my next words, and Dono frowned, his fingers peeling the label off his cider. It seemed everyone was watching my scene unfold.

"I didn't want anyone here to know that my parents died in a head-on collision three years ago. The same accident that left my sister paralysed from the waist down. The same accident that I caused by lying about where I was ..." my gaze cut back to Dane, "... and who I was with. I've kept my past a secret from everyone here at Oxley because I can't stand the pity, nor the sorrow I see in people's eyes when they look at me, nor the guilt in my heart when I think about that night. I lied to other important people too, about other things. Things that are worth more than the lies surrounding them made them out to be. Dane ..." I sought him out in the crowd again. "I love you, and I don't care what anyone thinks. You're more important to me than anything else ever could be."

"Right!" Tori jumped up onto the table and slid her arm around me.

Everyone cheered, but the expressionless way Dane looked at me made my knees weak. Finally, the whistles died down, and I needed to keep on talking.

"I'm tired of playing pretend. I want the real deal ... if you still want it, too."

He looked almost dumbstruck, standing there in his version of formal—suit pants and a button-down shirt that was almost hempy. With his hair pulled back into a topknot and the cream shirt showing off his bronzed skin, Dane was the sexiest he'd ever been … and he wasn't moving.

My heart thundered in my throat as the entire courtyard stared back and forth at the two of us. Slick hands trembled against my thighs, and I'd never felt so freaking unsure of myself.

I climbed down off the table, and the crowd parted as if I were Moses and they were the Red Sea. Dane finally reacted by taking a step forward, and my heart just about exploded. Before there was time to overthink it I was there, right in front of him, my hands on his firm chest. He took another step forward, dropping his head so his rough chin brushed against my tender one. He placed a light kiss right over my cheek, and something fluttered inside of me. I turned my head and captured his soft lips with my own, kissing the huge-hearted man with every ounce of strength I had in me. His strong hand spread over my back, and with a little shove he pulled us close, growling low in his throat when my tongue swept through his mouth. As if that were what woke him, Dane suddenly took control, not kissing but devouring my mouth as if every sweep of his tongue, every press of his lips was a declaration.

I didn't care where we were or who was watching. Honestly, for those few minutes I forgot about his battered face, his bruised chest, about everything but the way Dane made me feel and the obvious effect I had on him. My heart swelled to three times its normal size at just being with this man I loved more deeply than had to be humanly possible. Here I'd thought I'd always loved him, but what I felt now was entirely different. Now it felt as if the world had always been half asleep just waiting for us to wake it up. Dane wasn't just the man who lit up my days in all the best ways. He was my best friend. The one person I'd allowed to stand by me when I'd shut everyone else out. The only person with whom I'd never pretended.

He pulled away just long enough to growl in my ear. "We're ditching this bloody ball."

"Great idea." I devoured his kiss one last time before tearing myself away and looping a finger through his belt, which I used to lead him away from the party and upstairs.

CHAPTER THIRTY THREE

Savvy

The best thing about not going to the ball was having the entire dorm to ourselves. It didn't matter how loud or how quiet we were—no one was about to hear. That was probably why I was feeling a little sore and a whole lot sated as I sat in the front seat of Tori's Lancer the next day. My cousin kept sneaking little smirks my way between lulls in the conversation. If I had known she'd be this cool with Dane and me, things sure would have been different.

Him wanting to come home with us had been a pleasant surprise. Not that I should have been shocked. He'd always put his family first, and I didn't know all the details, but clearly he needed to be with them right now.

The indicator ticked its merry tune as Tori turned

the car into the driveway of her parents' two-storey home. She pushed the gearstick into park and climbed out, leaving the engine running. We all did a quick seat change and Tori grabbed her overnight bag from the backseat. "See you, Dane."

"Later."

I gave my cousin a heartfelt hug. "You're the best."

"Don't you forget it." She slapped me on the rear and trotted up to the porch while I settled into the driver's seat.

After reversing out the drive and into the street, I turned us onto the highway. It was only a short trip to Dane's house, but it had been so nice of Tori to allow us this time alone. He and I had talked long into the night, but we hadn't yet broached the topic of his dad's health and quite frankly, I was worried.

"Talk to me."

"You feeding me my own line, princess?"

I concentrated on the changing traffic lights and the pedestrians walking across the road, but out of my periphery I caught him pinching the bridge of his nose. Still, the silence stretched on while I drove the three short minutes to his house and parked on the street.

I killed the engine and Dane stepped out of the car, where he waited for me to walk around, and then he pounced. His lips moved hard and urgent over my own as his hands caught in my hair, and his hips pressed me against the side fender. My blood raced under my skin and I really wished we weren't standing out front of his parents' house, because I wanted to climb in the backseat and drag him with me. With more than just the late afternoon sun heating my zinging skin, we made out like a pair of horny teenagers, an age technically I'd been not too long ago.

A series of sharp honks from an amused passer-by pulled my raging hormones into line, and I moved my lips to his soft stubbled cheek. Dane's fingers loosened their death grip on my hair and the nape of my neck felt the absence of his warm touch. Our foreheads fell together and his shaky breath brushed my cheek. It took a few moments to regulate my heartbeat, but when I did, I said, "Hope your mum didn't see that from the window."

Dane chuckled low and husky before dropping a final lingering kiss on my over-sensitised lips. I sighed as he pulled away from the car and me, then moved toward his childhood home. There was something about the way he kissed me that made all the unsaid words clear. My man was hurting and maybe a little scared. I rushed to catch up and reaching back, Dane's fingers found mine a moment before he set a key to the lock and opened the front door. "Hello …" he yelled into the homely space that marked the living room and I followed him inside. Lovely and warm, the room was full of soft-coloured couches and timber unique furniture.

Roar bounded around the corner that led to the kitchen, his little paws just about reaching Dane's thighs when he jumped. Dane caught the tiny dog out of the air one-handed as Deanne appeared from the same direction, wiping her hands on a dishtowel. Her wide smile grew worried when she took in her son's injuries. In two strides she moved across the room to kiss him on the cheek. He set down Roar and pulled her into a one-armed hug, not dropping my hand, which was clasped so firmly in the undamaged hand on his sore arm that I thought I might just lose circulation.

"What a nice surprise. Your father will be so happy to see you." Deanne didn't let me off, placing a motherly kiss on my cheek too before turning away and shouting, "Stew! Dane's home."

Before I had time to draw breath, he yelled back, "I'm coming."

Dane's mum ushered us into the living room and disappeared just as Stew shuffled in. I'd only seen Stewart Beaumont once before, but the difference in him was so great it was like a whole different man stood before us. He looked a lot less like an older version of Dane than he had the last time I'd seen him. Despite the warm smile, in just a few months his cheeks had hollowed, as if he'd lost every ounce of spare weight he carried. Now, his skin was an awful white-grey, and although thinning before, his head was now completely bald.

Dane's grip on my fingers tightened, but as his father moved forward, right hand extended, my man let me go and clasped his father's thin hand instead, pulling the frail man into a man-hug. It didn't end there though, Stew's other hand finally stilled, settling on Dane's back, and they held each other for a good few minutes until Deanne returned, the tea tray rattling in her hold when she spotted their embrace. At the foreign noise they both dropped their arms and retreated.

"Pa ..." Dane snuck an arm around my waist, which he used to move me forward. "This is Savvy."

The older Beaumont beamed the exact same McFlirt smile I no longer loathed to love. "Why didn't you remind me she was this beautiful, Son?"

Dane barked out a laugh, and just like that the tension in the room fell away. Back in carer mode, Deanne steered her husband toward the sole recliner in the room and forced him to sit. Although he put on a show about the fuss, relief swept over his features when his legs were unburdened of the weight.

Now her husband was settled, Deanne turned her attention to her son. "Are you kids here for dinner, or just a quick visit?"

"I'm staying tonight, Ma. Tomorrow I'll organise a short leave of absence … few days."

I swear her shoulders dropped an inch, and her face softened at his news. I made a mental note to tell Dane she needed looking after, too.

"And Savvy as well?"

Now there was a thought. With another week of prac to go I wasn't headed back to Oxley, but there was no reason I couldn't stay here and swing by Aunt Rosy's in the morning on the way to work at East Coast Primary. I nodded. "Absolutely."

She bustled off to the kitchen, and I went to follow to see if she needed help, but Dane's huge hand settled on my thigh the second I started moving. The sideways look I gave him went unnoticed as his Dad began speaking. "That piece for Bonny Harris—"

"Don't you worry about it; I'm gonna look at that tomorrow."

Stew scowled, but his wife reappeared for long enough to place a hand over his, which smoothed his furrowed brow. "You need to rest, darling. Dane's more than capable, and while he's here you should let him help out."

Stew suddenly more tired. "Look, Son, the shop's not really holding up. I think maybe we need to wind things up."

Dane's easy slump disappeared, his entire body stiffening as he sat up straight in the couch. "Not gonna happen, old man."

"It was always a pipedream—"

"It was a real dream and one that'll flourish. In a few months I'll be done at uni, and back here full-time. It's a viable, profitable business, and no matter how long it takes we're going to work it, you hear me?"

Stew didn't look convinced. "It was never your thing, Son."

"You're right. It was our thing, and I say we're not giving it up."

Stew's beady glare held firm, as if he weighed up his son's declaration. Dane and I had never really talked futures, but I wasn't clueless. He wanted to help his father build a legacy, and since the younger Beaumont was business savvy, I had no doubt that was exactly what he would do.

The conversation seemed to end with their epic stare-off. Resolved or not, we moved onto lighter topics. The four of us talked and laughed the afternoon and later, the evening away. Just like their gorgeous son, these people were absolutely lovely, and I'd never felt more at home. In fact, I didn't think I'd been this comfortable anywhere for a really long time. Even Deanne's special meatballs made me feel as if I'd found my way home. It had been a long time since I'd found easy conversation while actually working in a kitchen.

It wasn't until Tori texted that I remembered her car was still parked out front, so I excused myself after dinner, gave Dane a kiss suitable for parental company and went back to my aunt and uncle's. After a quick 'I'm back' to Kody, I grabbed my work clothes and had Tori drop me back at the Beaumonts'. Stew had retired to bed, and Deanne was still bustling about the kitchen while Dane sat at the bench, his thighs pressed around the back of the bar stool and his good arm rest across the backrest while he chatted to her. I stood outside for a moment, not wanting to intrude, but Dane must have had some kind of radar because he turned around within a minute of me leaning against the door, hand poised to knock. He pushed up off his perch and swaggered over to me, placing his right hand on my waist, and as I looked up into those deep brown eyes my heart felt complete.

"Well, I'm beat. I think I might head to bed and see you kids in the morning."

Dane chuckled at his mother's less-than-subtle exit, while I mumbled, "G'night, Deanne. Thanks for dinner."

"Bed's a hell good idea." It only took a small tug with his strong arms to get my body flush against him and with an expertise that curled my toes, he kissed that spot where my jaw met my ear. Pretty sure I groaned before I squeaked out, "Not in your mother's house."

Of course my McFlirt didn't take that for an answer, but rather continued his ministrations, sucking the sensitive lobe of my ear into his warm mouth. He sure knew how to make me melt.

"I've got school tomorrow ..." the trail of kisses

continued, "... bigger kids. Grade six, so I need to have my wits intact."

"Thought you wanted kindergarten."

"Turns out the little ones aren't for me. The big kids though ..." Goosebumps broke out along the nape of my neck. "I'm pretty sure I'll love it."

Huge hands cupped my rear, lifting me off the ground with effortless ease. I wrapped my legs around his waist instinctively, and Dane walked while kissing the pulse point on the opposite side of my throat. My heart raced in an entirely pleasant way and my tummy tingled, making all thoughts of tomorrow evaporate. With a whimper I turned my head to meet his lips, capturing them with ones that were aching for his. His bandaged left arm disappeared from resting against me, so I tightened my thighs around his middle as the hall lights went out and a door opened then snicked closed behind us. The only warning before my back hit a firm mattress was the bending of Dane's knees. As he crawled over me, not breaking our kiss, the only thought I had was that without all the secrets, I felt free. This man made me happy in a way I'd never thought possible.

Life had never been more real.

EPILOGUE

Dane
4 months later

My calloused fingers ran along the smooth surface. There was a certain solidarity in working driftwood that I'd always felt. As I sat alone in the workspace out the back of Driftwood Creations, the same camaraderie that had been present when the seat across from me wasn't empty still lingered. Over the years, my father had slyly taught me his craft, passing along an expertise few carpenters ever mastered. At the time I hadn't realised that was what was happening, and now it was like he was still here with me, his spirit guiding my working hands.

The bell out front announced a customer arrival. Roar didn't even look up from his spot by the stack of scrap wood. I set the tools down and swiped the sawdust from my jeans as I wandered out. Most days Ma worked the front counter while I kept up with orders and the business end of things, but today she'd had an appointment with the travel agent. Her sister had insisted the two of them take a cruise, and although Mum had argued I couldn't do without her, in the end her argument hadn't been a match for her older sister, who thought she needed a distraction. I'd agreed. It'd be good for her to get out and live a little after the shit year we'd been dealt.

Standing in the middle of the shop was the man I'd grown up knowing as Pa's mate. With hands stuffed in his pockets, he looked around the small display.

"John." I offered up a friendly smile even though seeing him here in my father's space without the old man, stung. His weather-worn hand, used to holding a fishing line, dwarfed the lamp sitting by the counter. His thick finger, cracked from too much saltwater, smoothed over the spot where the timber stand joined the base. And that was the sign of true craftsmanship ... in only the best work was the seam invisible; a gem passed on from my father.

"You've done your old boy proud."

I tilted my head toward the staff entrance that led to the workshop out back. "You wanna see it?"

He tipped his sun-weathered chin, and I held the curtain aside while he entered my workspace. Giving him a little room, I waited by the door while John touched the piece as if it were made of glass. A low whistle let on just how much he thought of my work. "If I didn't know better, I'd think this was made by your father. It matches the other one like a twin." Trailing gnarled fingers over the backrest, he walked around the garden seat, checking it out from the rear. "Nice work, Dane."

"I had a good a teacher."

"That you did, Son."

Some days it seemed as though the hurt of Dad's passing would never dull, and in that moment it was as raw as when I'd first learned he was sick. That was why I'd thrown myself into working the shop. It had worked for a time. Now summer break was over and Savvy had gone back to college, his absence was multiplied by hers. I missed my blonde beauty something fierce, but with another year left in her studies, she was still at Oxley. We got together every other week and ran our phones flat daily, but it was times like this when I ached to see her smile at the end of the day.

John gave me one of his back slaps. When I was young, he'd always claimed that was the way real men showed they cared. "Thanks for this, kid."

I nodded. Making up the chair hadn't been hard when I had a set of solid plans to follow. My old man hadn't been sprouting shit when he'd told his fishing buddy he'd make the seat a matched set. He'd had a massive chunk of driftwood set aside and the plans all drawn up. Pity he'd never got to piece them together.

"I've got the truck backed up. You good for a lift?"

"Sure thing." I hit the remote to lift the automatic door, and we both watched it roll up. When it was all the way, John unclipped the tailgate on his truck and we each jumped on an end of the heavy seat, hefting it onto the waiting tray. John tossed a worn tartan blanket over the polished timber and strapped the furniture down.

After he left, I shut up shop and climbed in my Kia. A shiny red five-seater, it was a newer make than the Outlander, but I missed the old girl. I couldn't keep my board in the back, so it was relegated to the roof racks, which meant I didn't keep it with me all the time. Life needed a little more forethought than it had before anyway; the freedom of dropping into the water whenever I felt like it was long gone.

The trip up the mountains dragged. It didn't matter how many times I drove this road, when I knew my lady was waiting at the other end of the three-hour-drive, it seemed to take bloody forever. By the time I pulled up out front of Logan's apartment, my fingers tapped along to the music, and I was smiling for no other reason than the fact the long week since I'd last seen her was almost over.

I'd barely stepped foot out of the car when a squeal made my heart swell. A blonde blur shot my way, her body slamming into my chest. Lithe legs wrapped around my waist and slender fingers pressed against the back of my head, holding my mouth to hers. One of my hands found the crook of her neck while the other pressed against her lower back, trying to push us closer together even though it wasn't possible. After being apart for so long, I just wanted to wrap myself up in the sweet sensation that was Savvy, to kiss every last inch of her beautiful body, focusing on the most tender places, and when we were done with that, I wanted to catch up on all the shit we'd missed by being a few hundred clicks apart.

Next year couldn't come quickly enough. We had no idea where she'd be posted after she graduated, but Savvy was applying for all the schools within throwing distance of home. Not only for me, but for Kody too. Turned out Sav adored teaching sixth grade, and she was itching to get into a classroom again. Hopefully it'd be a classroom near home, but if that didn't work, we'd sort something out to get us closer than we were now.

"Leave me the fuck alone."

My hands faltered and Savvy slipped as I almost dropped her from shock at the curse shooting out of Molly's mouth as she crashed out from the front door. The chick was so old school; pretty sure I'd never heard her say shit, let alone drop an F-bomb. Savvy's forehead fell onto mine, and she sighed. I stepped away from the car, letting her thin body slide to the ground. She righted her skirt and smoothed out her top before slinking an arm around my waist.

One F-bomb wasn't enough.

Molly continued cussing as she stormed down the street in the direction of Oxley. She left a dude standing on the lawn in her wake, dragging his hands through his dark hair. I'd never seen the guy before, and he sure wasn't the type this group usually hung with. Dressed in tailored jeans and cowboy boots, and holding an Akubra, he looked as if he'd just stepped off a farm. Or straight out of the university's agriculture department.

"I don't know why he's even here." Savvy's voice vibrated against my shoulder, where she'd rested her cheek. "It's not like Molly even likes being in the same room as him."

"Who the hell is he?"

"The guy that followed her all the way here from home just to *talk*."

I raised a brow. The cowboy had a lot more than talking on his mind if he'd followed her to a college bash. Pretty sure the hike from her hometown to college wasn't a light one either.

"Yup."

"To a barbeque at Logan's?"

"I know, right?" Savvy tossed me a wink that set my pulse racing, then she hooked an arm around my waist, sliding her hand into the back pocket of my dusty work jeans. The curve of her palm against my arse cheek did nothing to help the urge to throw her on a bed, so I spun around, pinning her against the car again. She chuckled low in her throat as our lips met, my tongue seeking out every inch of her mouth.

The squeaky front door slamming closed drew us apart just in time to see Molly's friend duck inside. Jordan appeared in his place a moment later. "If you need a room ..."

I grinned at the younger of the Hays brothers, who in his red Mozzarella's polo had propped himself against the doorjamb. He seemed to have settled down. Logan attributed the change to the pizza shop's owner, who'd recently taken a liking to Jordan and treated him as a son.

The smirk kicking up one side of Jordan's mouth was a dead giveaway of the punch line he had set up. Of course, Savvy bit. "It's not like we've got no restraint."

"Well, if you do need a *room*, don't use mine." And there it was.

With a hand near the top of the screen, he held the door open for us to duck inside, offering an impressed smirk. The mouth-watering tang of cooking meat hung in the air. It smelled delicious. I hadn't stopped to eat more than a muesli bar all day. I'd been flat out getting John's garden chair finished.

On the way through the tiny kitchen, I grabbed one of the James Squires I'd asked Savvy to put in the fridge and followed the smell. I pushed the back door open, and Logan looked up from his spot by the grill, waving giant tongs. "You made it."

"Yeah, not a bad run either." I raised the beer. "Cheers, mate."

"Hi Dane." Olivia smiled as she fussed over what looked to be a brand new outdoor table, where Molly's mystery man sat brooding with one leg kicked up on his knee.

"Liv." I gave her a quick hug. "How's that sports centre gig working out?"

"Fabulously. You should swing by sometime, make Savvy hit the gym."

My girl snorted from her spot tucked under my arm. She wasn't much for sports, unless they were of the bedroom kind. Then, bedroom sports could happen anywhere. "Savvy and I have been pretty active recently. At the beach … in the car, the shop. Logan's bathroom …" I caught her attention with a pointed wink. "Why not?"

"See? You'll like it, Savvy." Olivia continued rearranging the salad bowls and sauce bottles. Honestly, she had no clue our sports weren't technically sports, but my girl laughed along with me.

I pulled out a chair and Savvy plopped herself in my lap, leaning back into my chest and circling her arm around my shoulders. Her phone buzzed and fishing it out of her pocket, she picked up.

"Hey, chickpea. What's up?"

I placed a kiss on her neck and smiled at me, while nodding as if Kody could see her. "Sure thing. I'm going to be home next weekend—"

Sav fell suddenly silent and frowning, she tapped her foot off the table leg. "Not unless she accepts Dane coming too. I love you, Kody, and I'm busting to see you again, but I'm not putting up with the way she treats him. So no family dinners, but I'll pick you up and we can go out for ice cream. Maybe spend the night watching a movie at that new under-stars cinema. What do you say?"

Sav wound her fingers into my shirt and pulled my lips to hers. The best thing about time apart was how neither of us could stand an inch between us when we were finally in the same town.

"Sounds perfect, see you then."

I dragged my attention to the poor cowboy sitting there peeling the label off his beer. "Mate ... I don't believe we've met."

"Callan Hunter." He tipped his chin. "And you've got to be Dane."

I took a slug of beer. "Yep."

My arm fit around Savvy, resting in the curve of her waist, and as I sat there watching my college family I knew that although things had been tough this year, they were only going to get better. I had the girl of my dreams by my side, and we no longer had to pretend.

Continue the Oxley College Saga

With Jordan and Hex in

WAIT!

It's time to play truth or dare.

Jordan Hays knows just how precious life is; that's why he has his own mapped out. He'll work to pay his way through university while he studies hard, regardless of the constant distractions. Because when it comes to becoming a nurse, he's deadly serious. He won't fail to save someone again.

But Hex Penton is way too similar to the sister he lost, and even though the only thing more fun than stupid dares is the crazy girl who sets them, Jordan needs to make a choice. Hex believes every moment is important; every opportunity must be taken, because you never know when the world will be yanked out from underneath you. With the foundations he's based his life on shaken, Jordan must discover what's more important: making sure Hex's life isn't wasted, or remembering how to live his.

Meet Molly and Callan in an Oxley College Saga spinoff.

STOLEN SANCTUARY

Is home really where the heart is?

The one thing that keeps Oxley College's Molly McLean calm amidst midterm exams and keg parties is knowing she's got a quiet place to land in her hometown of Bindarra Creek. But even from college, Molly's heard rumours about her small country hometown's big city makeover. She knows reviving tiny Bindarra Creek will draw in more tourists—so while home for the summer, she sets out to convince her conservative parents to spruce up their motel in order to cash in on the influx of new business that will surely come.

However, Molly never thought the town's makeover would have a negative impact on her little slice of home until she returns to the stables were she's worked every summer since she was thirteen. Sexy city boy Callan Hunter is turning the tranquil property she loves into another churn-people-through tourist spot. Butting heads with the business-minded hottie is the last way Molly thought she'd be spending her holidays, but there's no way she can stand around and allow the stables her pop hand-built to be torn down. If she can't convince Callan to ease up on the bulldozing, Bindarra Creek will no longer be a sanctuary. It'll be a concrete jungle.

His sexy arrogance might have everyone else ensnared, but Molly's already been there, done that. Now she's immune. Or is she?

Acknowledgements

It has been a rough year for me and because of that Pretend… is the book I thought would never be finished, so it's such a wonderful feeling to not only have reached *the end*, but also to have it polished and published. There are so many wonderful people who helped me through this year and I am grateful to have each and every one of them in my life.

My mum is the best in whole the world. Truly she is. From her unwavering support to her chicken broths, and handholding, I truly am blessed. Thank you for being you, and letting me be well … me.

My husband is also pretty darn good and if it weren't for his undying support and gentle encouragement, many of my words would still be in my head rather than on the page. We were lucky enough to meet each other in our college years and in many ways the Oxley books remind me of that special time.

ST, Lauren, Anabel ... my gosh, I've said it before, but I could not do this writing gig without each of you. You truly are my rocks. Thank you for the hours of brainstorming, sound boarding, emailing, texting, chatting, plot and cover anguishing and just well, everything. You girls are the best.

My writers' groups are both filled with such supportive ladies, who are always available to share ideas, suggestions, and cups of hot tea. Thank you for all the laughs and wonderful support, Story Queens and Hunter Romance Writers.

To my wonderful street team, the Nash-aholics, and all my amazing friends in the bookish community, thank you for sticking by me when I fell off the face of the internet. There have been many days in the past nine months when I just wasn't able to respond the way I usually had in the past. You are all such beautiful people, who give so much. Thank you supporting my writing endeavours and for continuing to read and enjoy my books.

Xx

About the author

Stacey Nash calls the Hunter Valley of New South Wales, Australia home. An area nestled between mountains and vineyards, its history and culture have always called to her. Stacey has loved reading for as long as she can remember, so it's no wonder she finally opened a word document and wrote chapter one. Stacey made her publishing debut in 2014 with a young adult novel titled *Forget Me Not*. Writing for the young and new adult market, Stacey's books are all adventure filled stories with a lot of adventure, a good dose of danger, a smattering of romance, and plenty of KISSING!

You can connect with Stacey via

Facebook
Twitter
Goodreads
Instagram

To stay up to date with new releases and upcoming titles be sure to sign up for Stacey's newsletter at the www.stacey-nash.com